Once upon a time...

HEARTLESS PRINCE

A GRAPHIC NOVEL

STORY & ILLUSTRATIONS BY
ANGELA DE VITO

WRITTEN BY
LEIGH DRAGOON

HYPERION

Los Angeles   New York

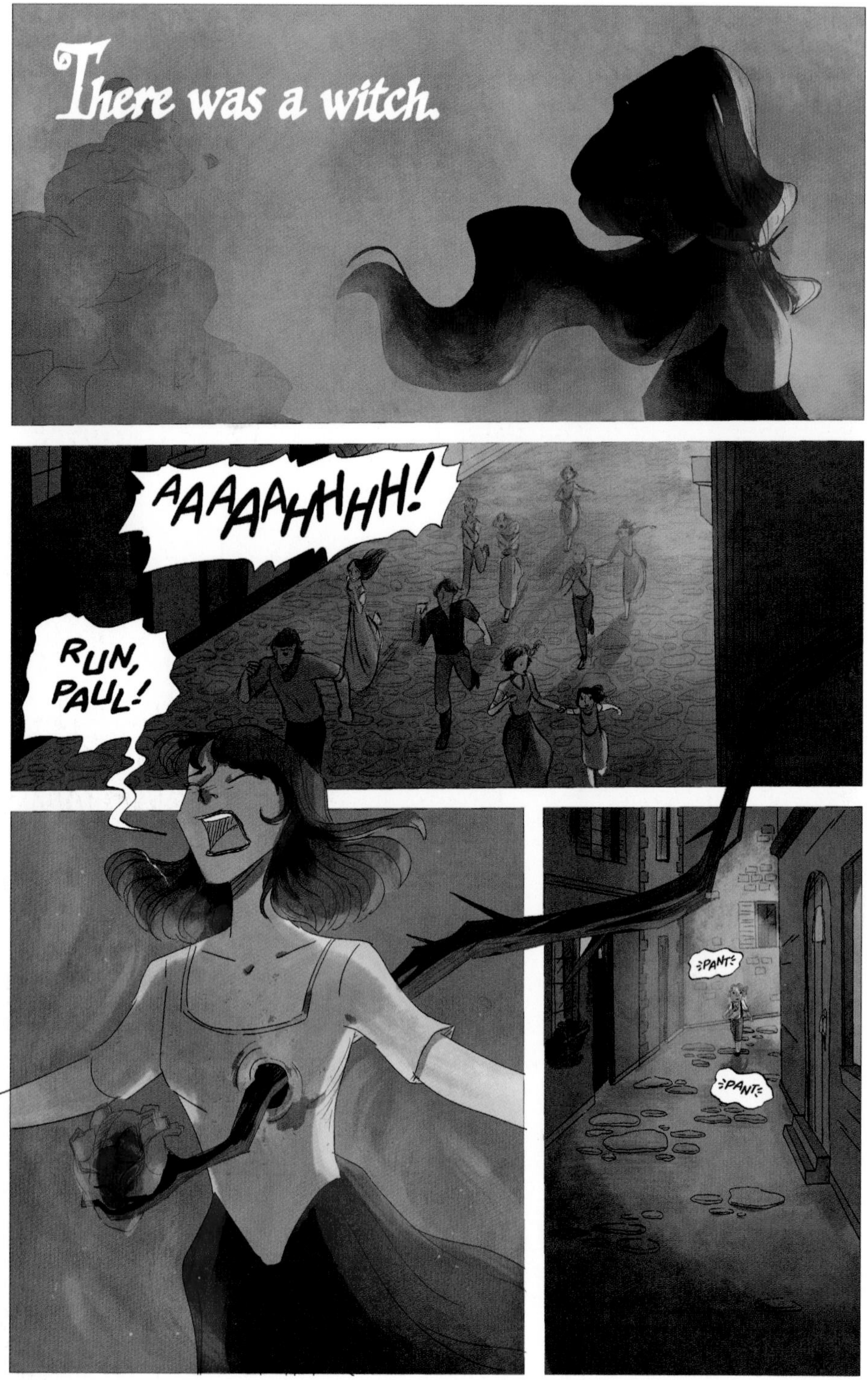
There was a witch.
AAAAAHHHH!
RUN, PAUL!
PANT
PANT

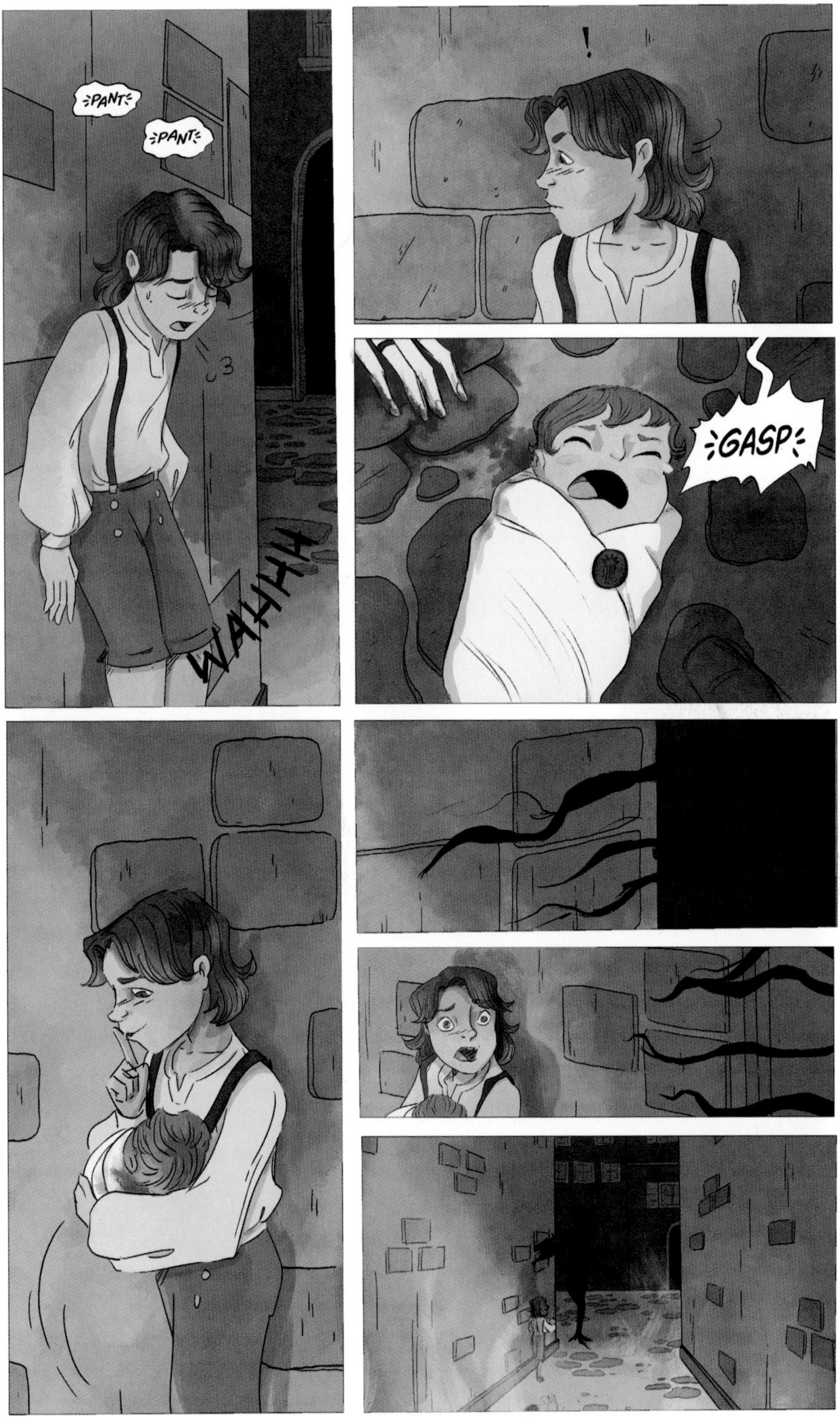
PANT
PANT
WAHHH
!
GASP

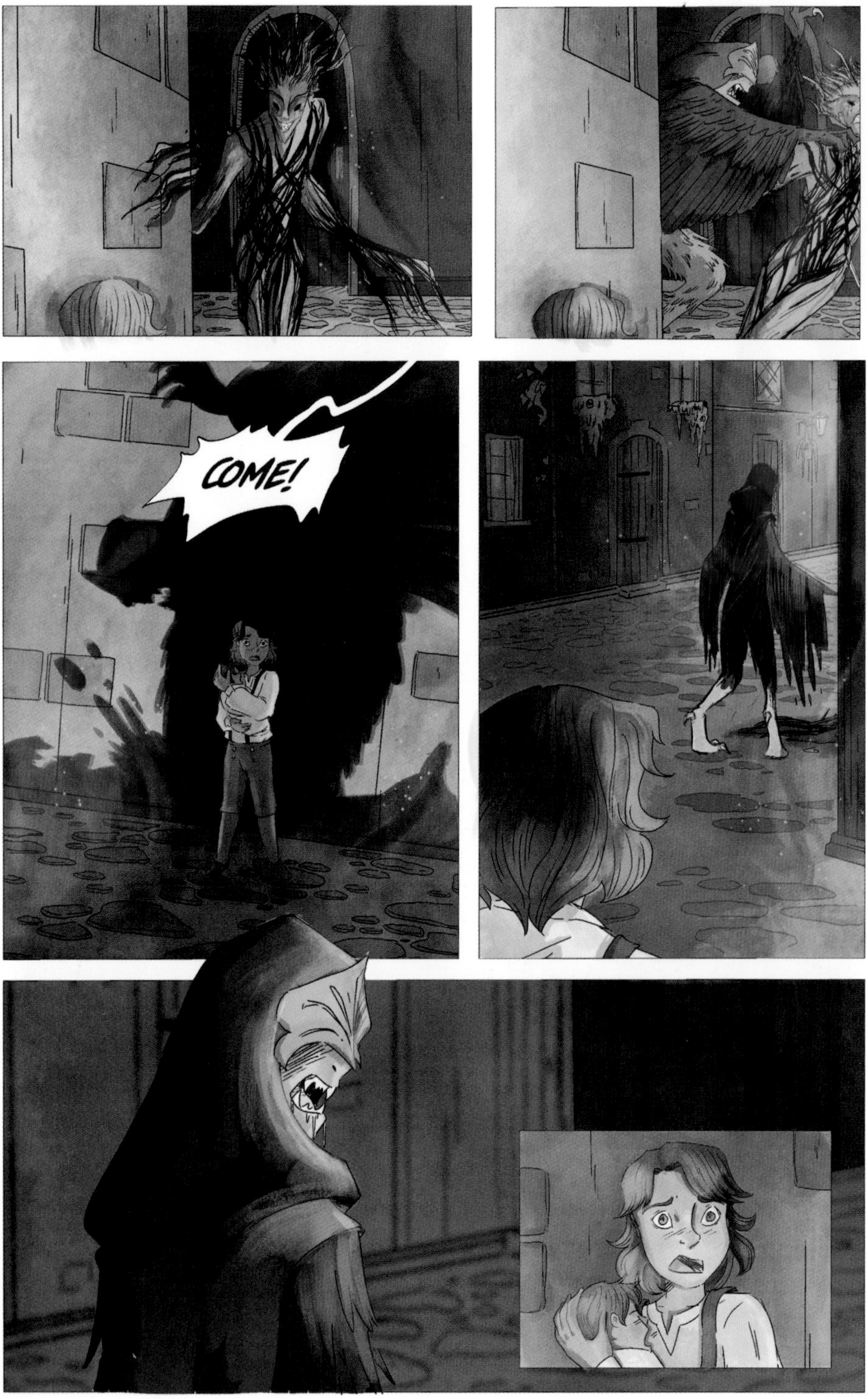
COME!

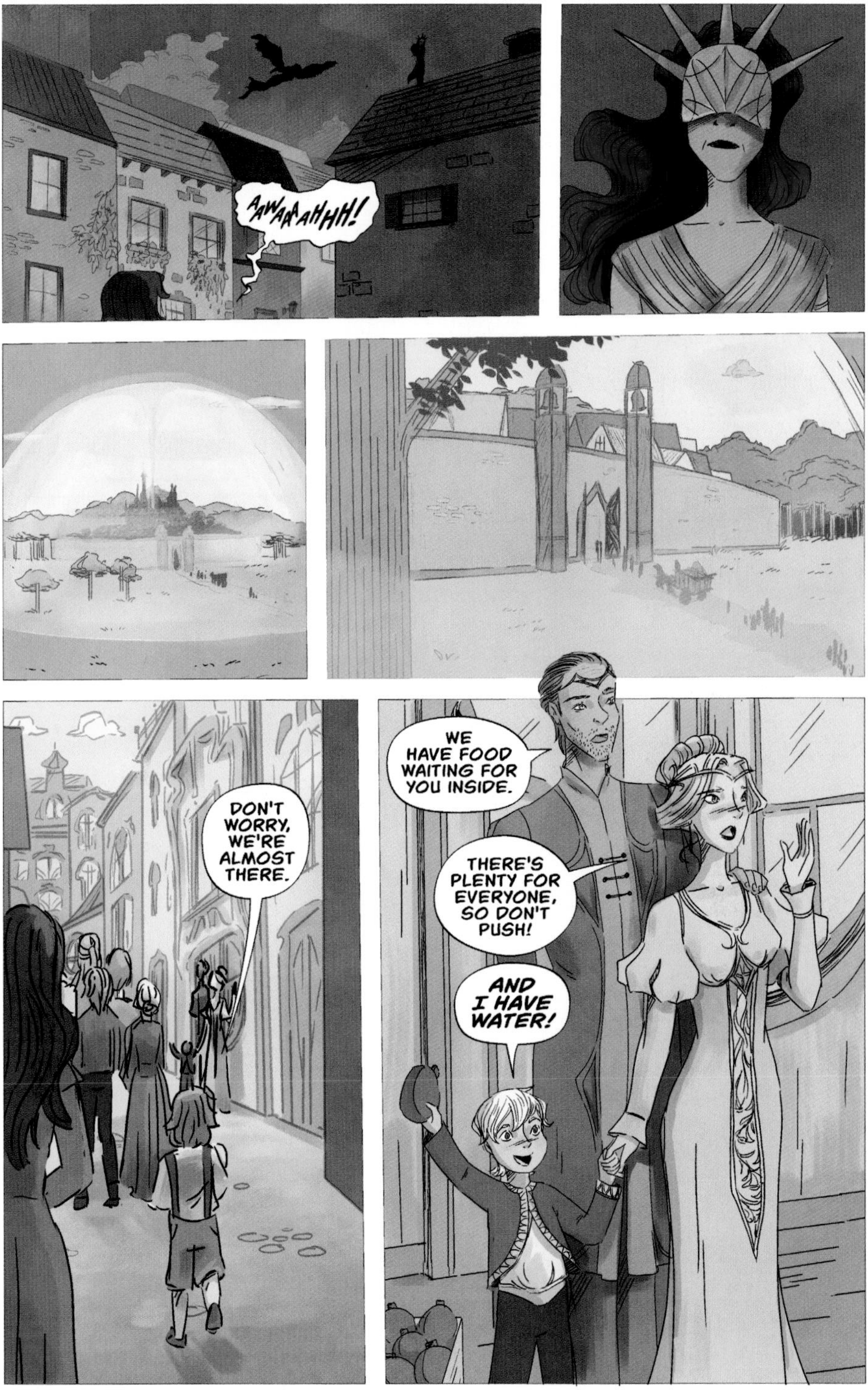
AAWAAAAHHH!
DON'T WORRY, WE'RE ALMOST THERE.
WE HAVE FOOD WAITING FOR YOU INSIDE.
THERE'S PLENTY FOR EVERYONE, SO DON'T PUSH!
AND I HAVE WATER!

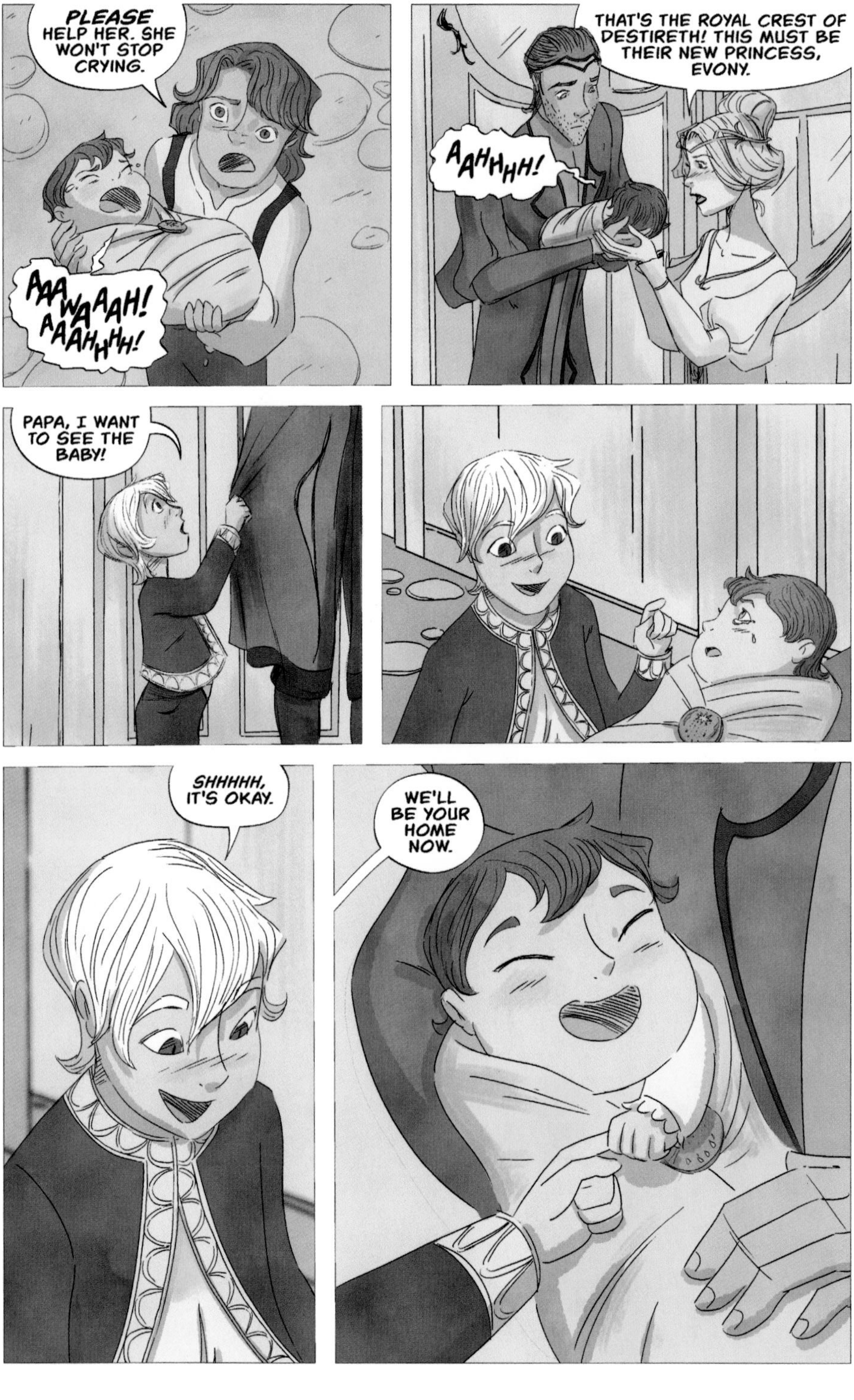
PLEASE HELP HER. SHE WON'T STOP CRYING.
AAAWAAAH! AAAHHHH!
THAT'S THE ROYAL CREST OF DESTIRETH! THIS MUST BE THEIR NEW PRINCESS, EVONY.
AAHHHH!
PAPA, I WANT TO SEE THE BABY!
SHHHHH, IT'S OKAY.
WE'LL BE YOUR HOME NOW.

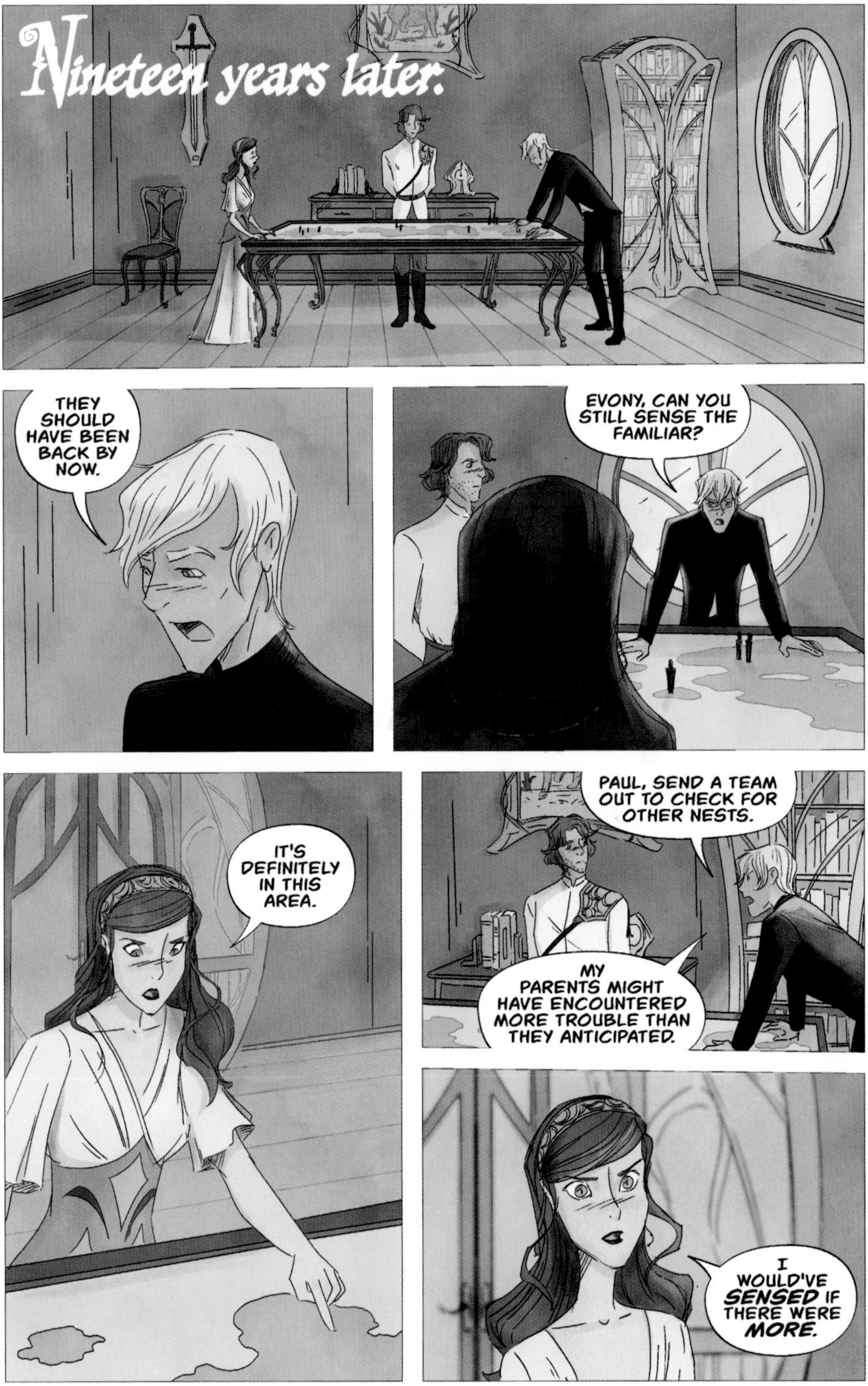
Nineteen years later.
THEY SHOULD HAVE BEEN BACK BY NOW.
EVONY, CAN YOU STILL SENSE THE FAMILIAR?
IT'S DEFINITELY IN THIS AREA.
PAUL, SEND A TEAM OUT TO CHECK FOR OTHER NESTS.
MY PARENTS MIGHT HAVE ENCOUNTERED MORE TROUBLE THAN THEY ANTICIPATED.
I WOULD'VE *SENSED* IF THERE WERE *MORE.*

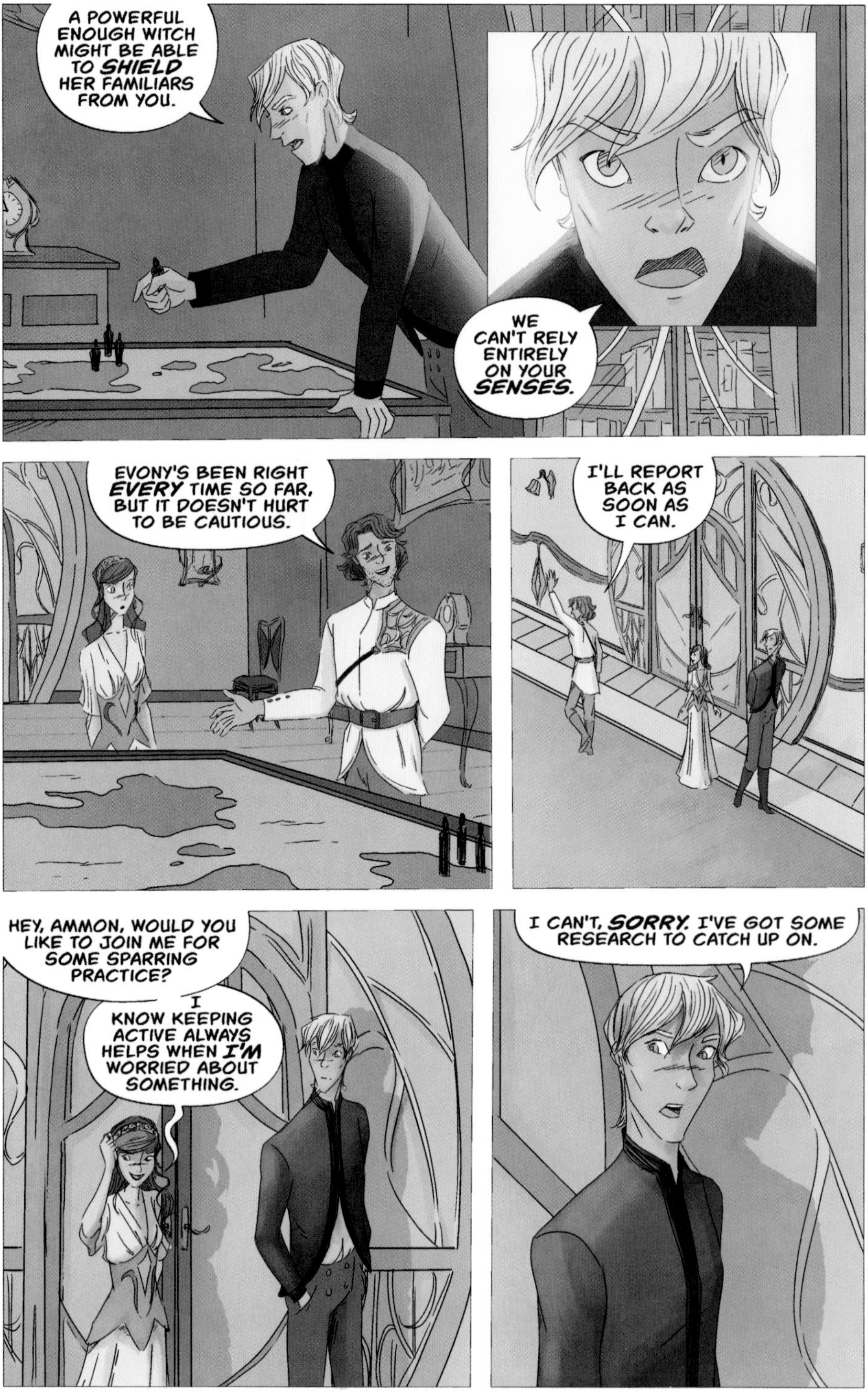
A POWERFUL ENOUGH WITCH MIGHT BE ABLE TO SHIELD HER FAMILIARS FROM YOU.
WE CAN'T RELY ENTIRELY ON YOUR SENSES.
EVONY'S BEEN RIGHT EVERY TIME SO FAR, BUT IT DOESN'T HURT TO BE CAUTIOUS.
I'LL REPORT BACK AS SOON AS I CAN.
HEY, AMMON, WOULD YOU LIKE TO JOIN ME FOR SOME SPARRING PRACTICE?
I KNOW KEEPING ACTIVE ALWAYS HELPS WHEN I'M WORRIED ABOUT SOMETHING.
I CAN'T, SORRY. I'VE GOT SOME RESEARCH TO CATCH UP ON.

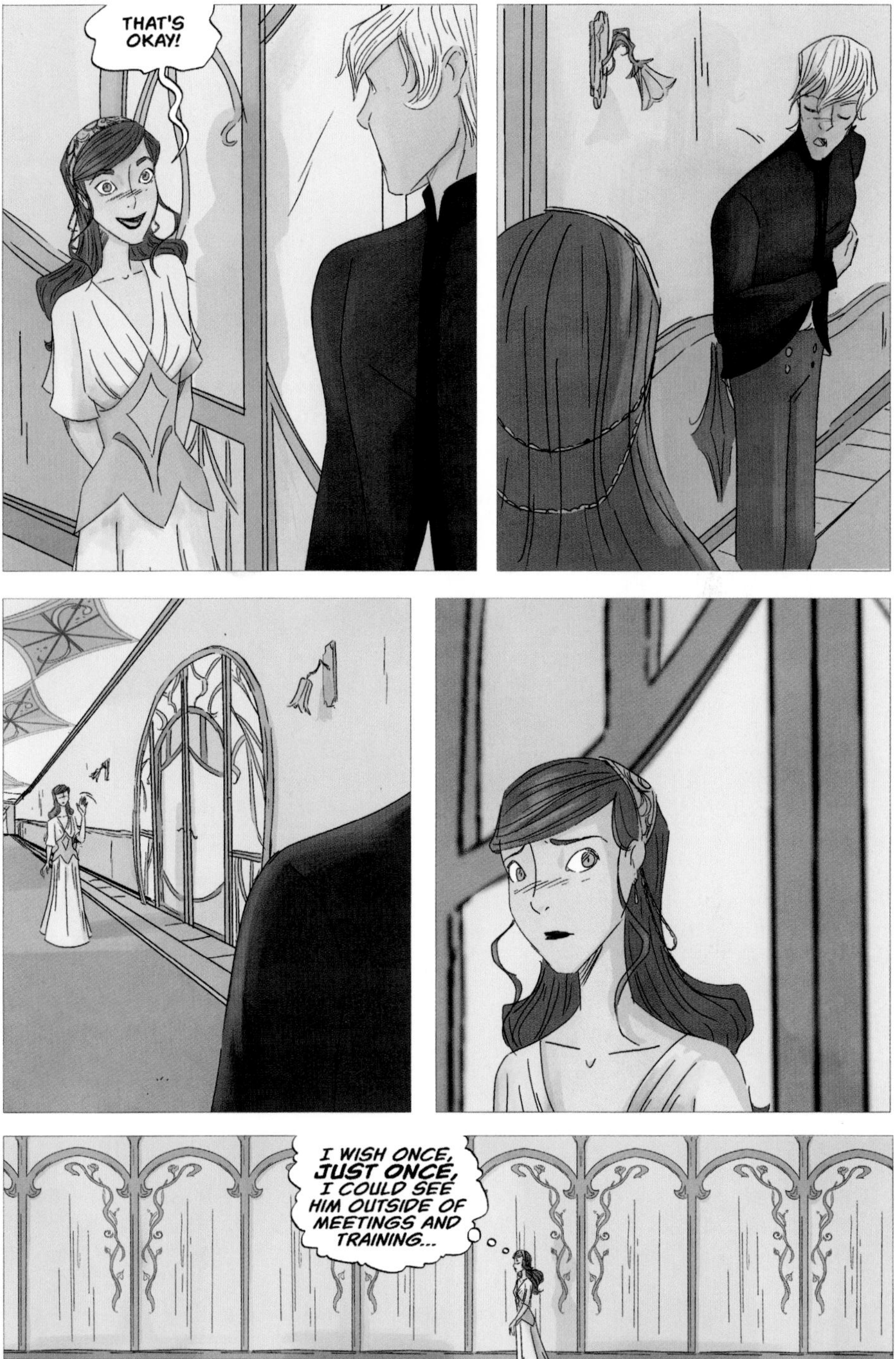
THAT'S OKAY!
I WISH ONCE, **JUST ONCE,** I COULD SEE HIM OUTSIDE OF MEETINGS AND TRAINING...

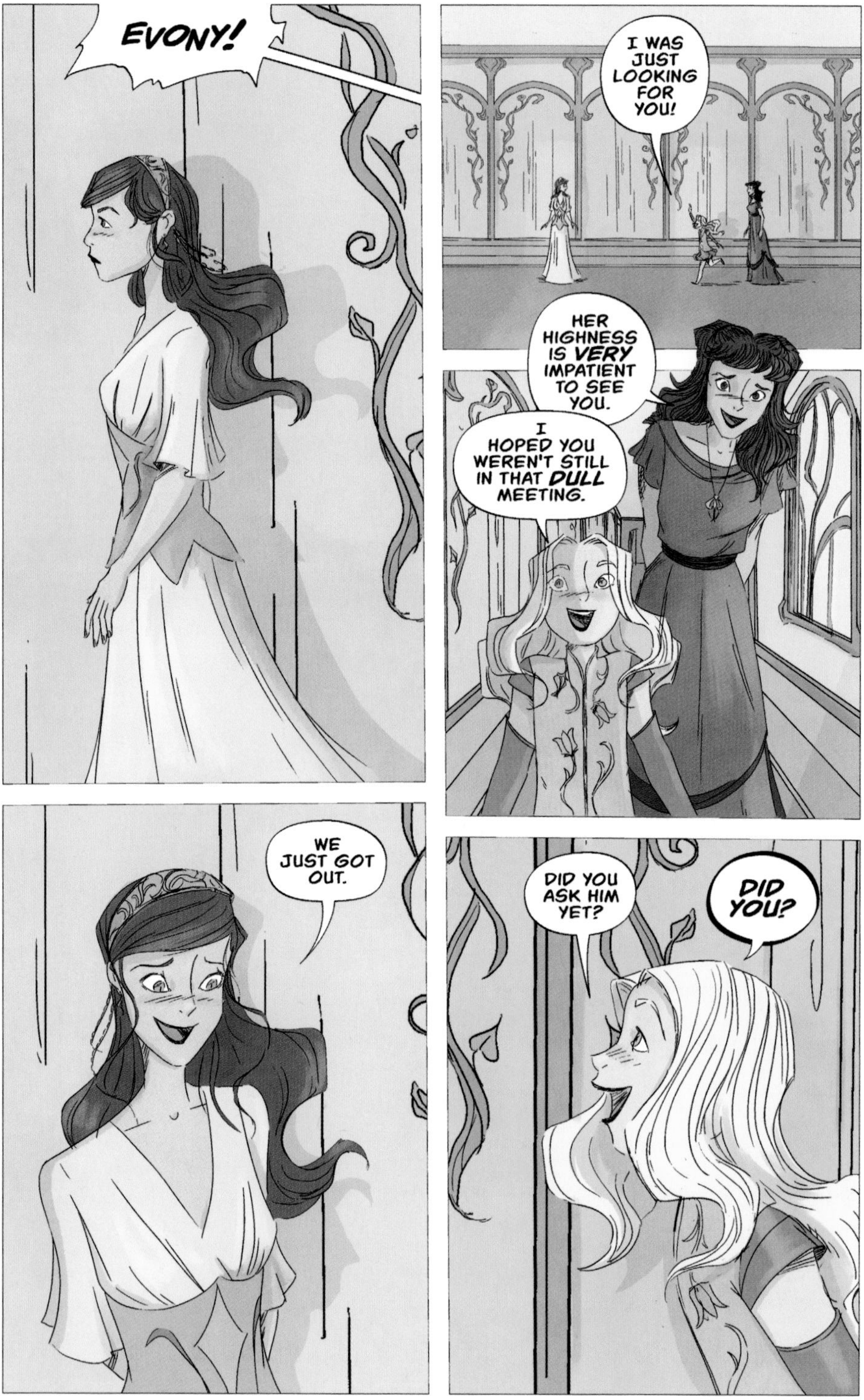
EVONY!
I WAS JUST LOOKING FOR YOU!
HER HIGHNESS IS VERY IMPATIENT TO SEE YOU.
I HOPED YOU WEREN'T STILL IN THAT DULL MEETING.
WE JUST GOT OUT.
DID YOU ASK HIM YET?
DID YOU?

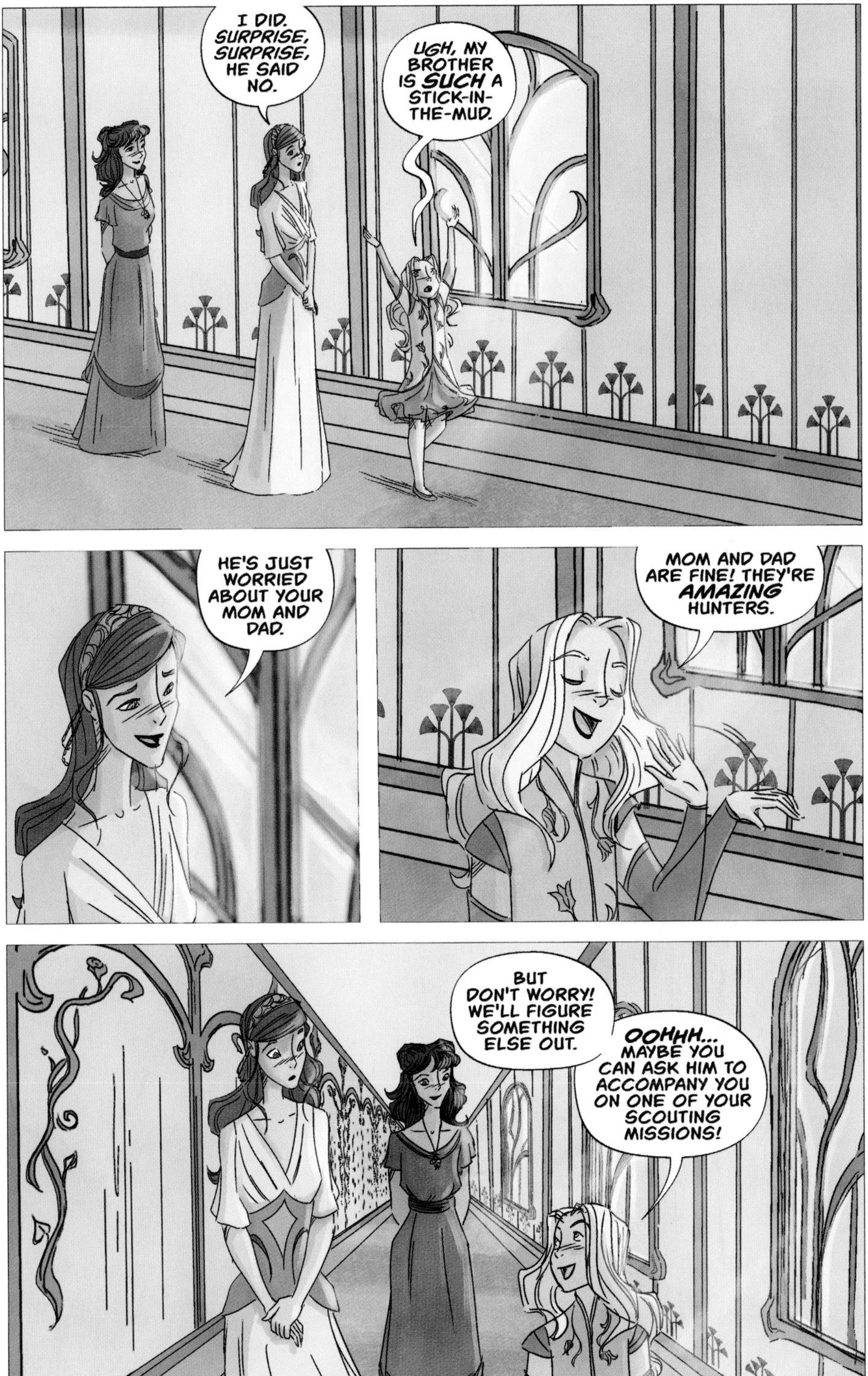
I DID. SURPRISE, SURPRISE, HE SAID NO.
UGH, MY BROTHER IS SUCH A STICK-IN-THE-MUD.
HE'S JUST WORRIED ABOUT YOUR MOM AND DAD.
MOM AND DAD ARE FINE! THEY'RE AMAZING HUNTERS.
BUT DON'T WORRY! WE'LL FIGURE SOMETHING ELSE OUT.
OOHHH... MAYBE YOU CAN ASK HIM TO ACCOMPANY YOU ON ONE OF YOUR SCOUTING MISSIONS!

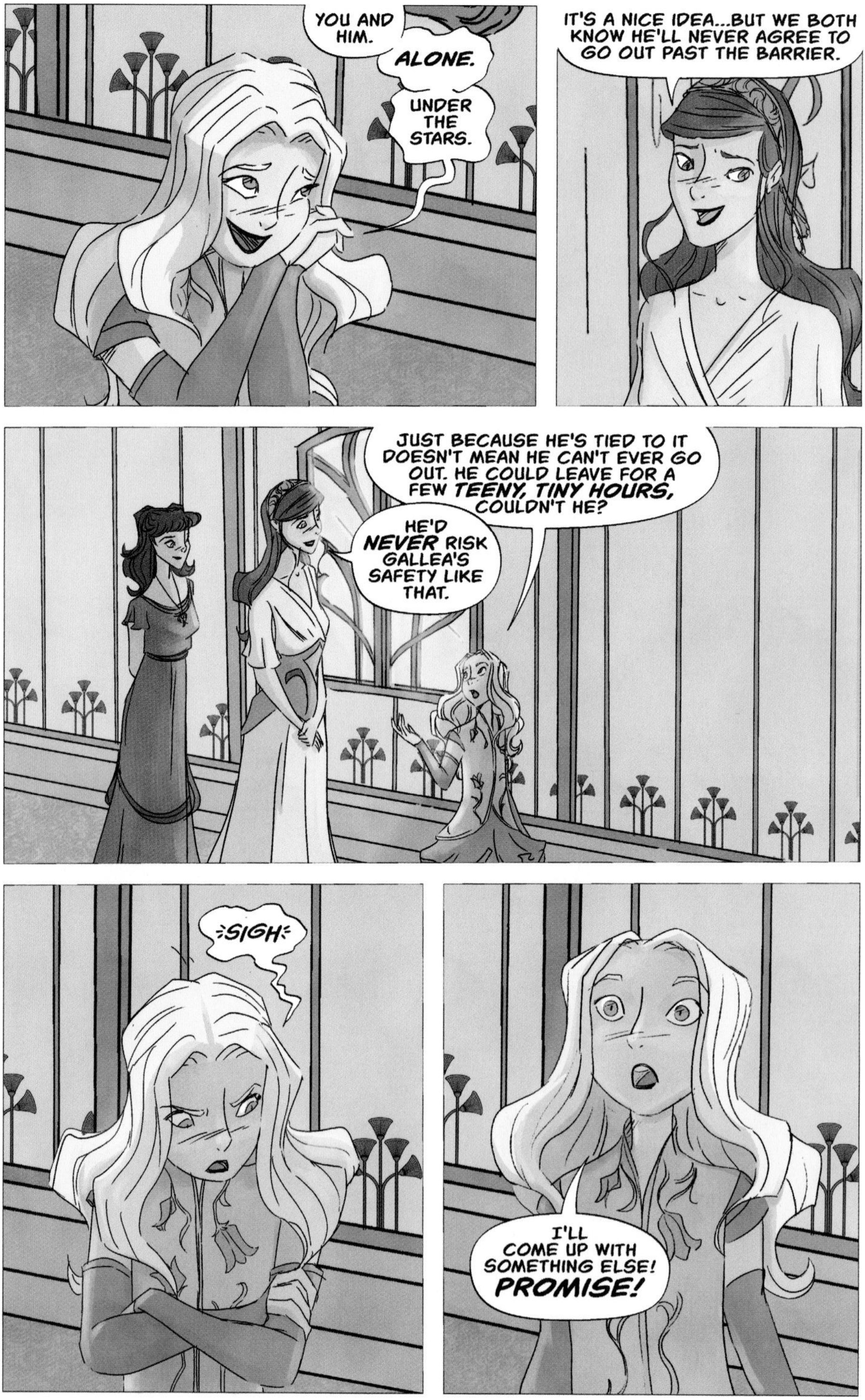
YOU AND HIM.
ALONE.
UNDER THE STARS.
IT'S A NICE IDEA...BUT WE BOTH KNOW HE'LL NEVER AGREE TO GO OUT PAST THE BARRIER.
JUST BECAUSE HE'S TIED TO IT DOESN'T MEAN HE CAN'T EVER GO OUT. HE COULD LEAVE FOR A FEW TEENY, TINY HOURS, COULDN'T HE?
HE'D NEVER RISK GALLEA'S SAFETY LIKE THAT.
SIGH
I'LL COME UP WITH SOMETHING ELSE! PROMISE!

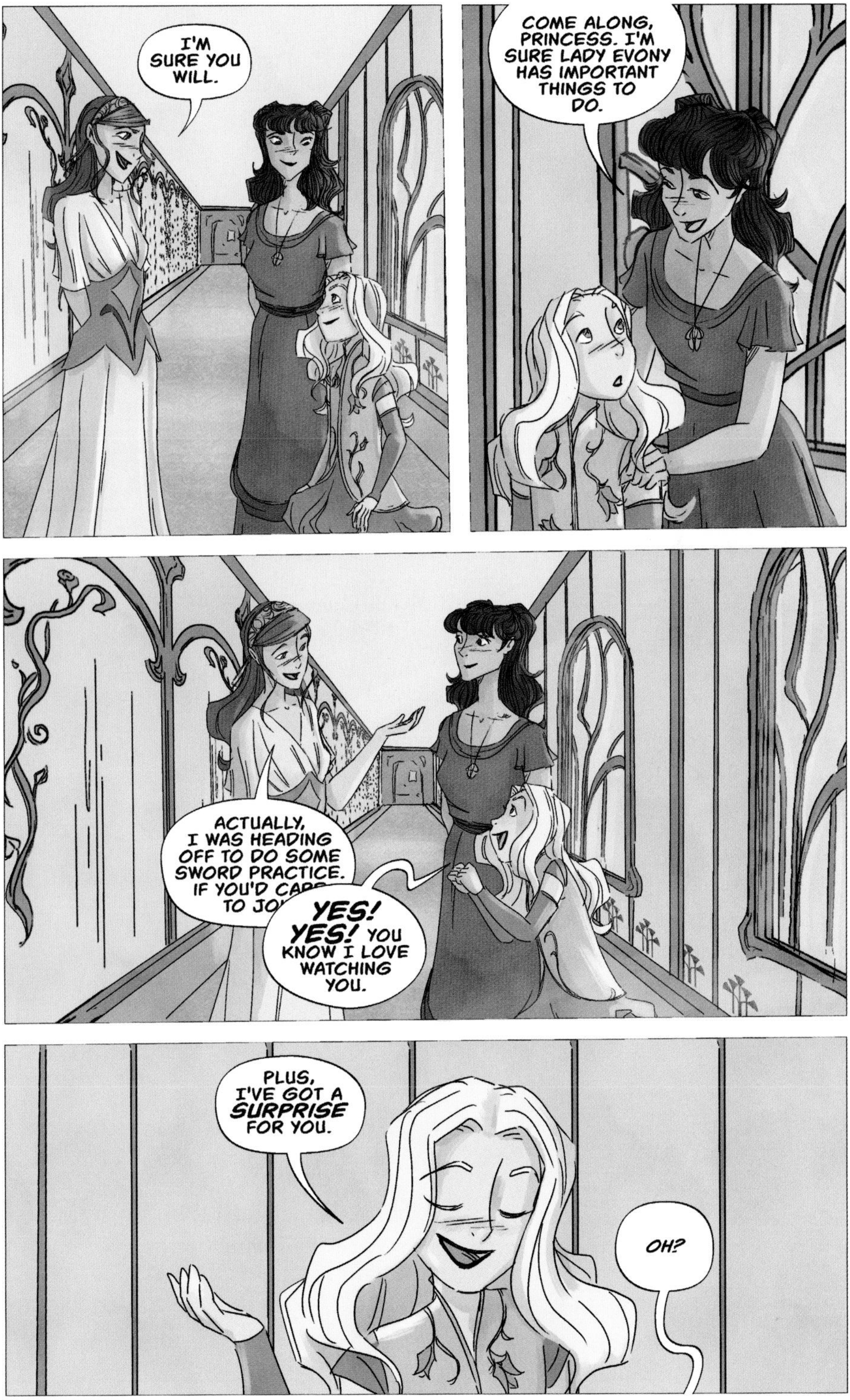
I'M SURE YOU WILL.
COME ALONG, PRINCESS. I'M SURE LADY EVONY HAS IMPORTANT THINGS TO DO.
ACTUALLY, I WAS HEADING OFF TO DO SOME SWORD PRACTICE. IF YOU'D CARE TO JO
YES! YES! YOU KNOW I LOVE WATCHING YOU.
PLUS, I'VE GOT A SURPRISE FOR YOU.
OH?

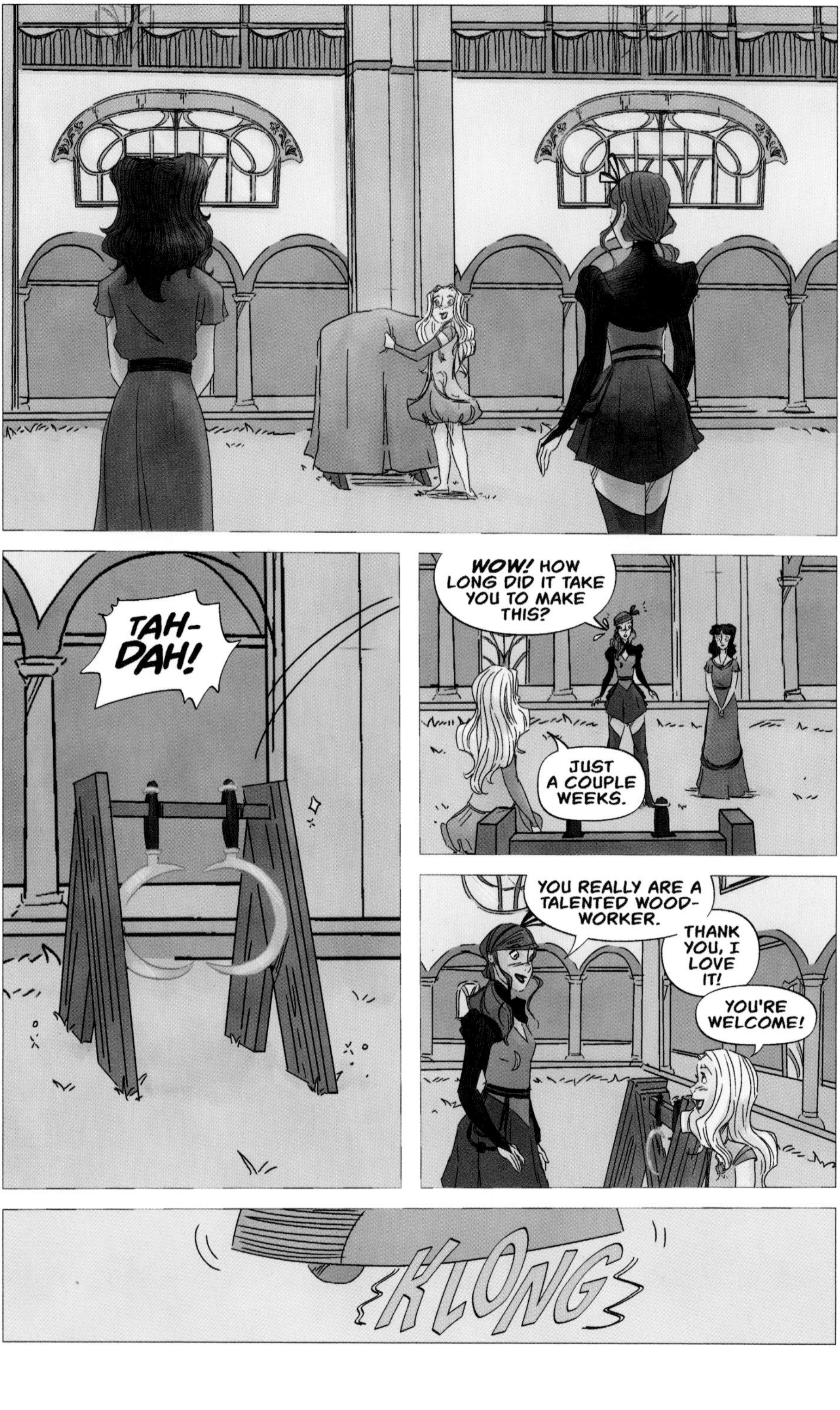
TAH-DAH!
WOW! HOW LONG DID IT TAKE YOU TO MAKE THIS?
JUST A COUPLE WEEKS.
YOU REALLY ARE A TALENTED WOOD-WORKER.
THANK YOU, I LOVE IT!
YOU'RE WELCOME!
KLONG

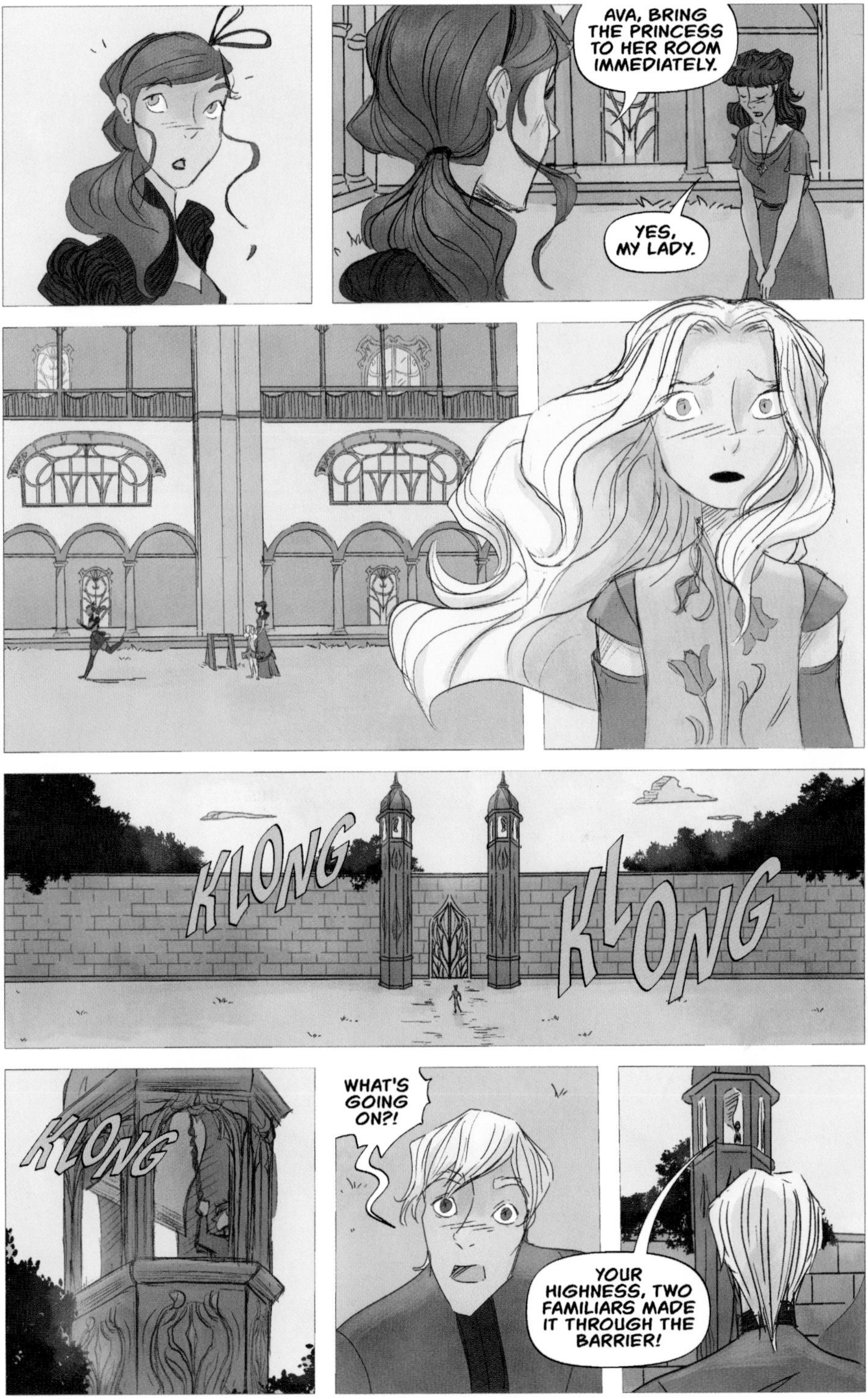
AVA, BRING THE PRINCESS TO HER ROOM IMMEDIATELY.
YES, MY LADY.
KLONG
KLONG
KLONG
WHAT'S GOING ON?!
YOUR HIGHNESS, TWO FAMILIARS MADE IT THROUGH THE BARRIER!

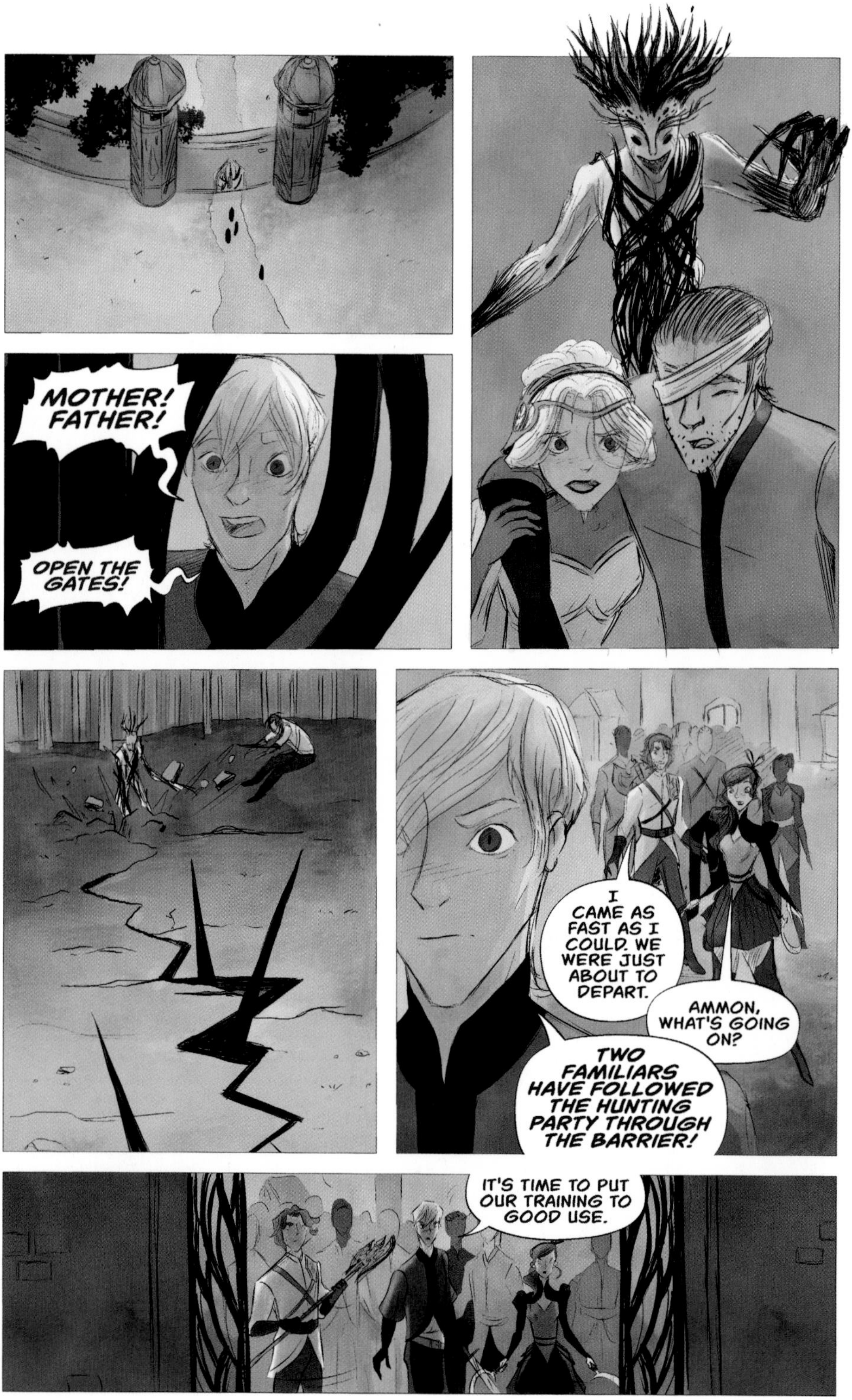
MOTHER! FATHER!
OPEN THE GATES!
I CAME AS FAST AS I COULD. WE WERE JUST ABOUT TO DEPART.
AMMON, WHAT'S GOING ON?
TWO FAMILIARS HAVE FOLLOWED THE HUNTING PARTY THROUGH THE BARRIER!
IT'S TIME TO PUT OUR TRAINING TO GOOD USE.

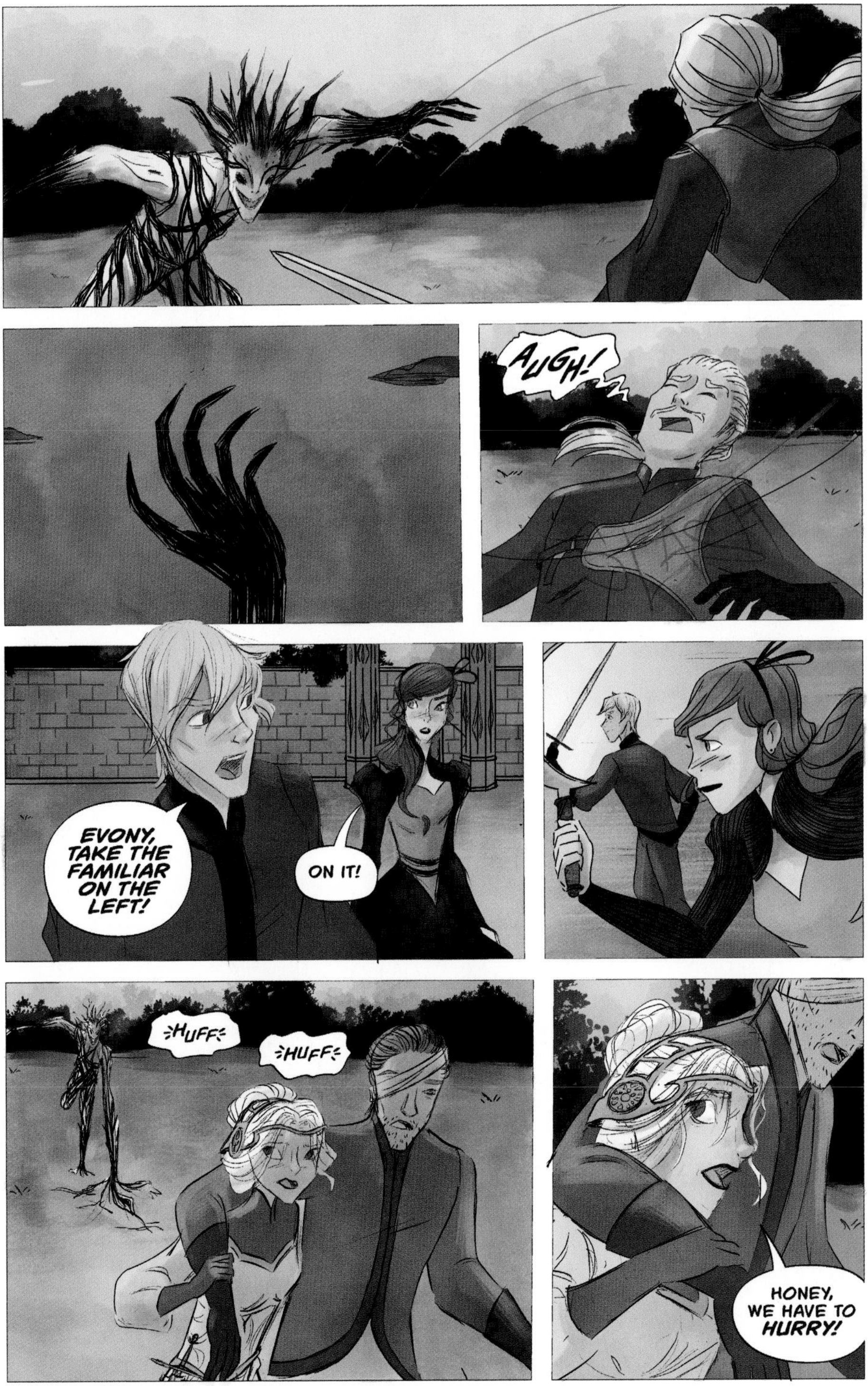
AUGH!
EVONY, TAKE THE FAMILIAR ON THE LEFT!
ON IT!
HUFF
HUFF
HONEY, WE HAVE TO HURRY!

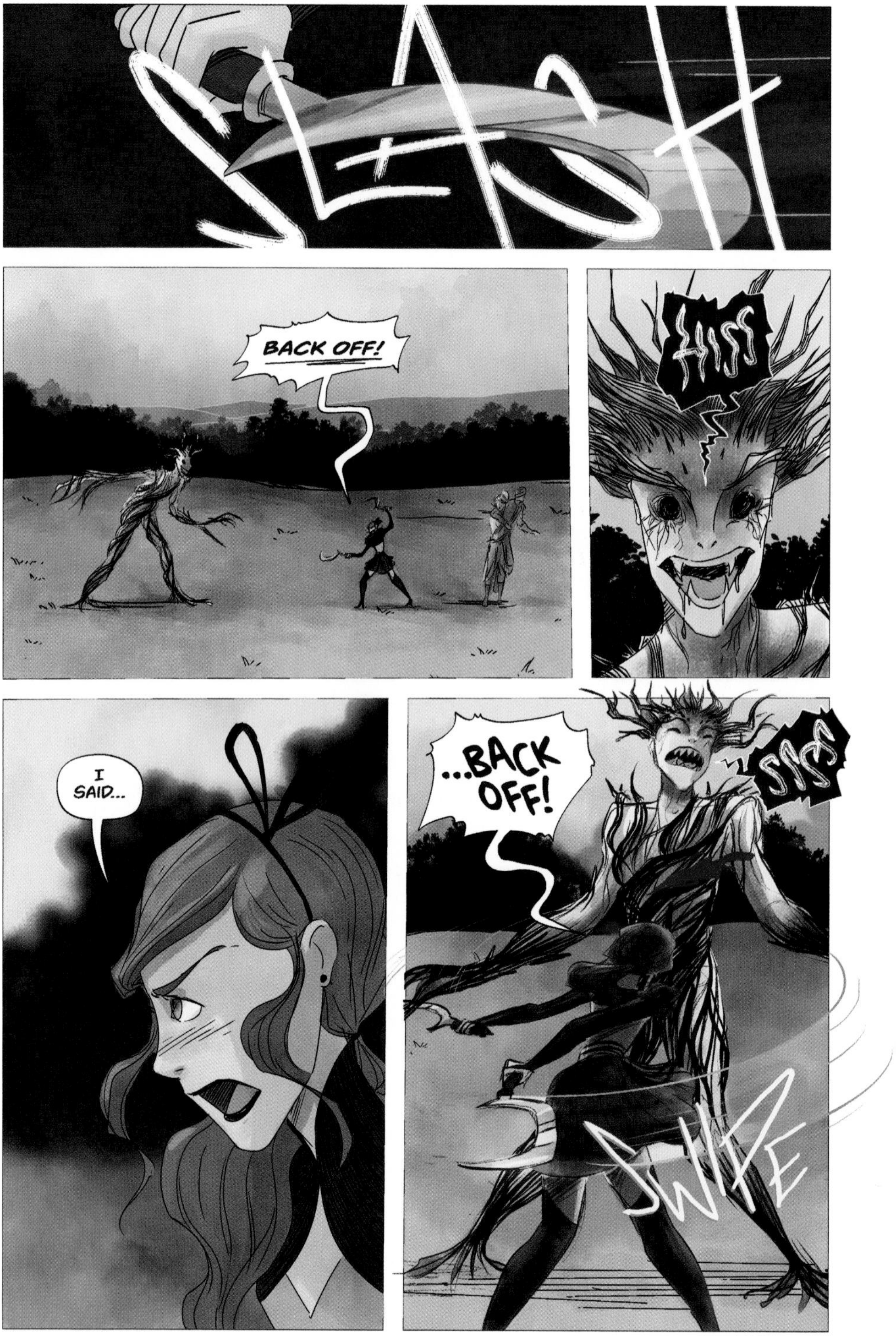
SLASH
BACK OFF!
HISS
I SAID...
...BACK OFF!
SSSS
SWIPE

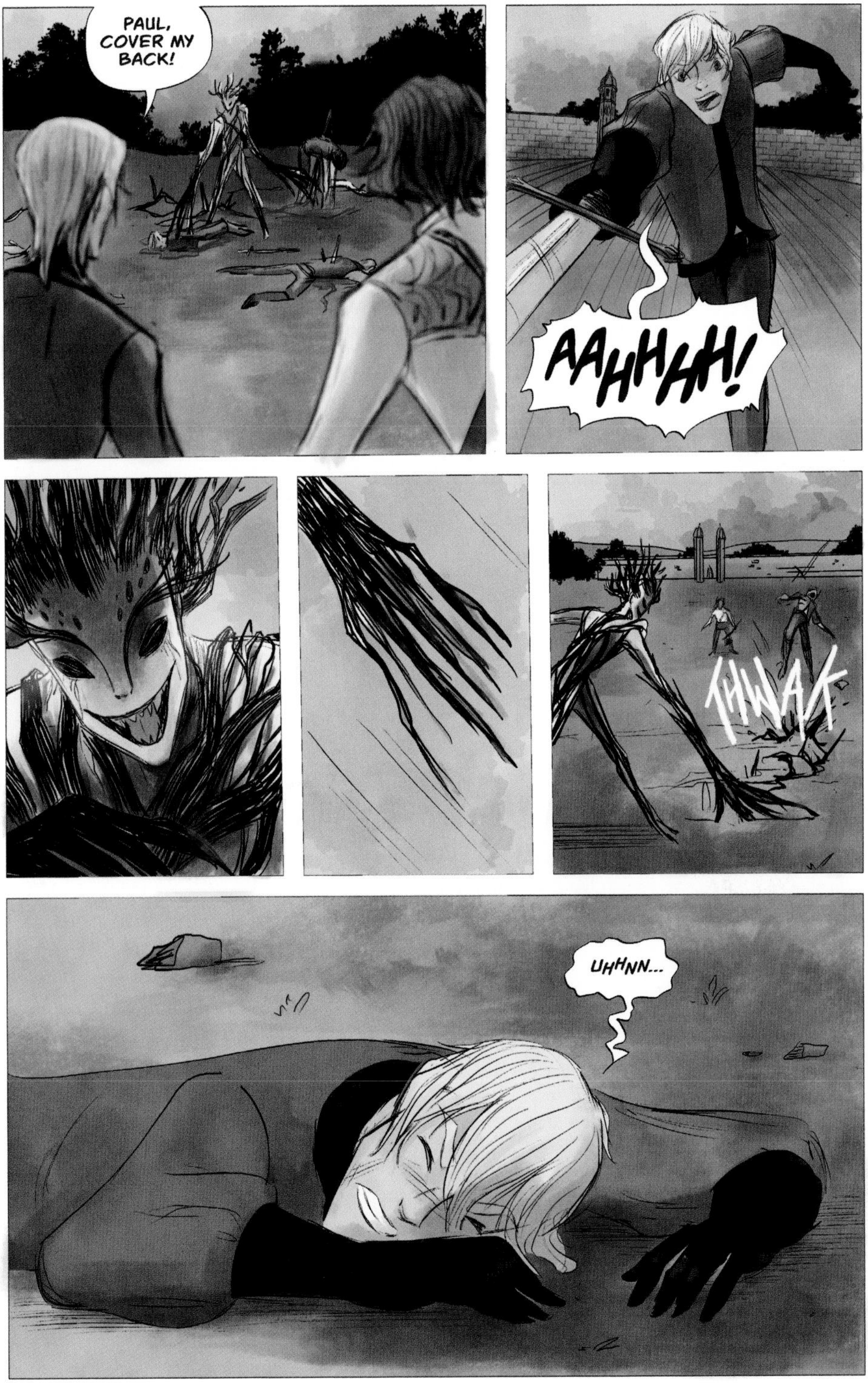
PAUL, COVER MY BACK!
AAHHHH!
THWAK
UHHNN...

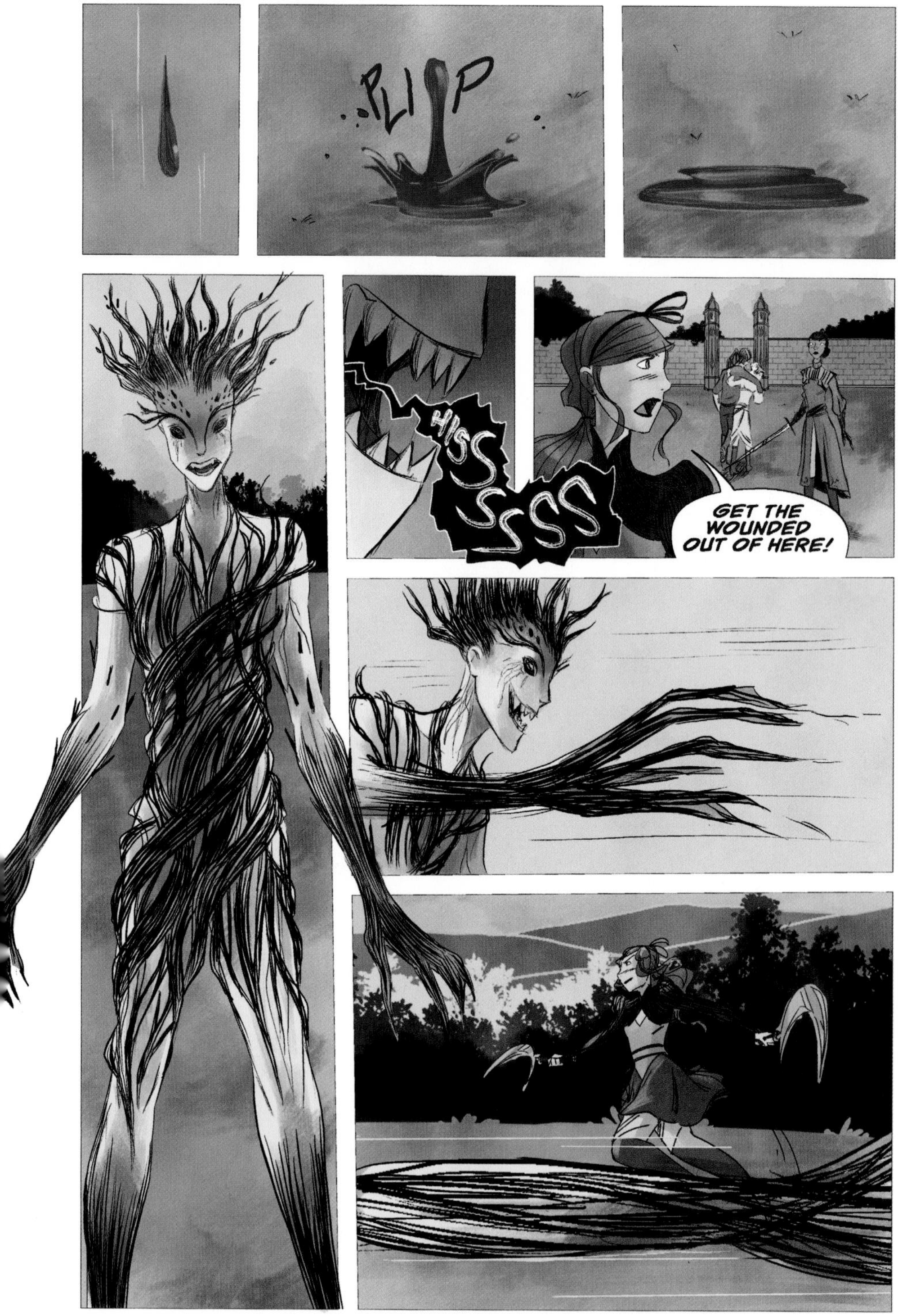
PLIP
HISSSSSS
GET THE WOUNDED OUT OF HERE!

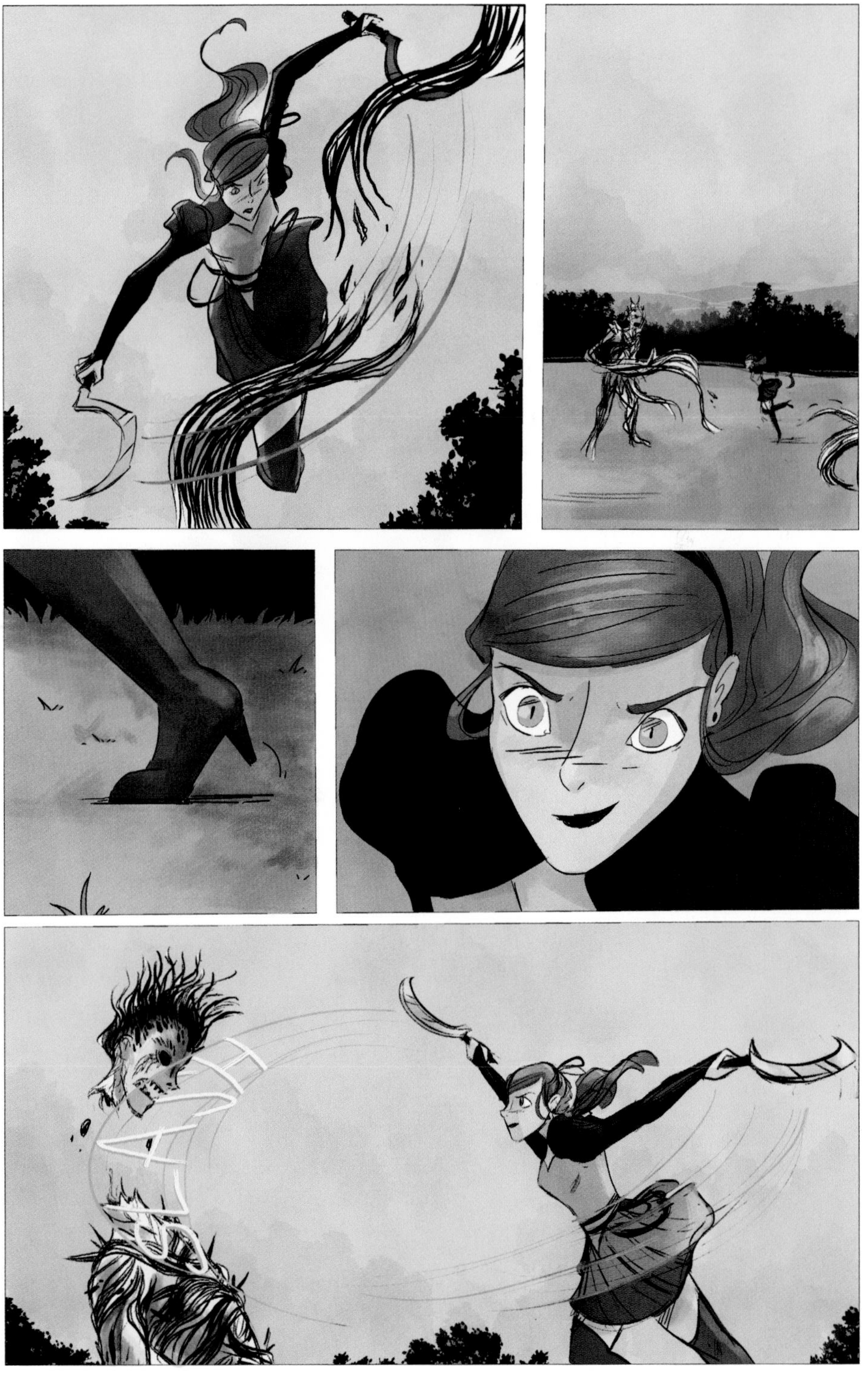
SLASH

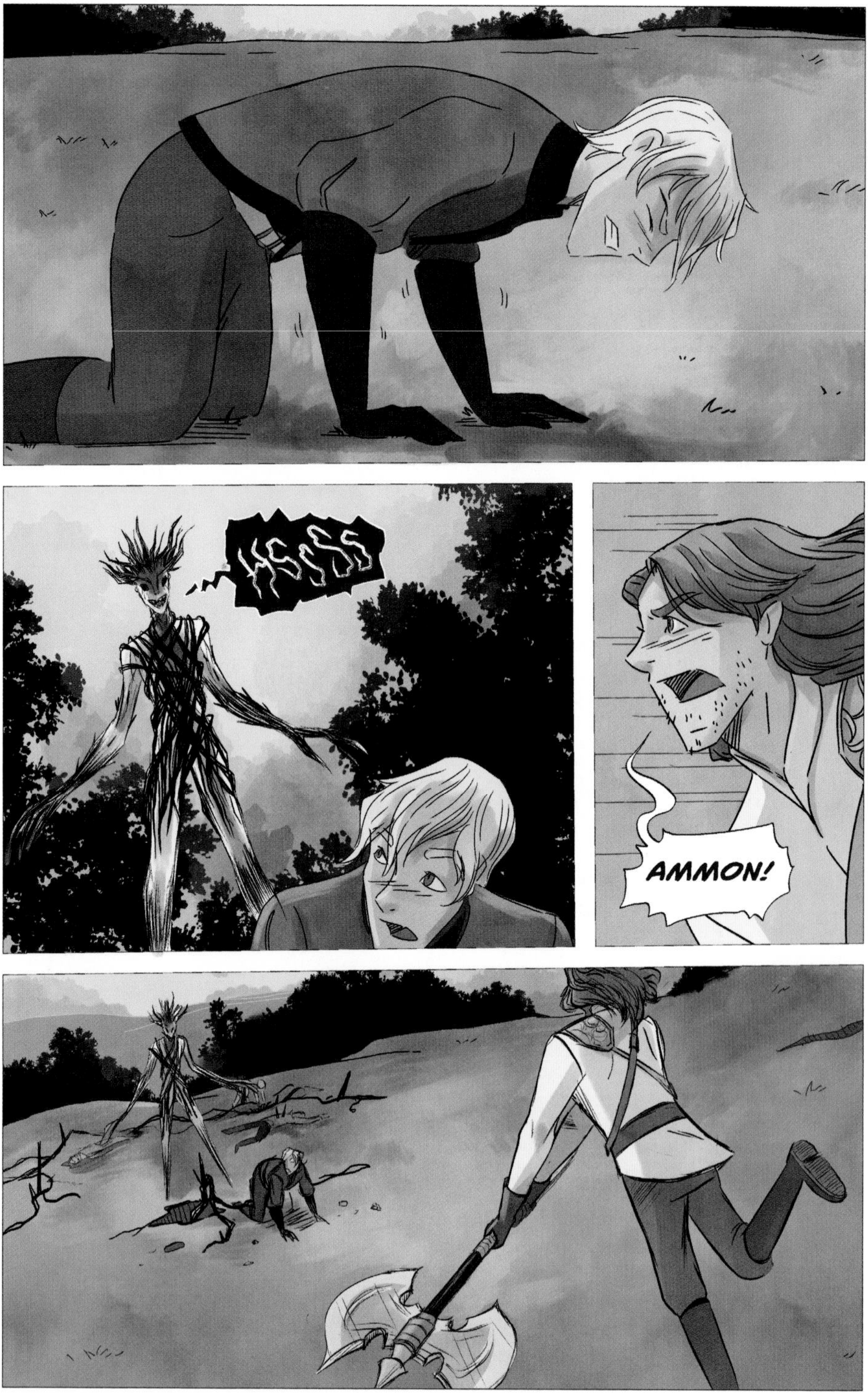
HSSSS
AMMON!

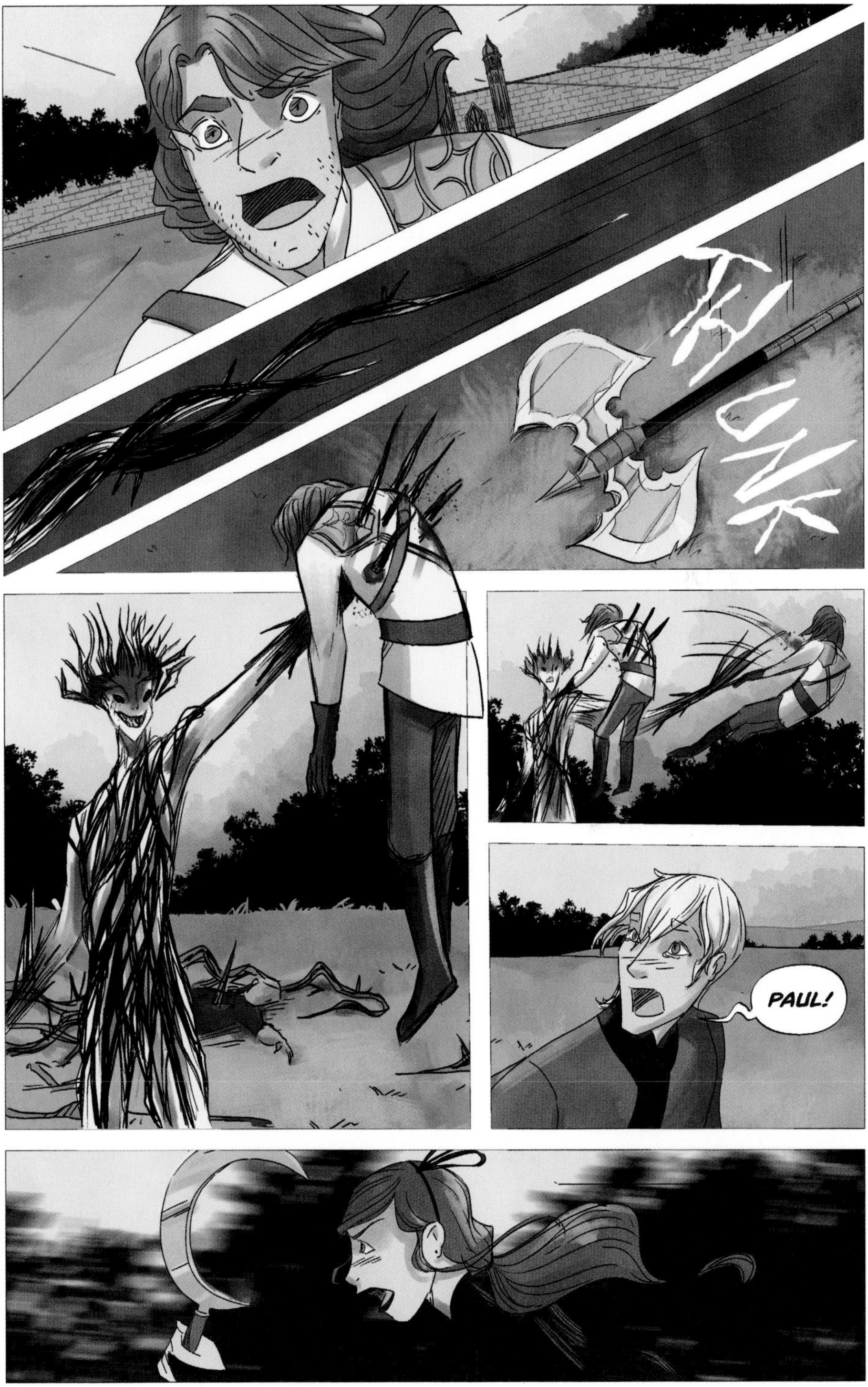
THUNK
PAUL!

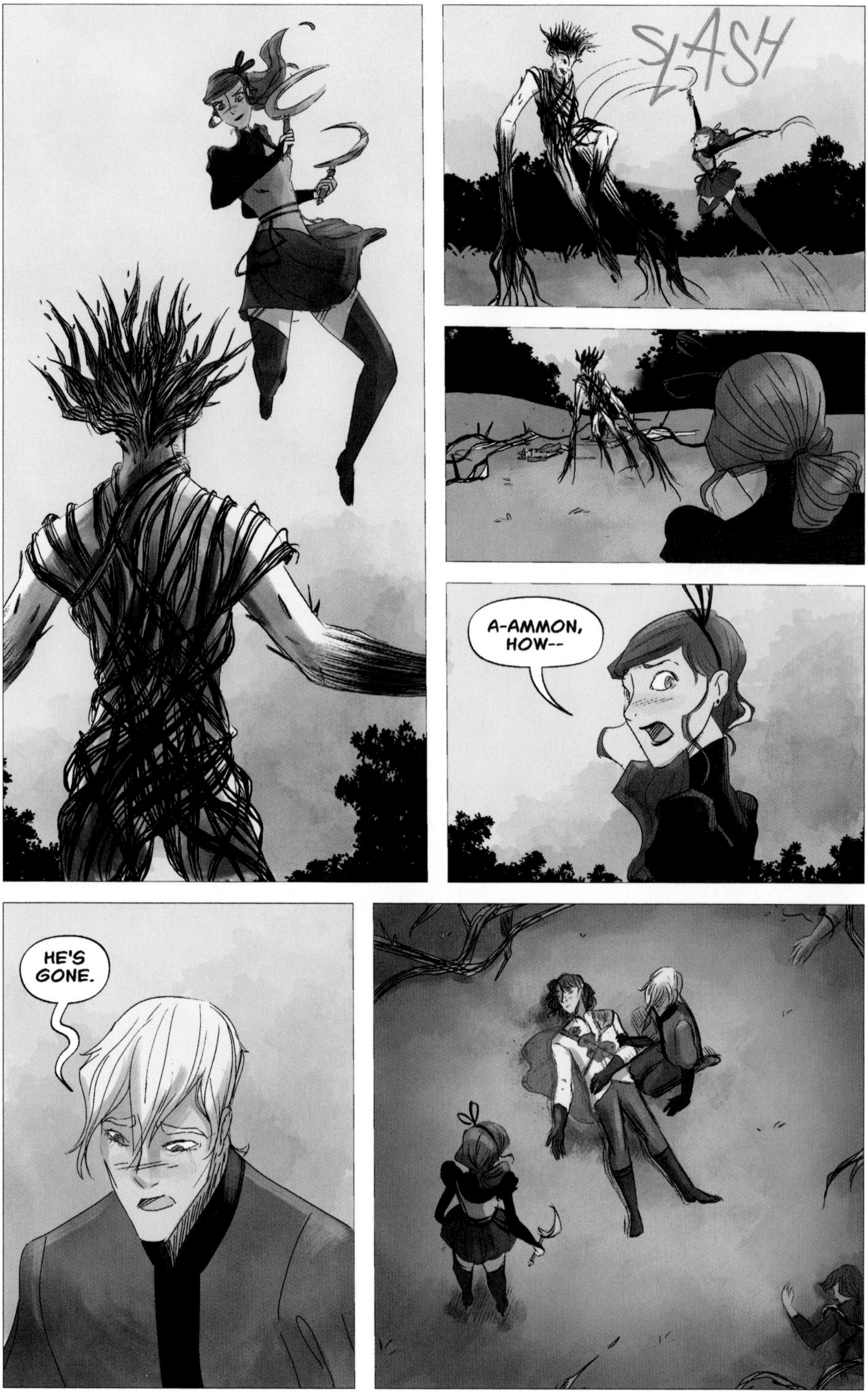
SLASH
A-AMMON, HOW--
HE'S GONE.

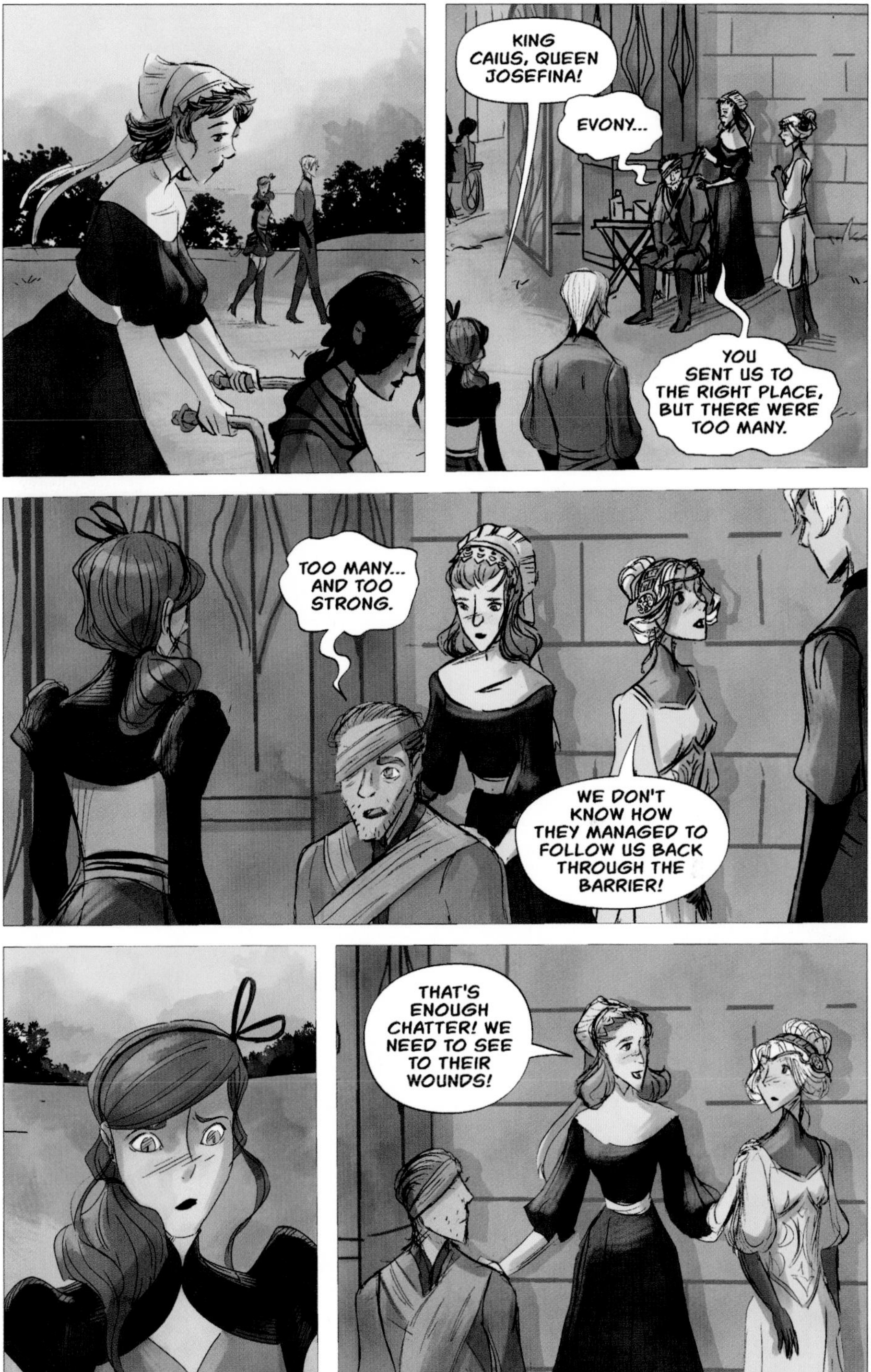
KING CAIUS, QUEEN JOSEFINA!
EVONY...
YOU SENT US TO THE RIGHT PLACE, BUT THERE WERE TOO MANY.
TOO MANY... AND TOO STRONG.
WE DON'T KNOW HOW THEY MANAGED TO FOLLOW US BACK THROUGH THE BARRIER!
THAT'S ENOUGH CHATTER! WE NEED TO SEE TO THEIR WOUNDS!

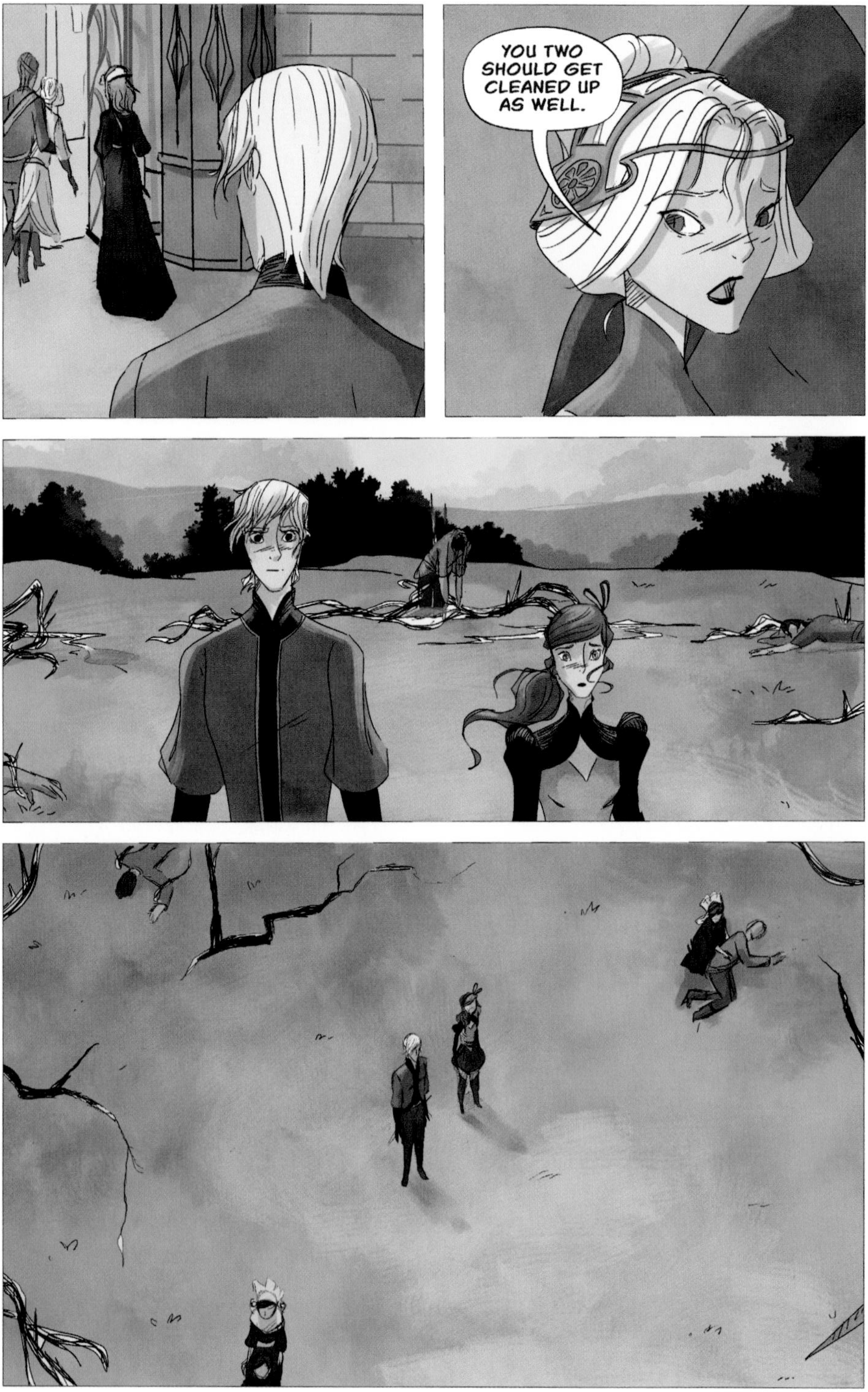
YOU TWO SHOULD GET CLEANED UP AS WELL.

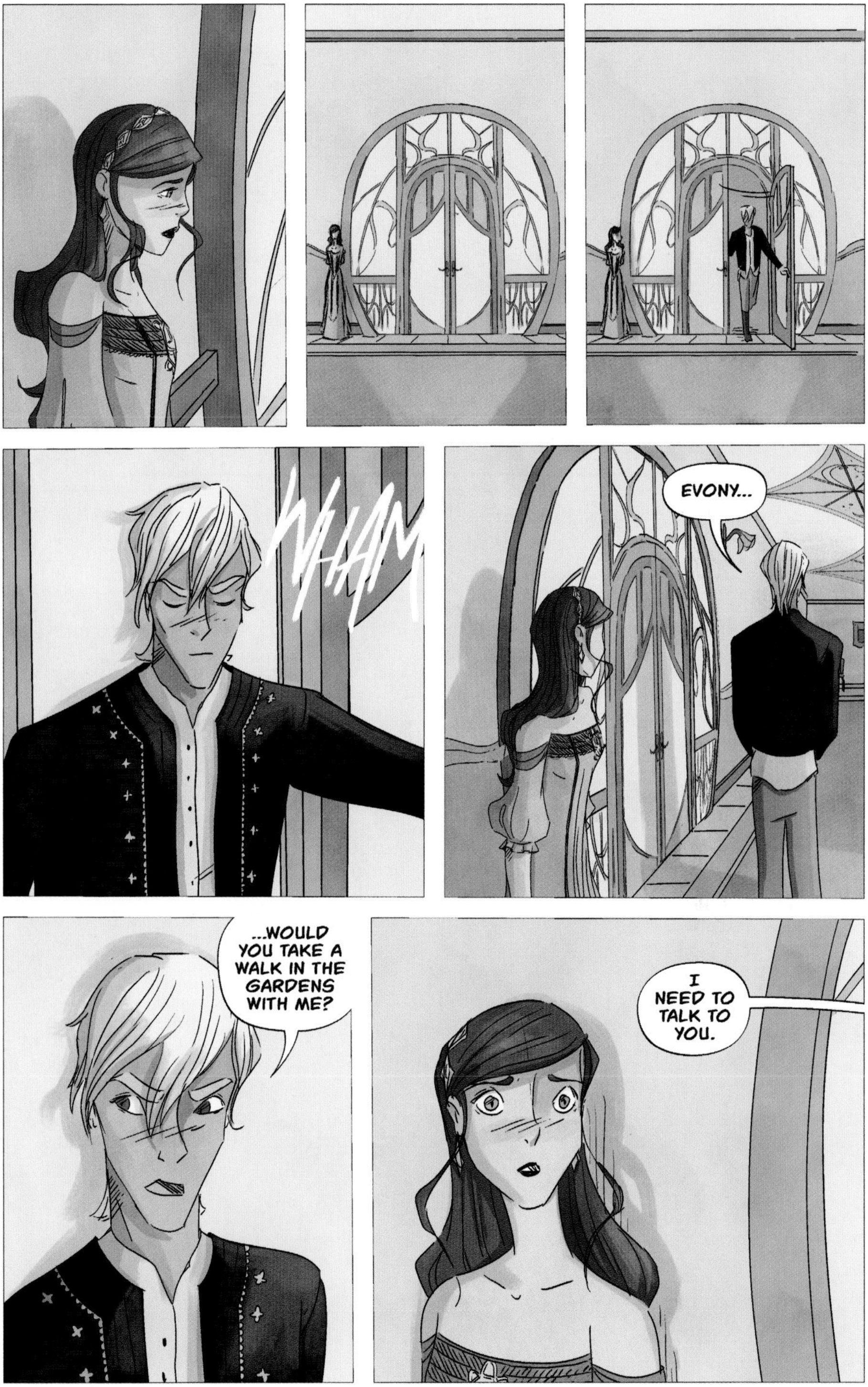
WHAM
EVONY...
...WOULD YOU TAKE A WALK IN THE GARDENS WITH ME?
I NEED TO TALK TO YOU.

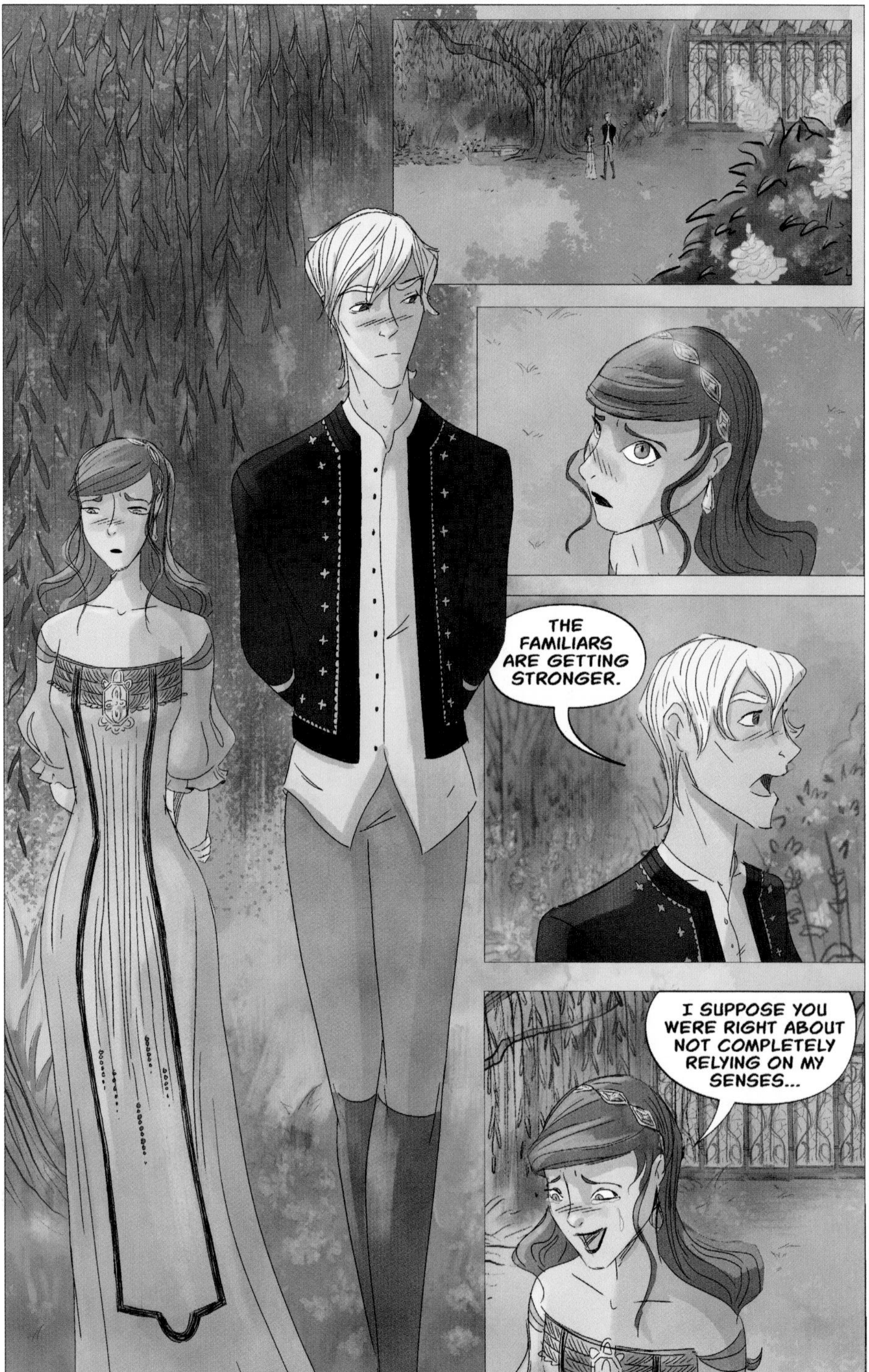
THE FAMILIARS ARE GETTING STRONGER.
I SUPPOSE YOU WERE RIGHT ABOUT NOT COMPLETELY RELYING ON MY SENSES...

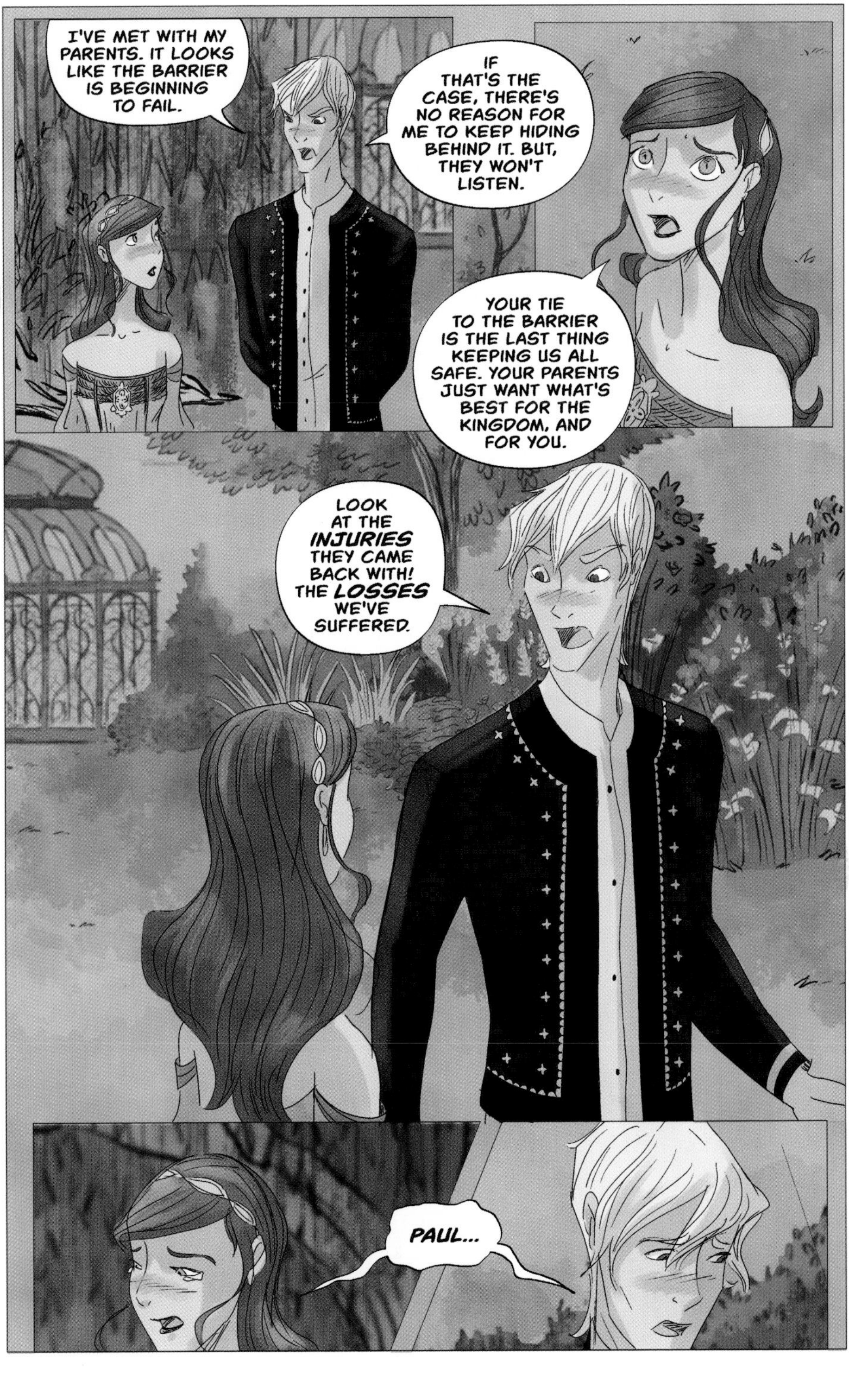
I'VE MET WITH MY PARENTS. IT LOOKS LIKE THE BARRIER IS BEGINNING TO FAIL.
IF THAT'S THE CASE, THERE'S NO REASON FOR ME TO KEEP HIDING BEHIND IT. BUT, THEY WON'T LISTEN.
YOUR TIE TO THE BARRIER IS THE LAST THING KEEPING US ALL SAFE. YOUR PARENTS JUST WANT WHAT'S BEST FOR THE KINGDOM, AND FOR YOU.
LOOK AT THE *INJURIES* THEY CAME BACK WITH! THE *LOSSES* WE'VE SUFFERED.
PAUL...

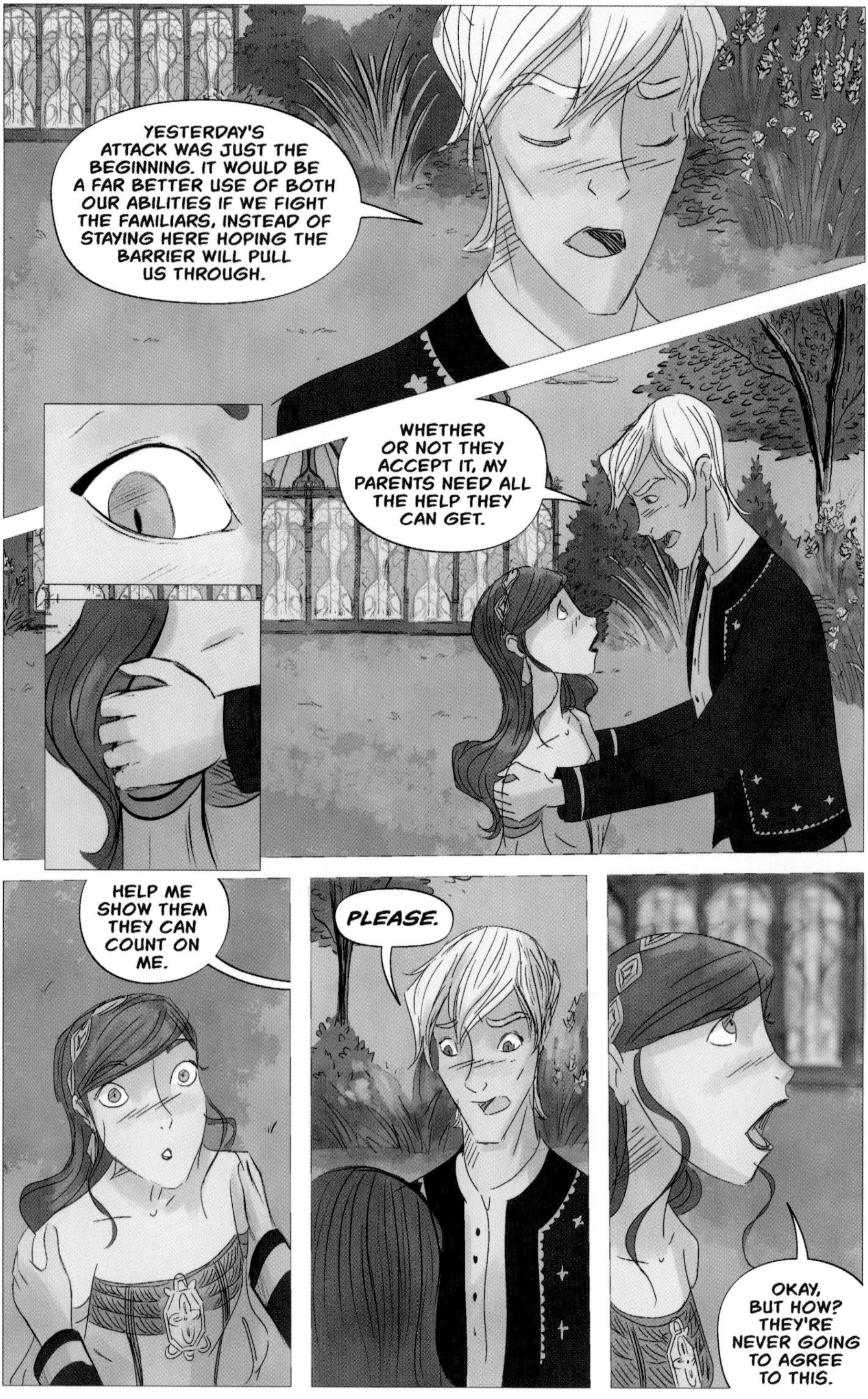
YESTERDAY'S ATTACK WAS JUST THE BEGINNING. IT WOULD BE A FAR BETTER USE OF BOTH OUR ABILITIES IF WE FIGHT THE FAMILIARS, INSTEAD OF STAYING HERE HOPING THE BARRIER WILL PULL US THROUGH.
WHETHER OR NOT THEY ACCEPT IT, MY PARENTS NEED ALL THE HELP THEY CAN GET.
HELP ME SHOW THEM THEY CAN COUNT ON ME.
PLEASE.
OKAY, BUT HOW? THEY'RE NEVER GOING TO AGREE TO THIS.

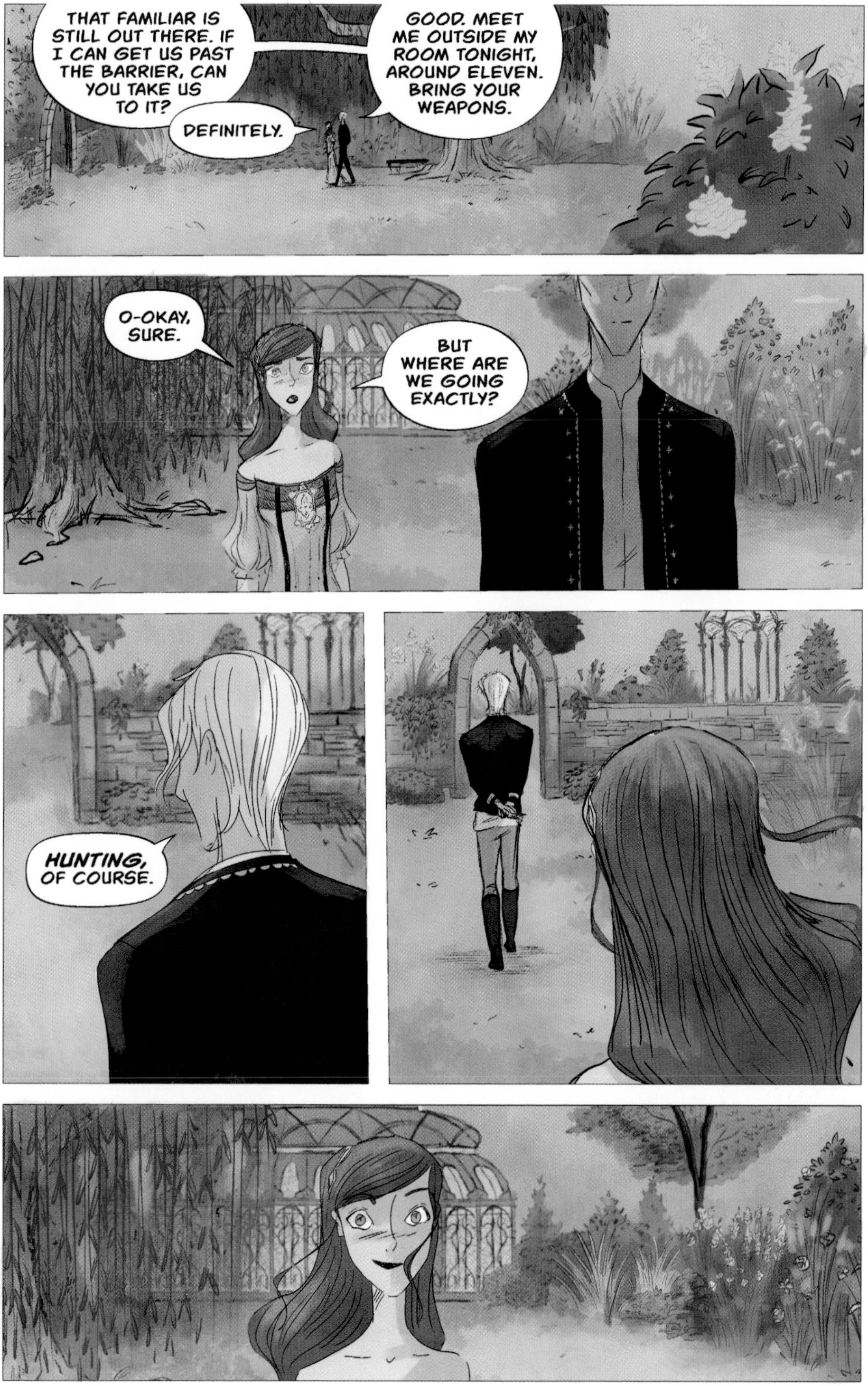
THAT FAMILIAR IS STILL OUT THERE. IF I CAN GET US PAST THE BARRIER, CAN YOU TAKE US TO IT?
DEFINITELY.
GOOD. MEET ME OUTSIDE MY ROOM TONIGHT, AROUND ELEVEN. BRING YOUR WEAPONS.
O-OKAY, SURE.
BUT WHERE ARE WE GOING EXACTLY?
HUNTING, OF COURSE.

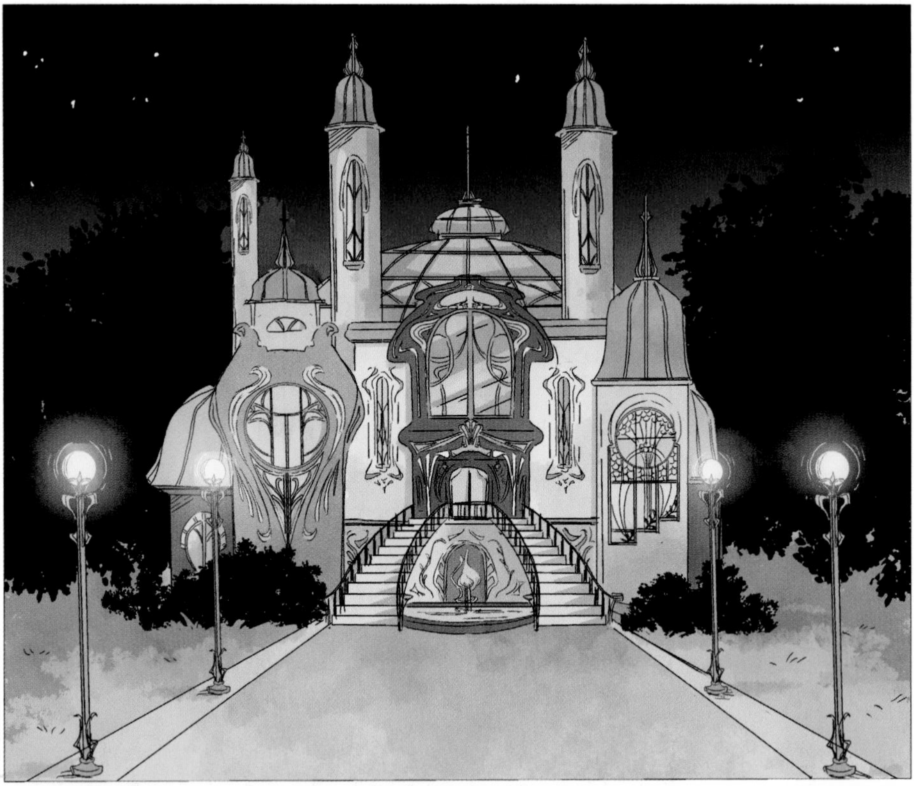

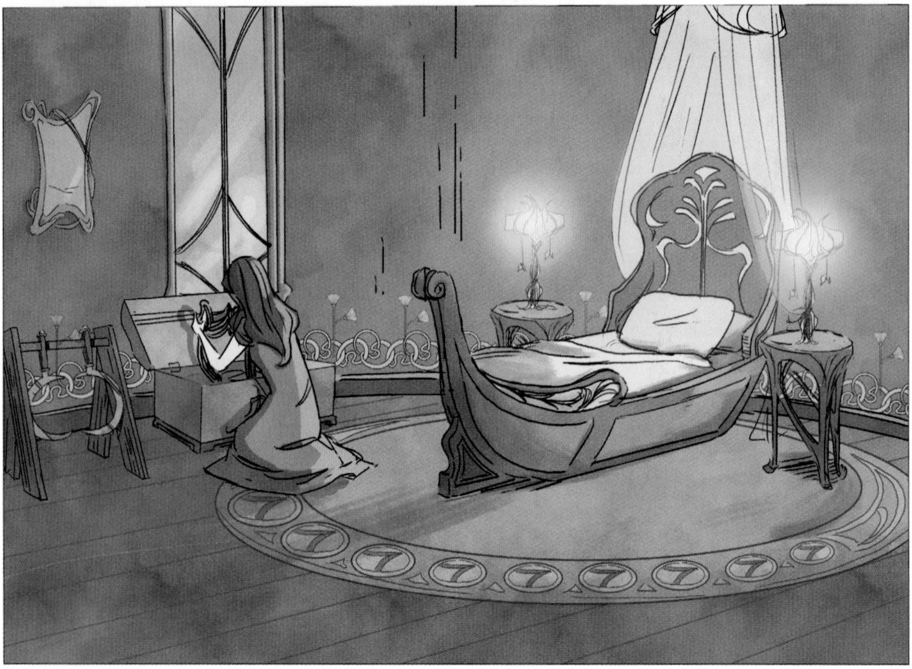

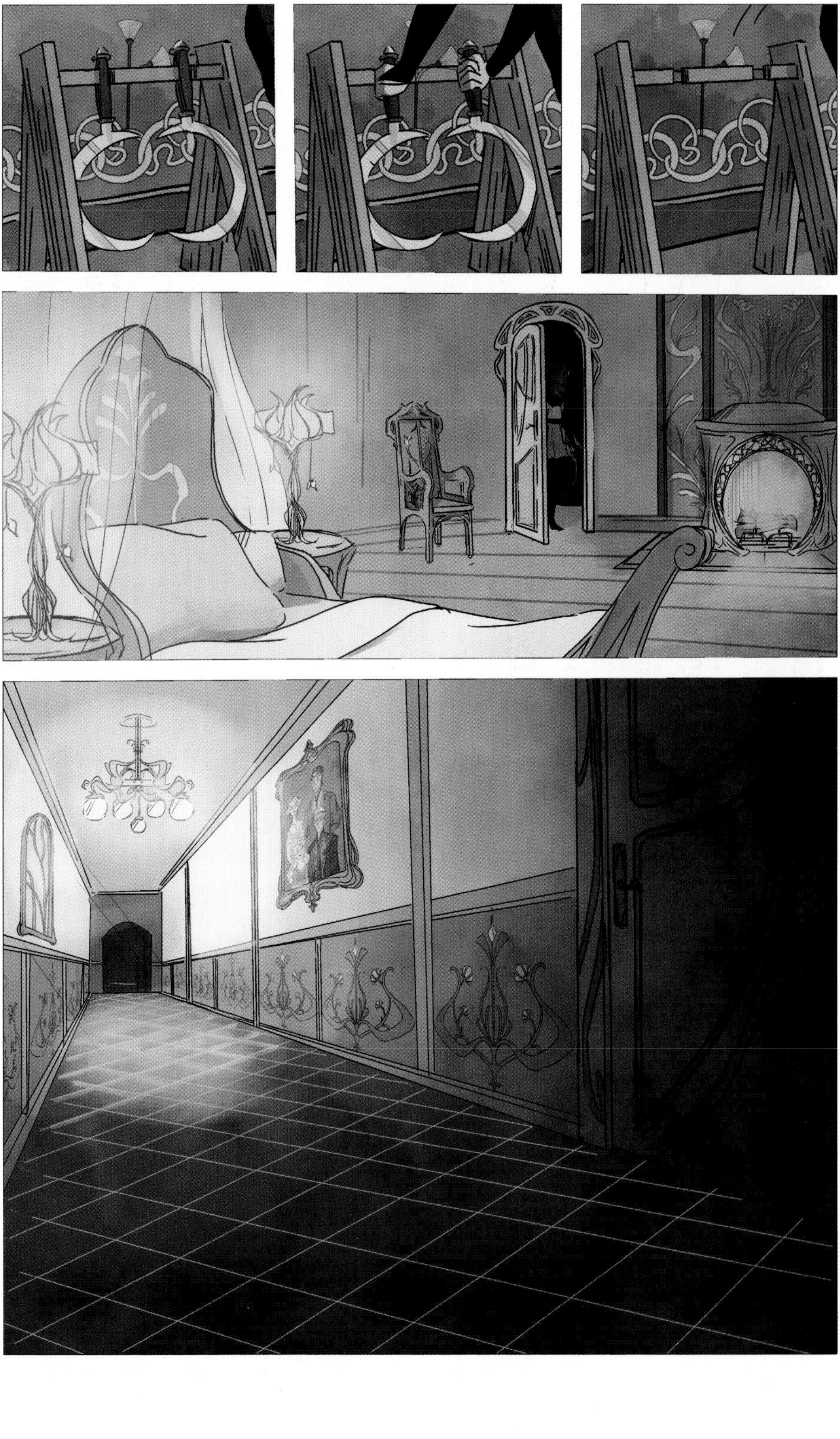

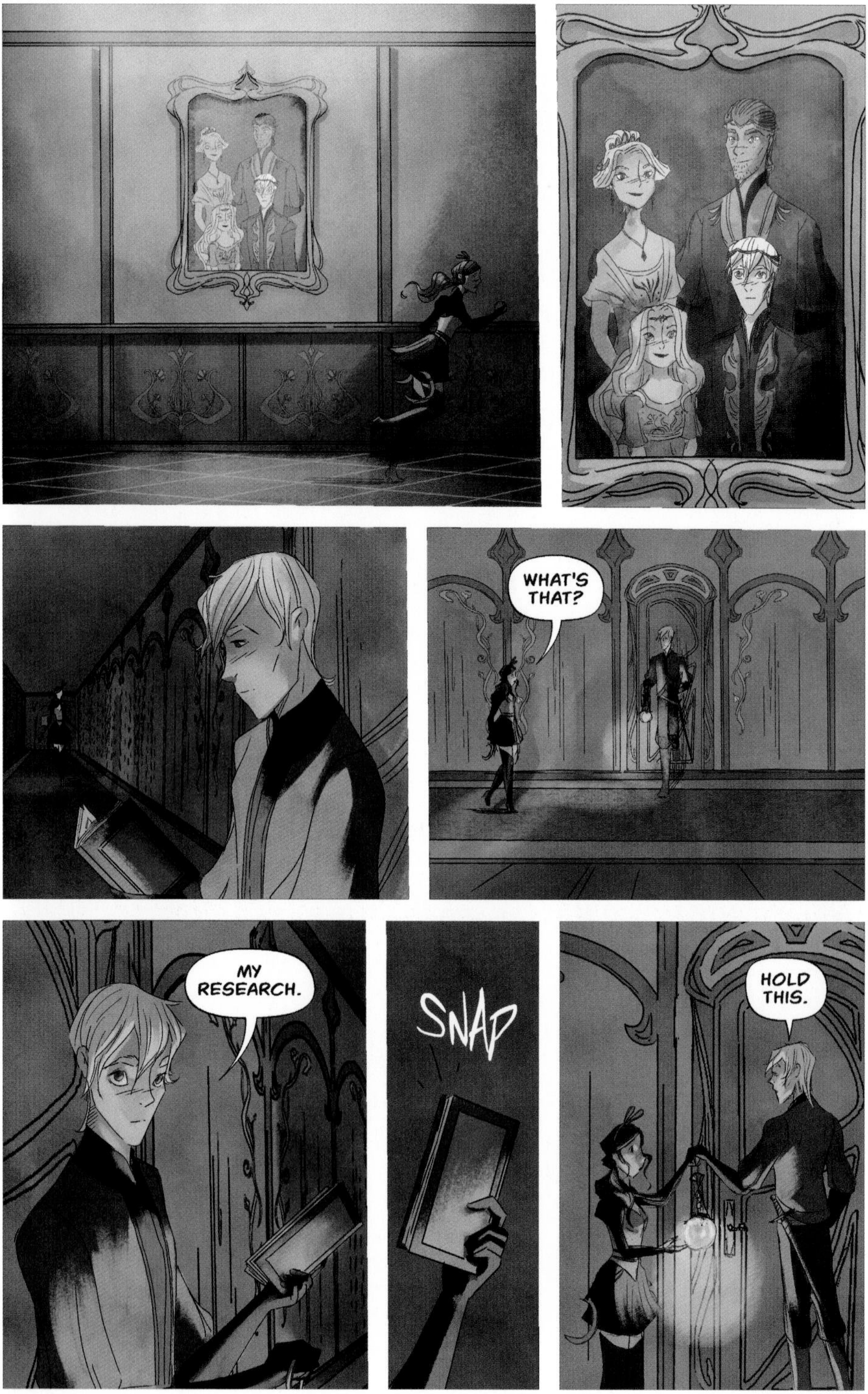
WHAT'S THAT?
MY RESEARCH.
SNAP
HOLD THIS.

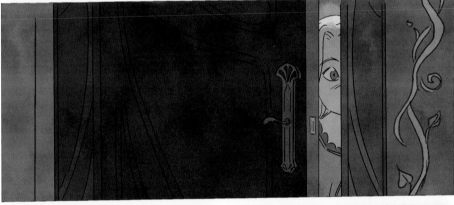

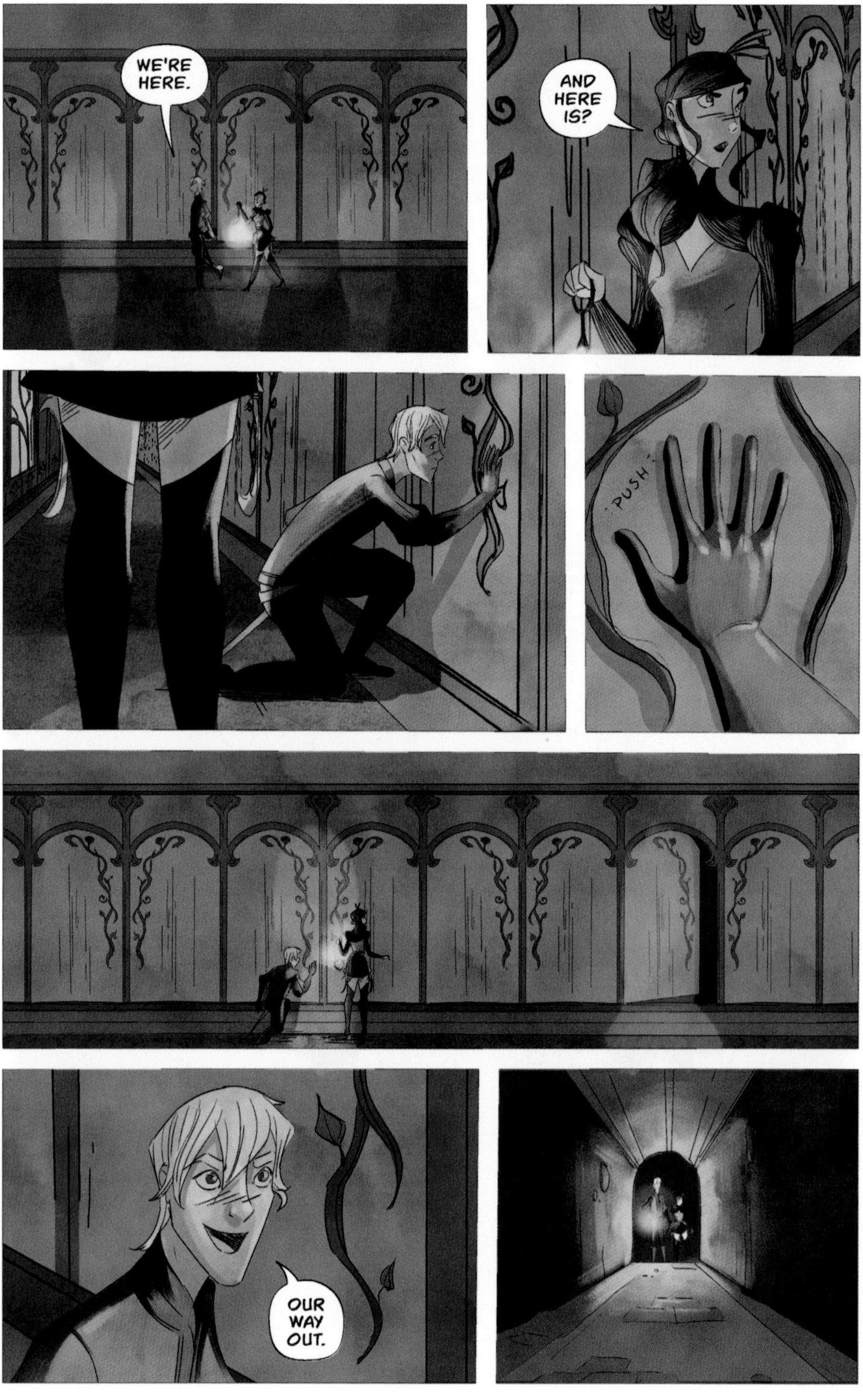
WE'RE HERE.
AND HERE IS?
PUSH
OUR WAY OUT.

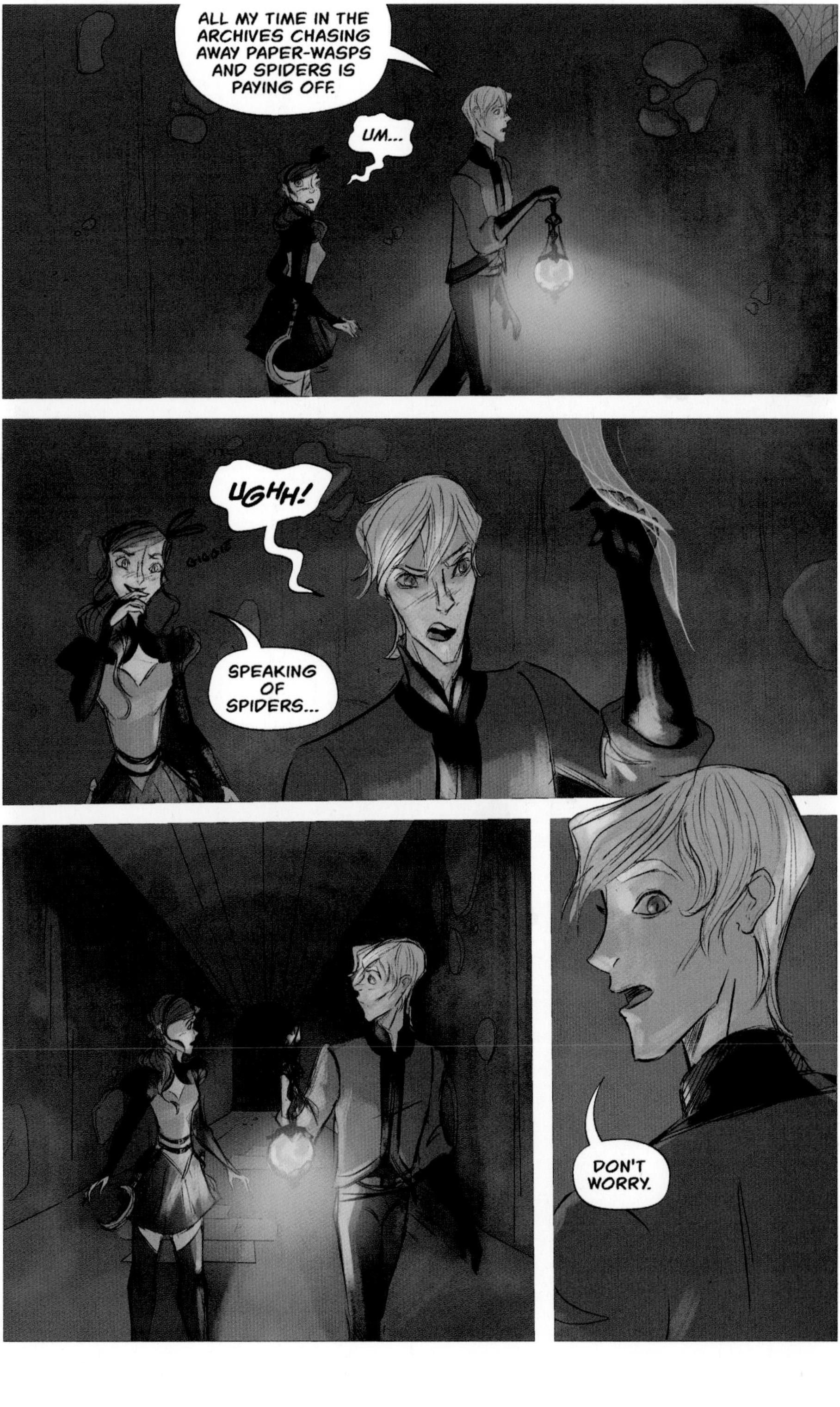
ALL MY TIME IN THE ARCHIVES CHASING AWAY PAPER-WASPS AND SPIDERS IS PAYING OFF.
UM...
UGHH!
GIGGLE
SPEAKING OF SPIDERS...
DON'T WORRY.

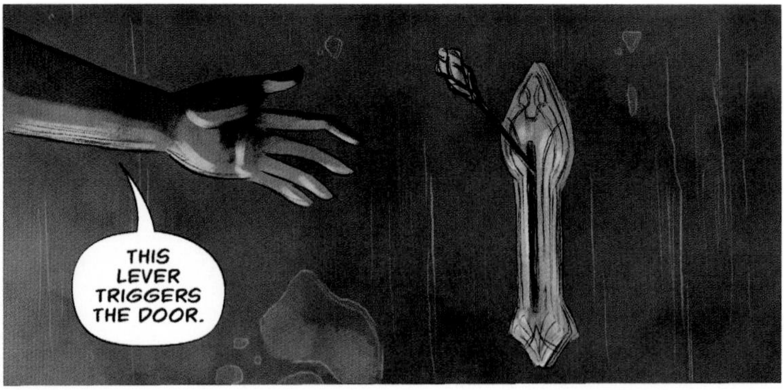
THIS LEVER TRIGGERS THE DOOR.

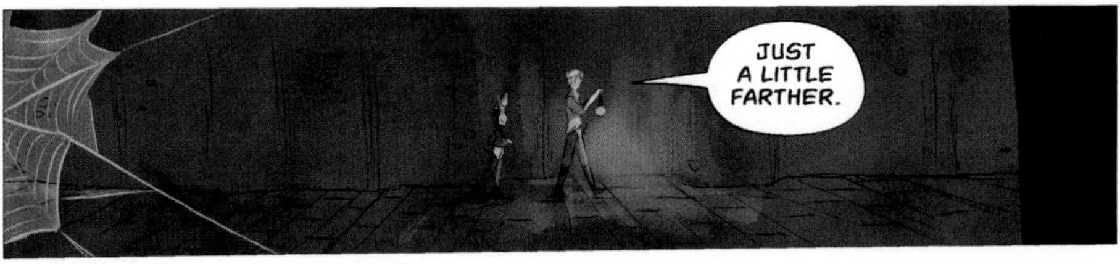
JUST A LITTLE FARTHER.

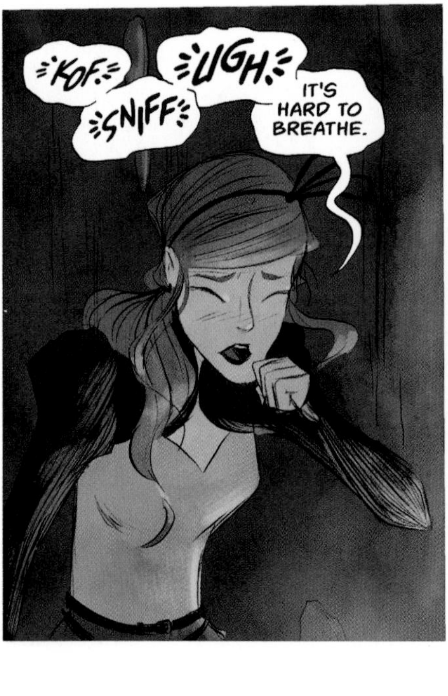
KOF
SNIFF
UGH
IT'S HARD TO BREATHE.

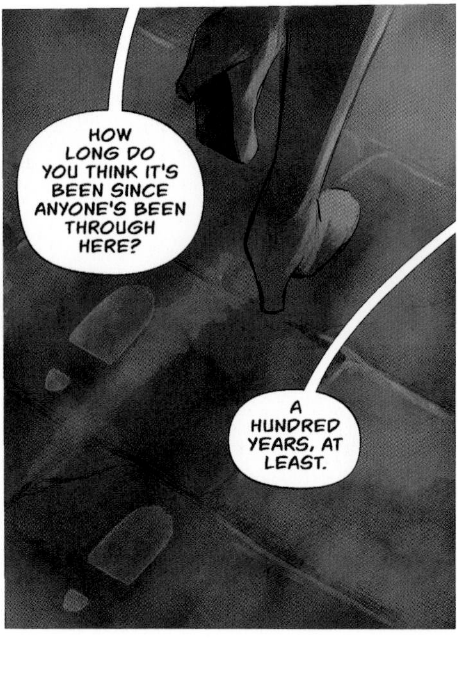
HOW LONG DO YOU THINK IT'S BEEN SINCE ANYONE'S BEEN THROUGH HERE?
A HUNDRED YEARS, AT LEAST.

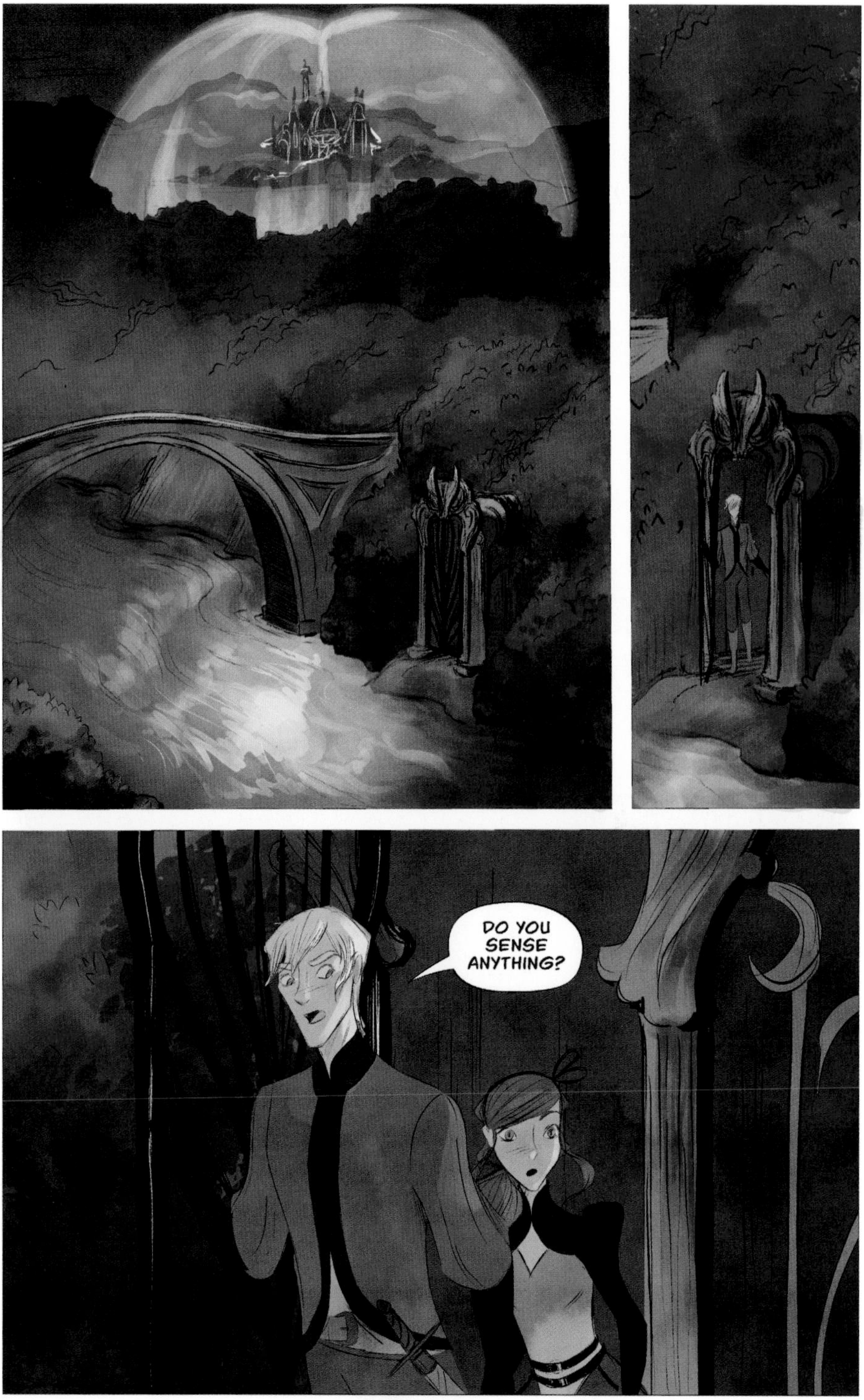
DO YOU SENSE ANYTHING?

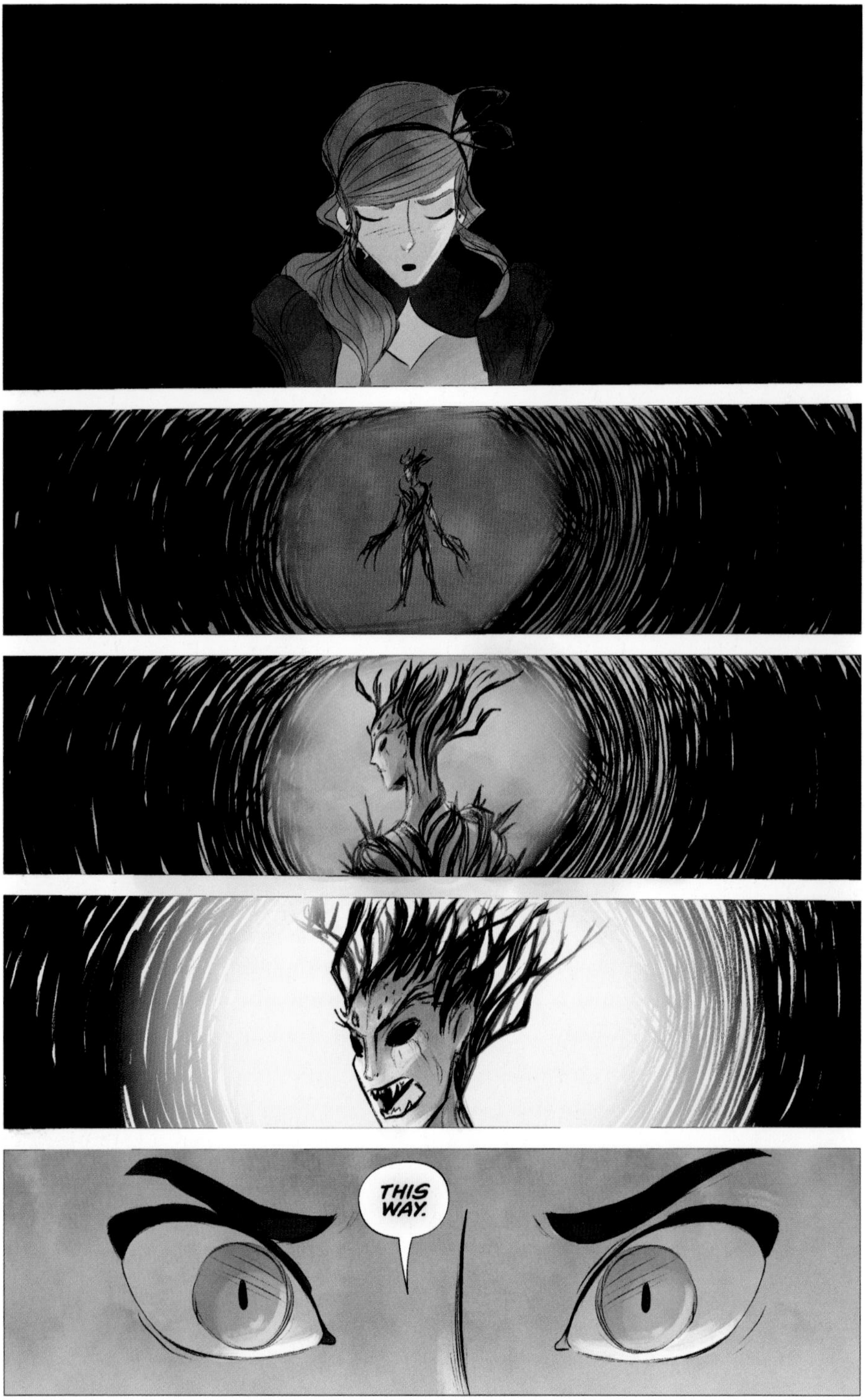
THIS WAY.

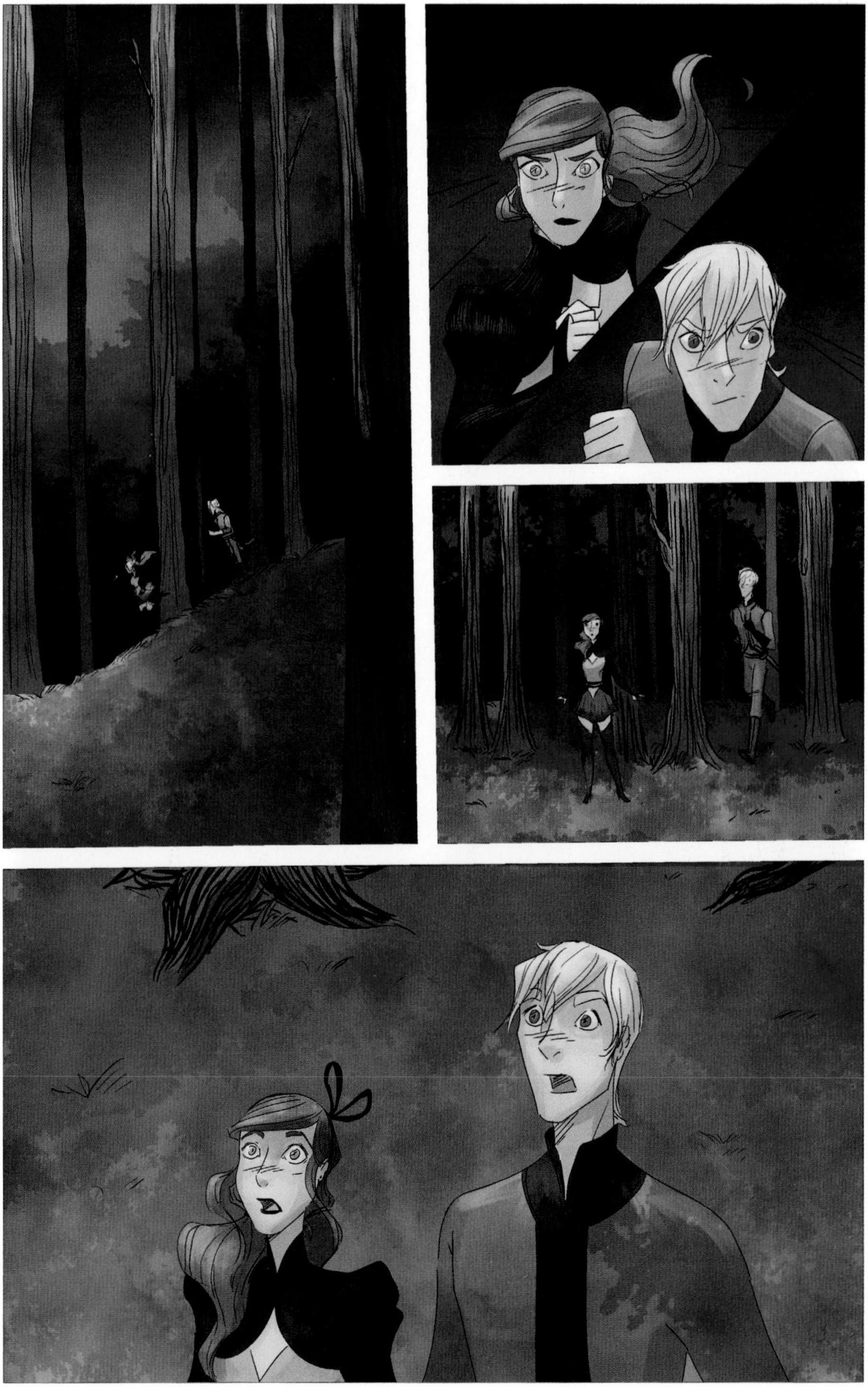

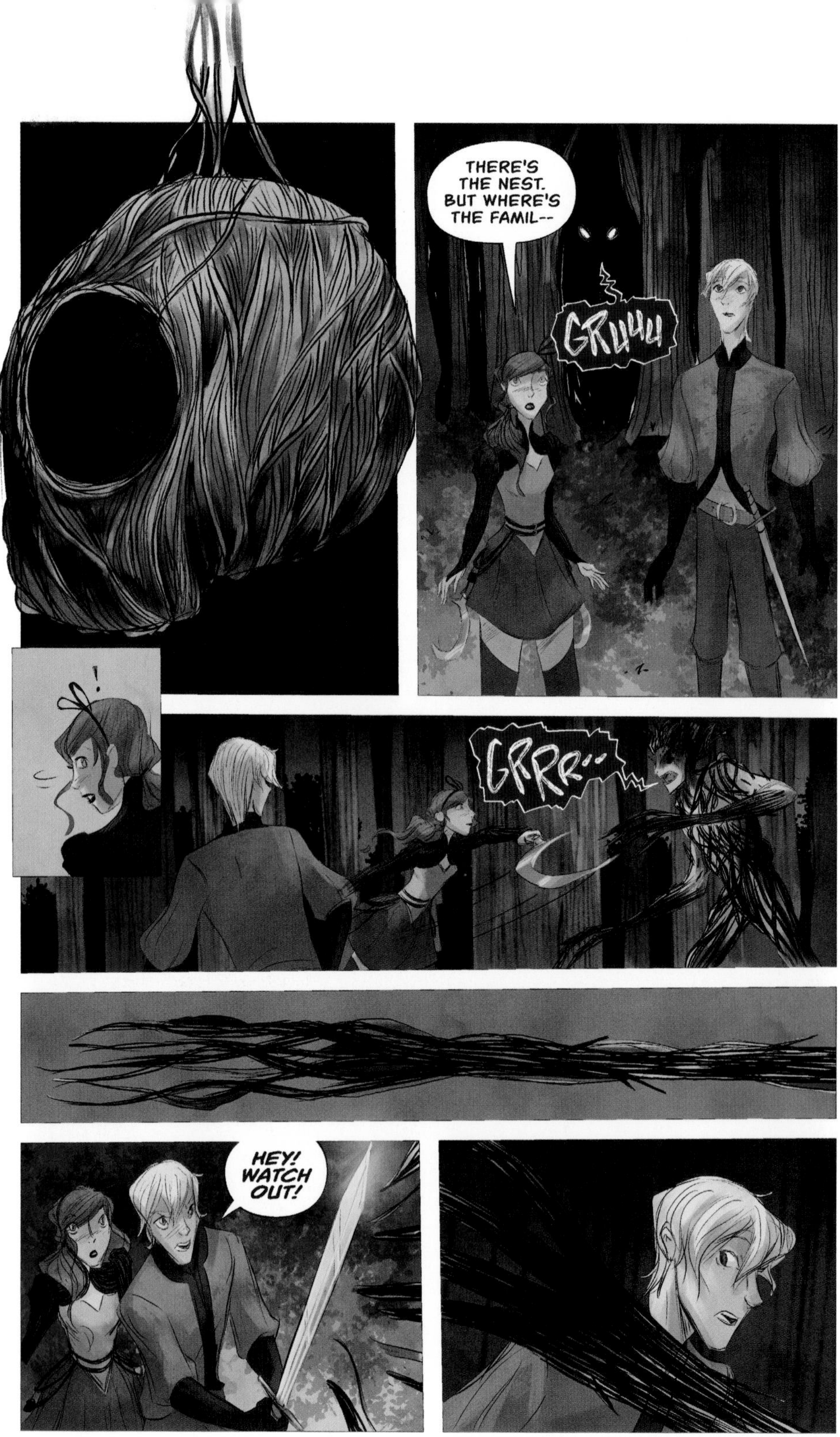
THERE'S THE NEST. BUT WHERE'S THE FAMIL--
GRUUU
!
GRRR..
HEY! WATCH OUT!

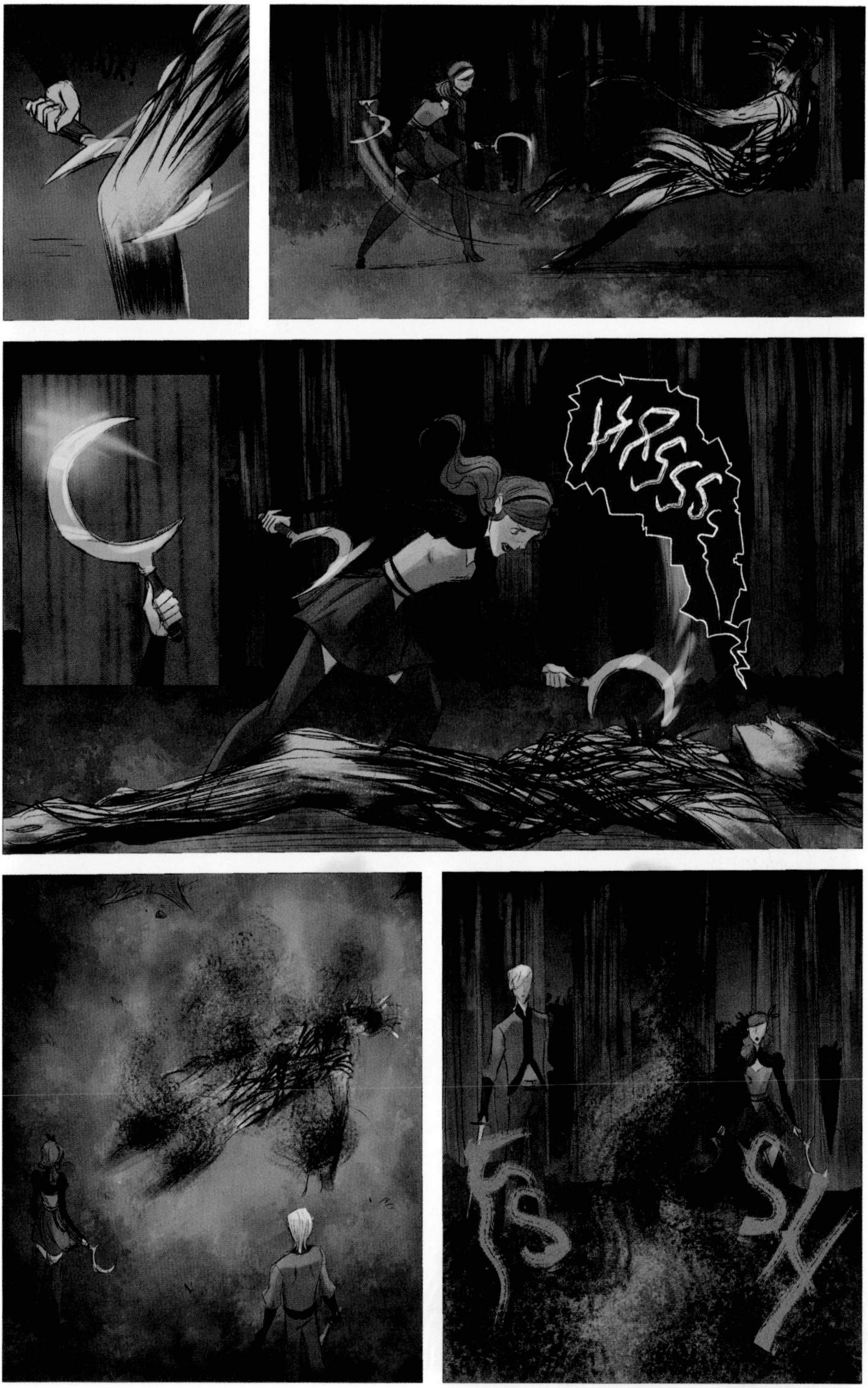
HISSSS

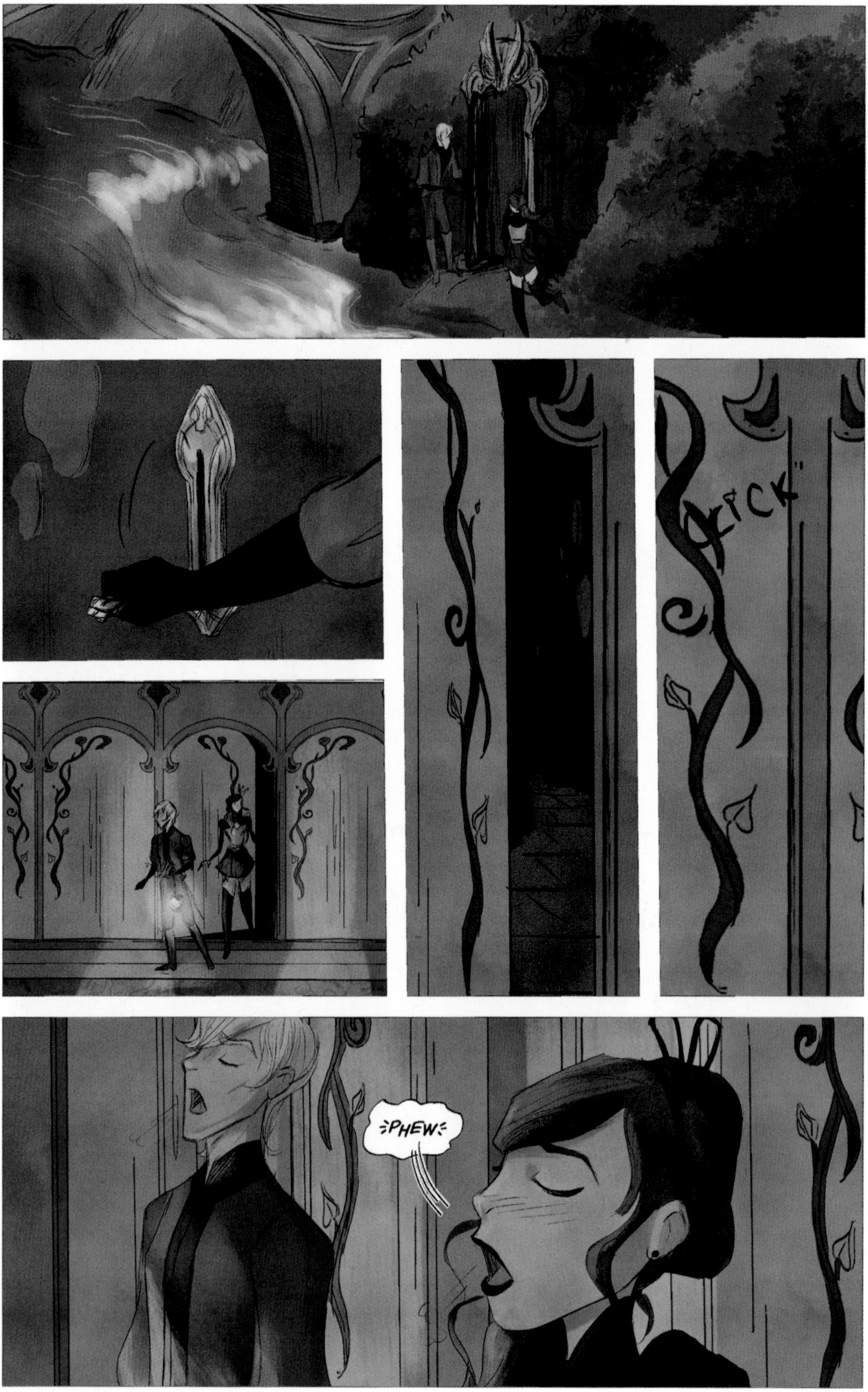
CLICK
PHEW

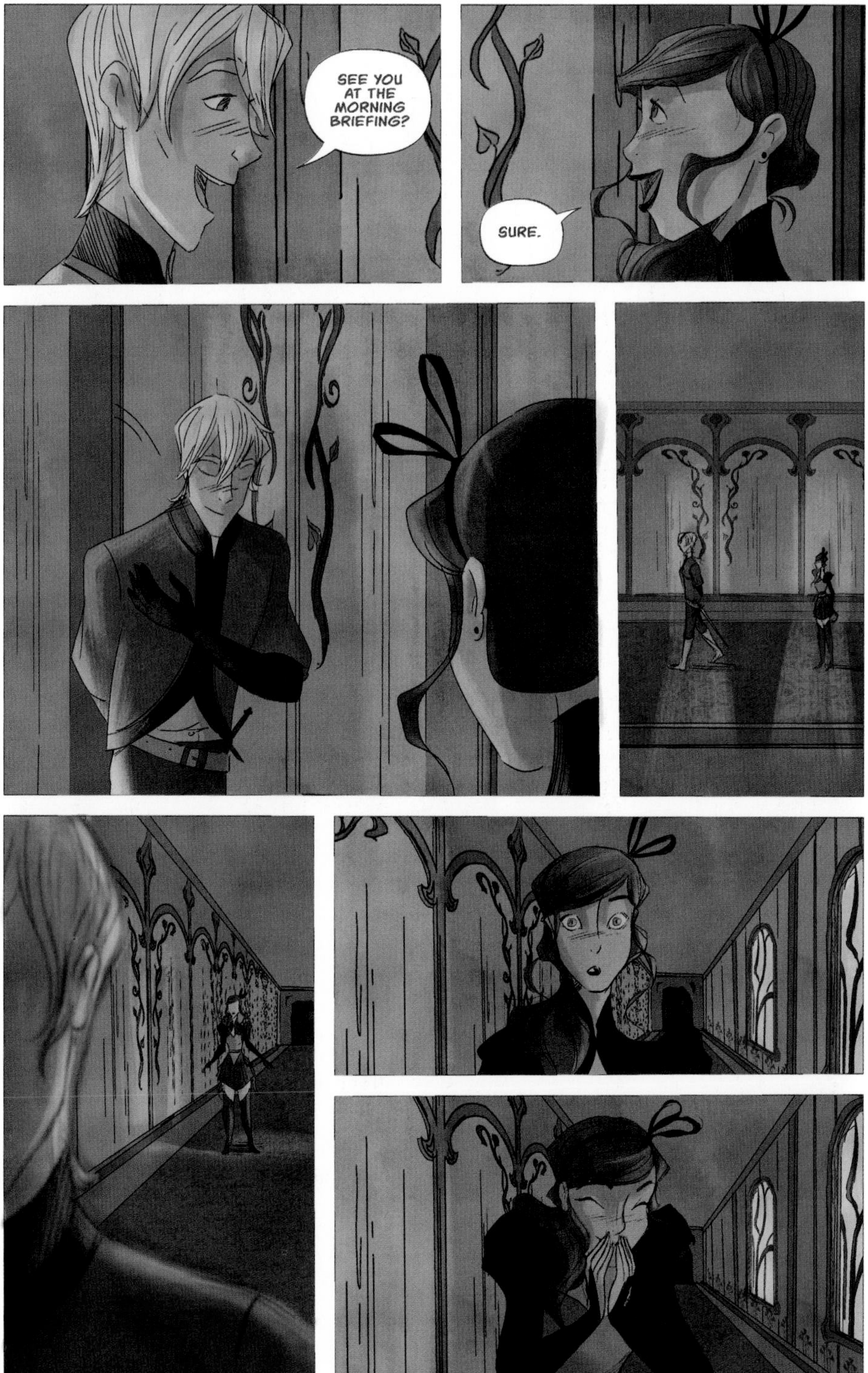
SEE YOU AT THE MORNING BRIEFING?
SURE.

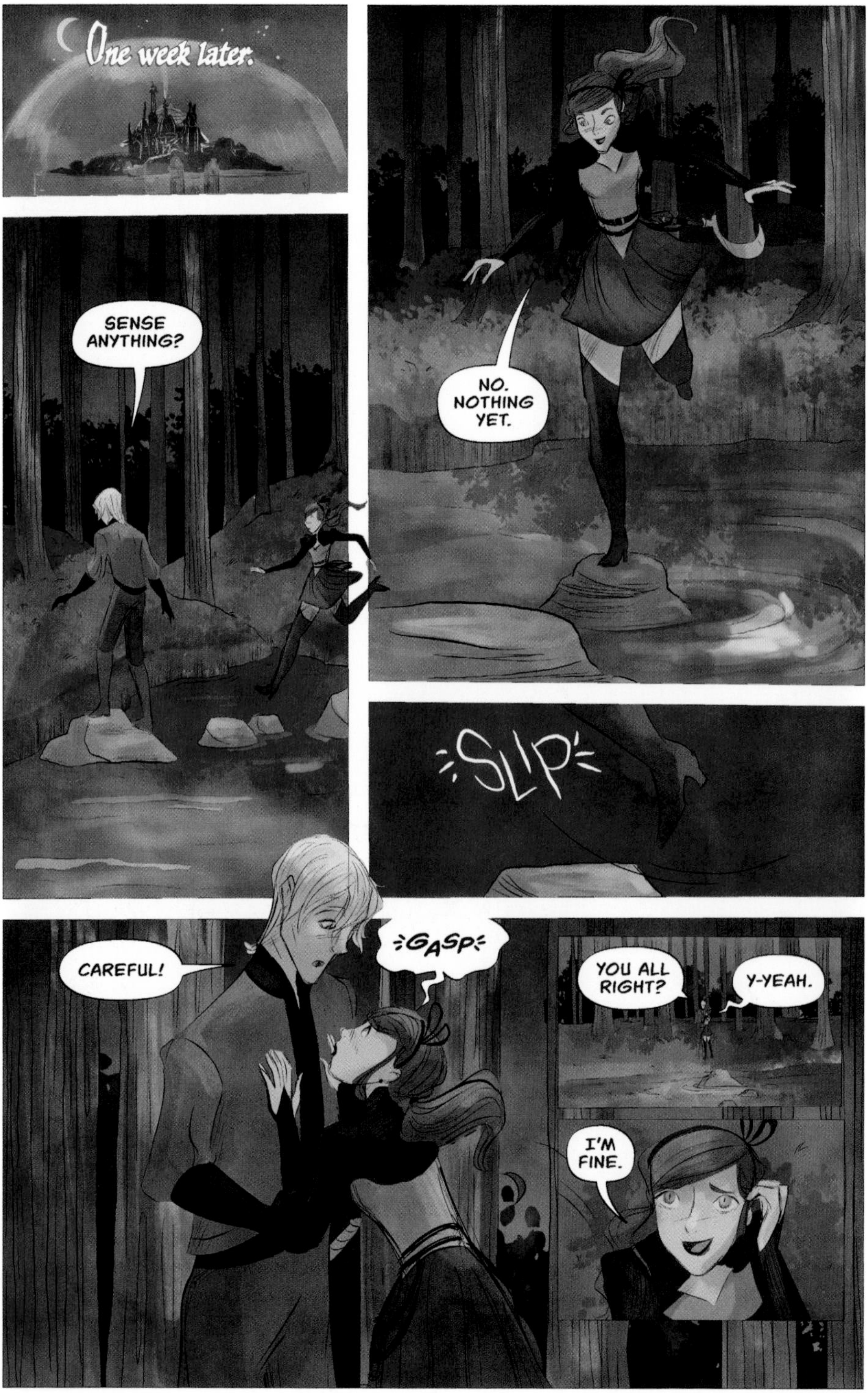

One week later.
SENSE ANYTHING?
NO. NOTHING YET.
SLIP
CAREFUL!
GASP
YOU ALL RIGHT?
Y-YEAH.
I'M FINE.

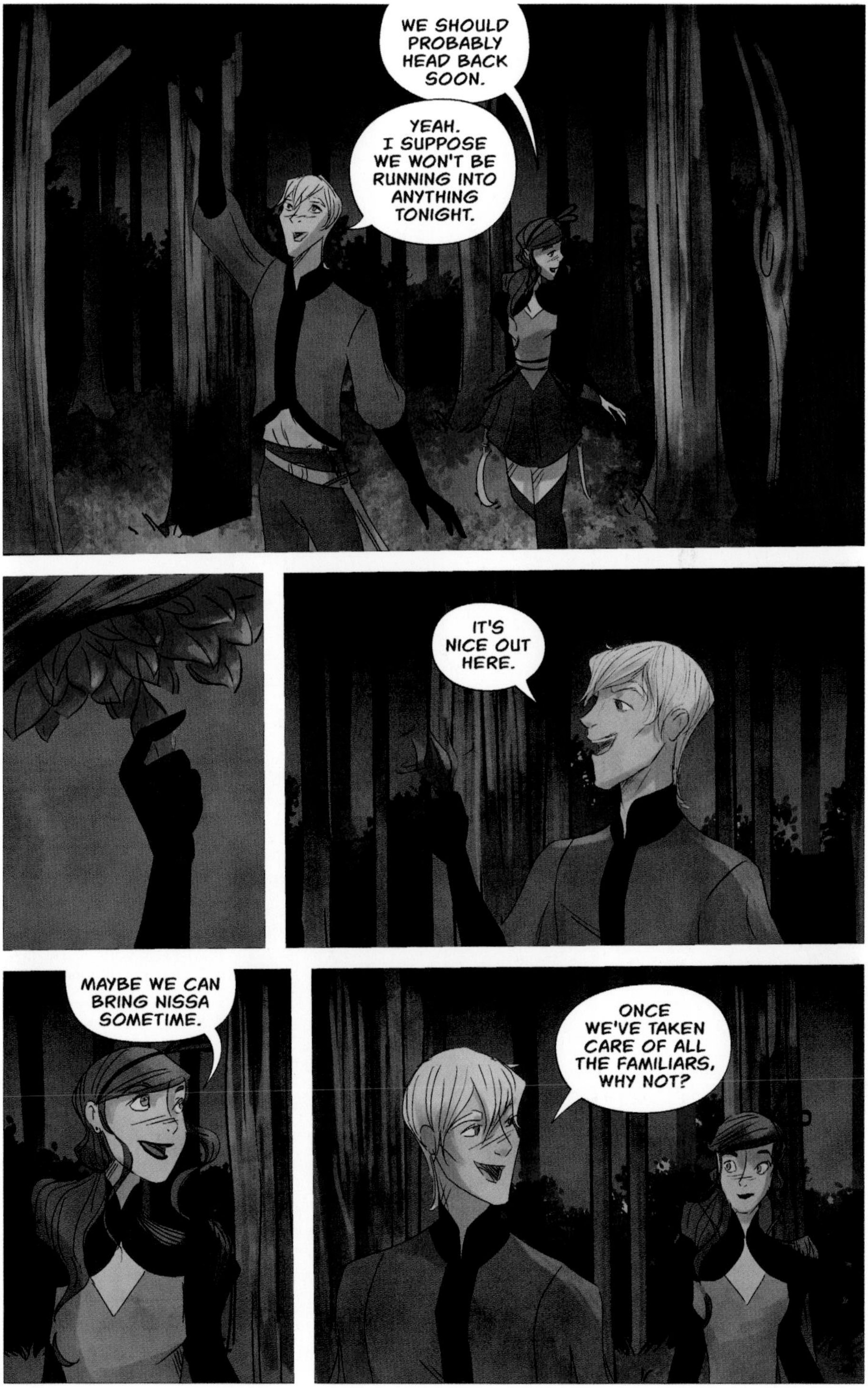
WE SHOULD PROBABLY HEAD BACK SOON.
YEAH. I SUPPOSE WE WON'T BE RUNNING INTO ANYTHING TONIGHT.
IT'S NICE OUT HERE.
MAYBE WE CAN BRING NISSA SOMETIME.
ONCE WE'VE TAKEN CARE OF ALL THE FAMILIARS, WHY NOT?

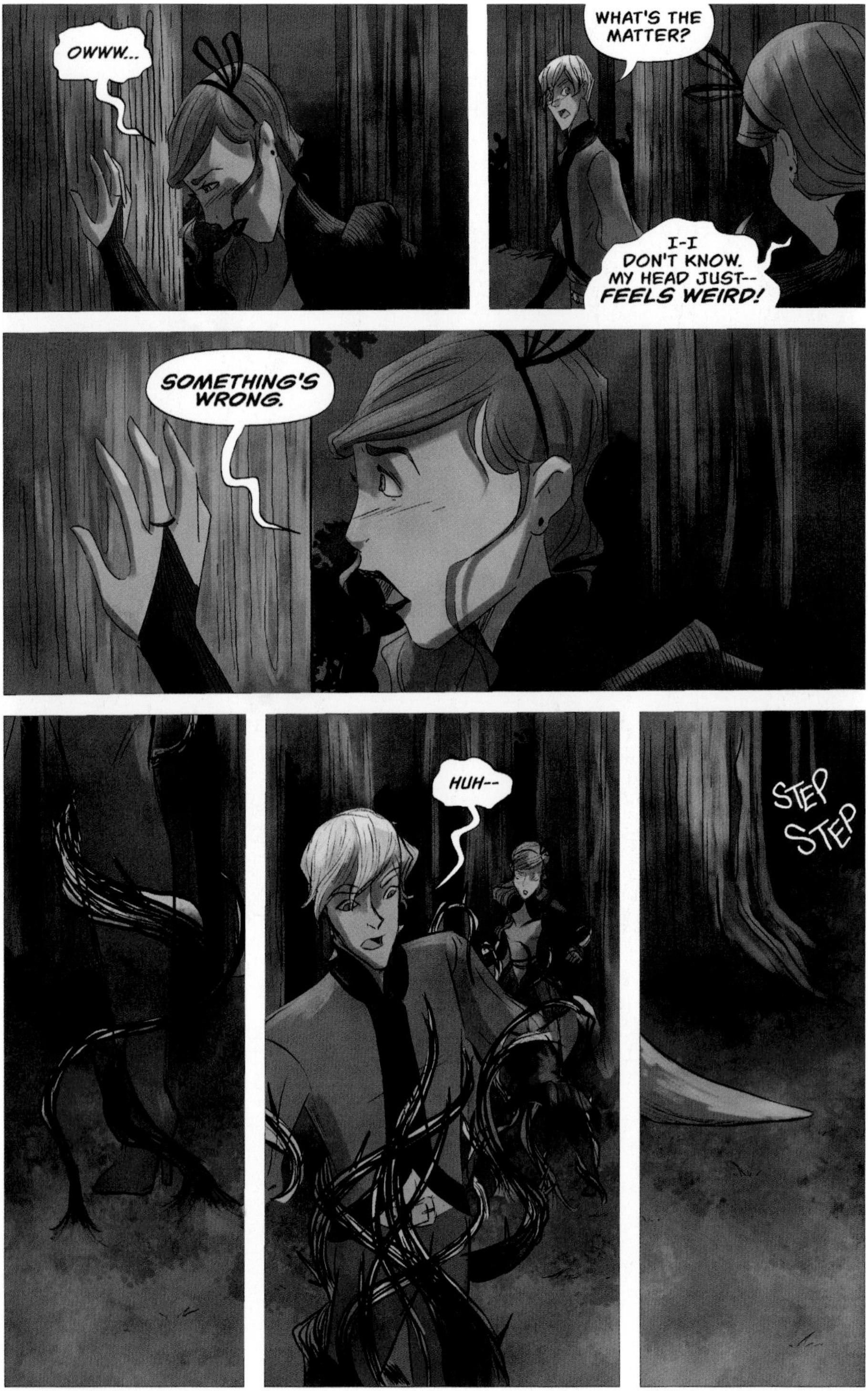
OWWW...
WHAT'S THE MATTER?
I-I DON'T KNOW. MY HEAD JUST-- FEELS WEIRD!
SOMETHING'S WRONG.
HUH--
STEP STEP

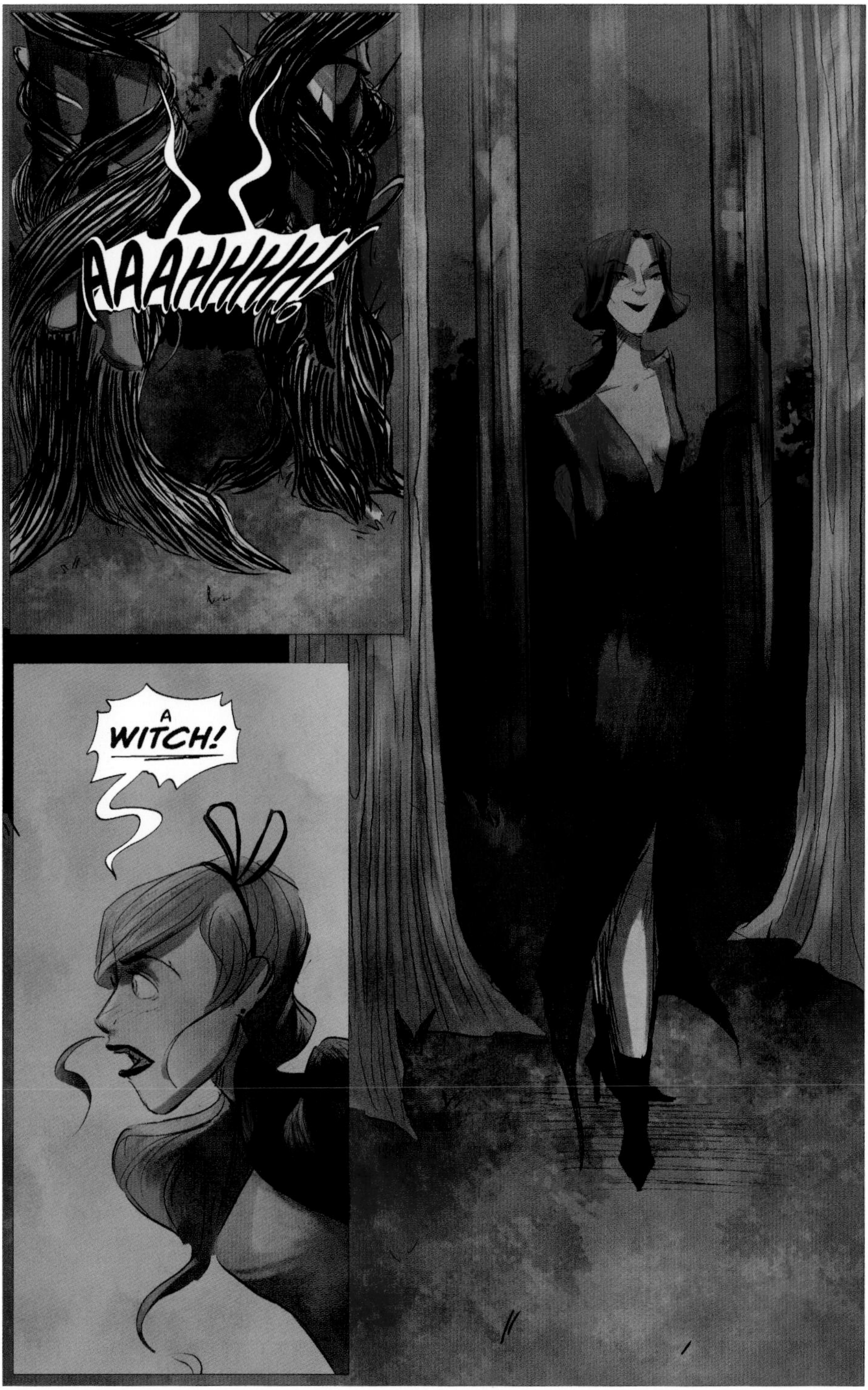
AAAHHHH!
A WITCH!

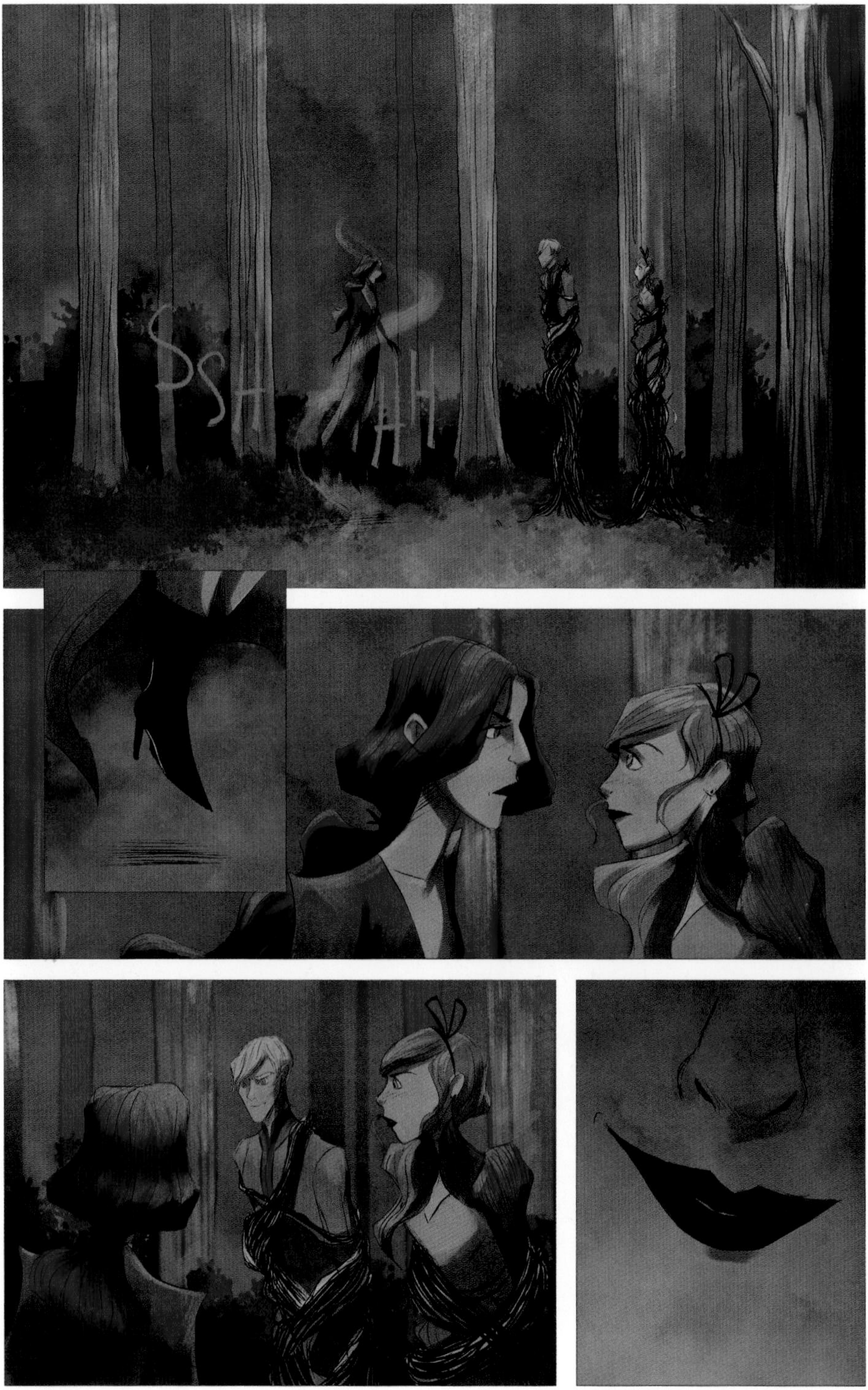
SSHHH

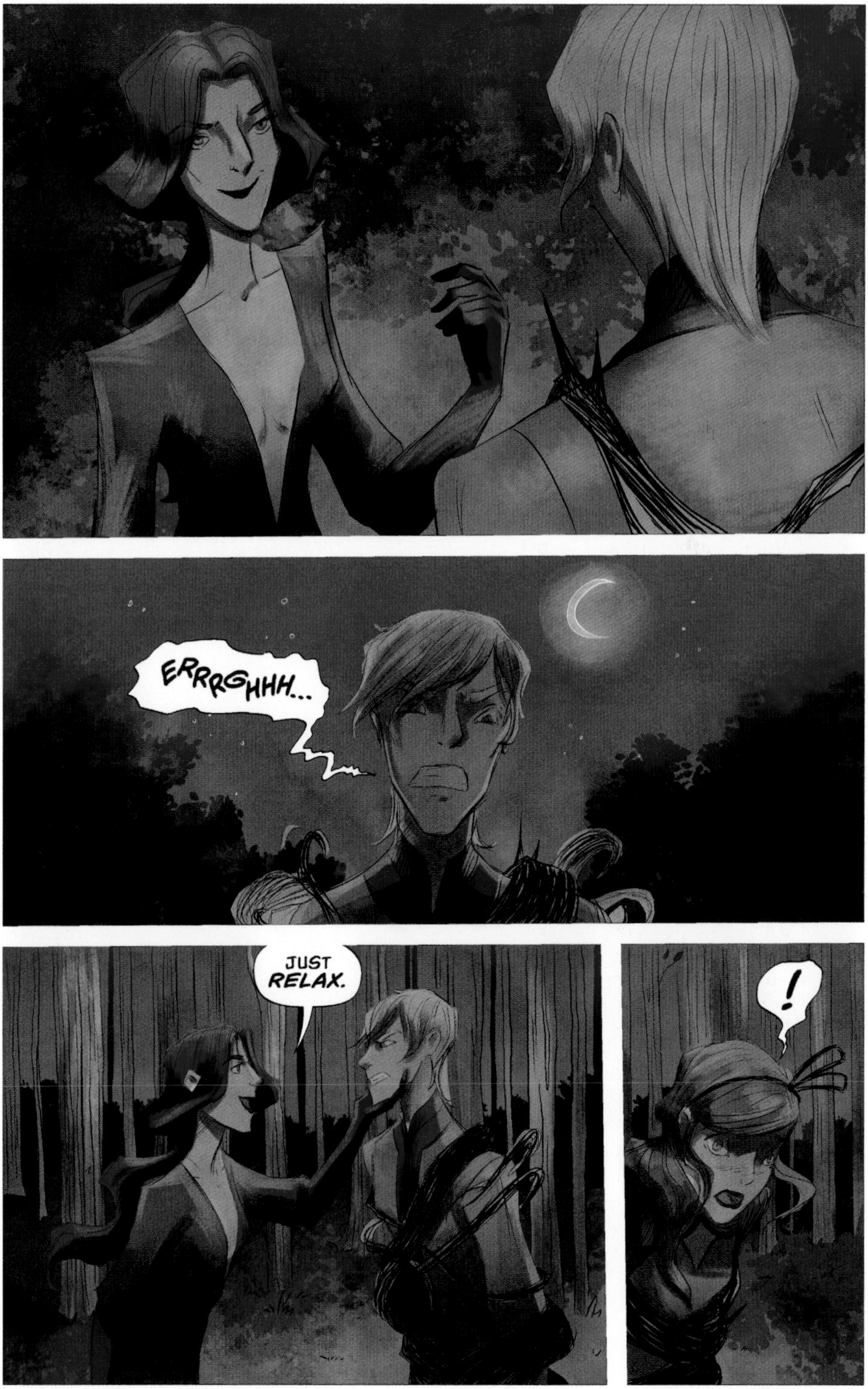
ERRRGHHH...
JUST RELAX.
!

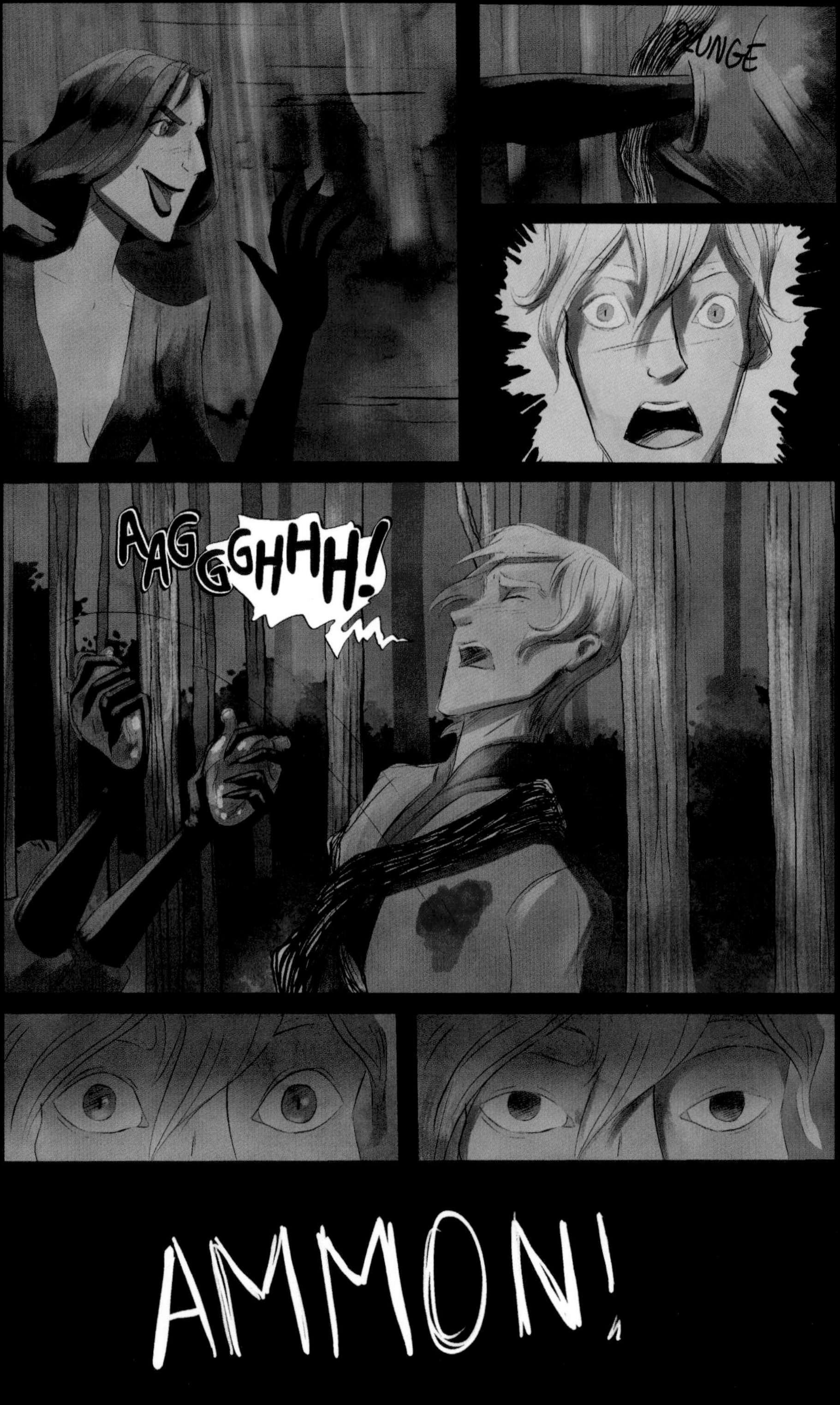
PLUNGE
AAGGGHHHH!
AMMON!

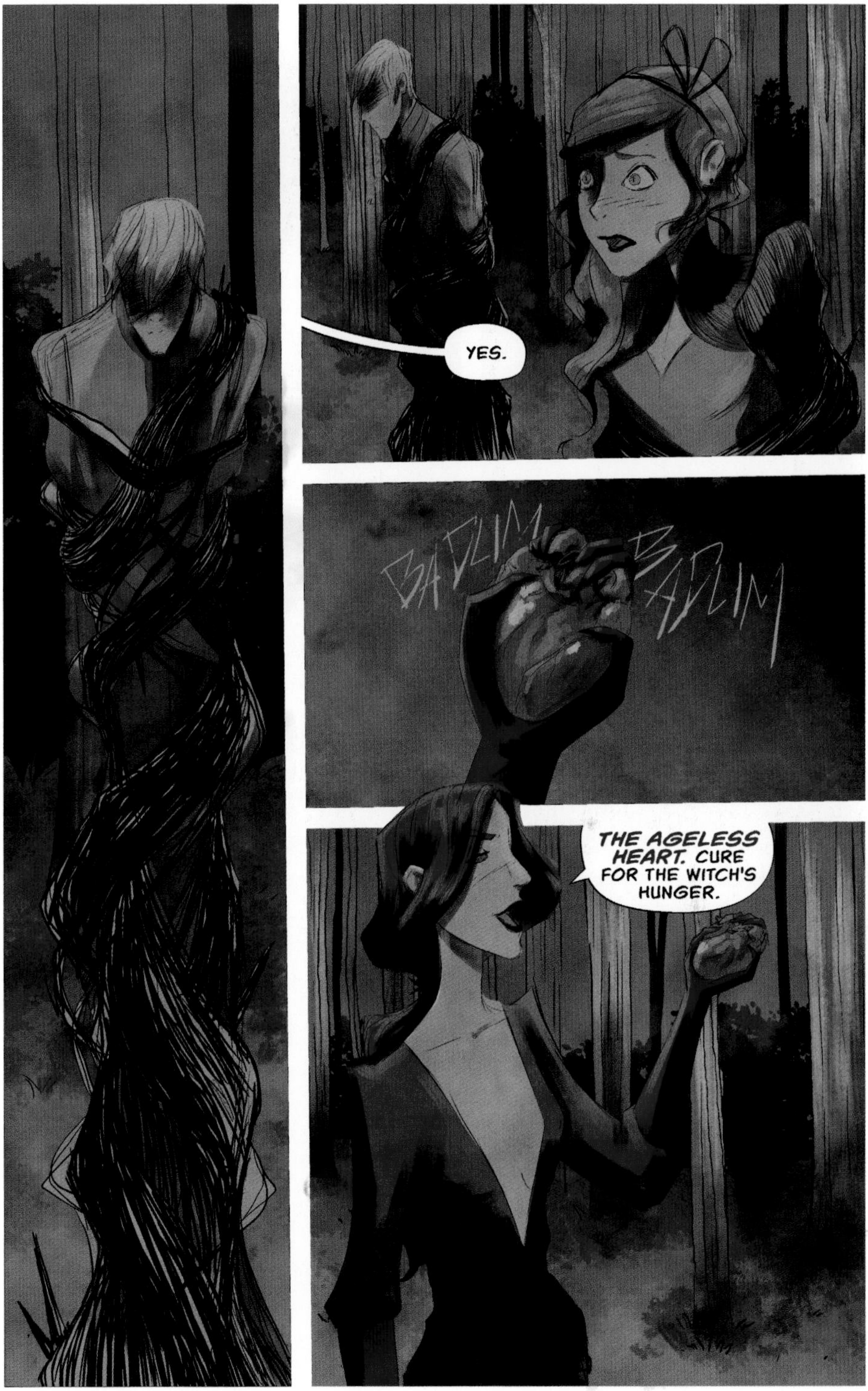
YES.
BA-DUM BA-DUM
THE AGELESS HEART. CURE FOR THE WITCH'S HUNGER.

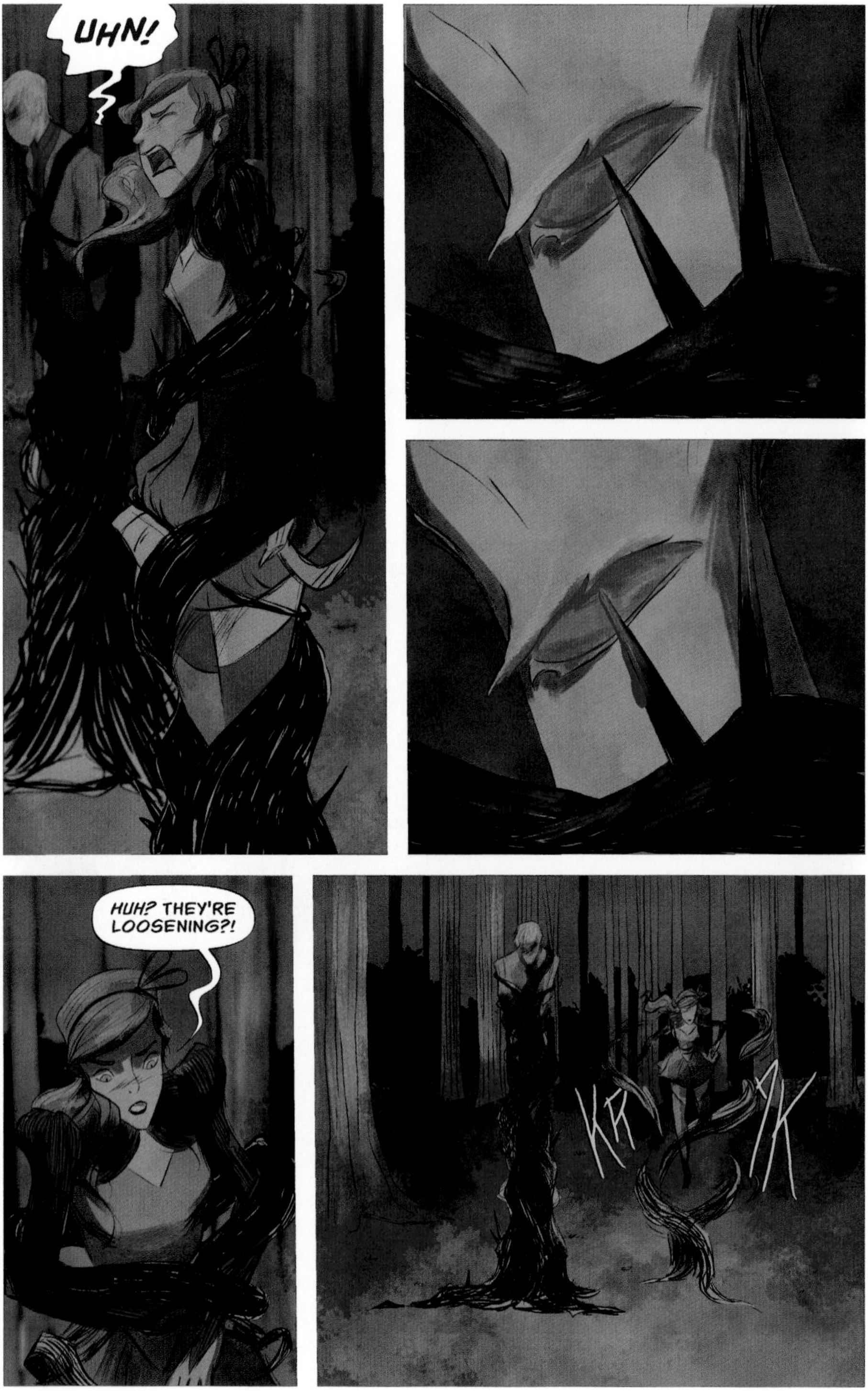
UHN!
HUH? THEY'RE LOOSENING?!
KR
ZK

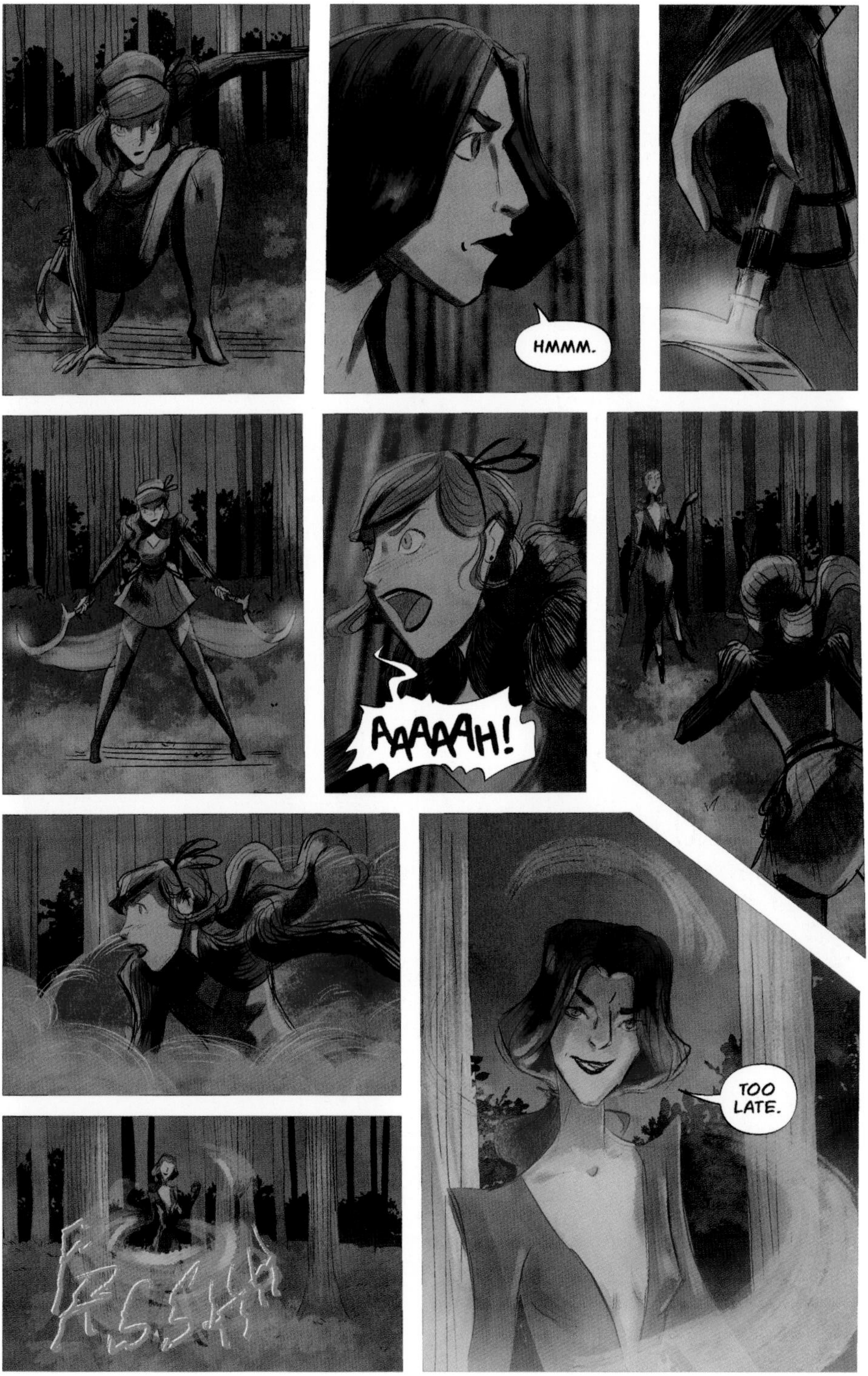
HMMM.
AAAAAH!
TOO LATE.
FSSSHH

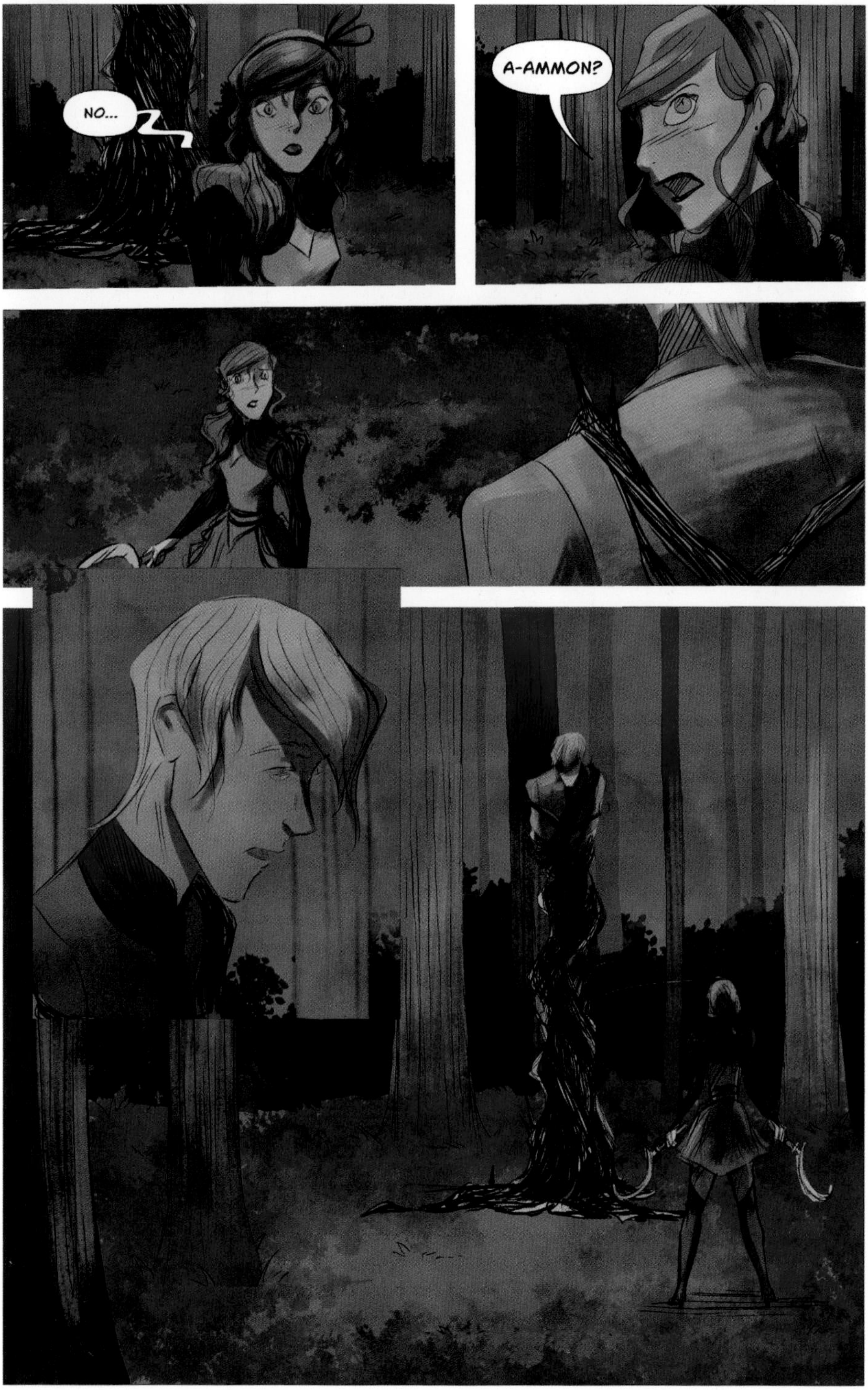
NO...
A-AMMON?

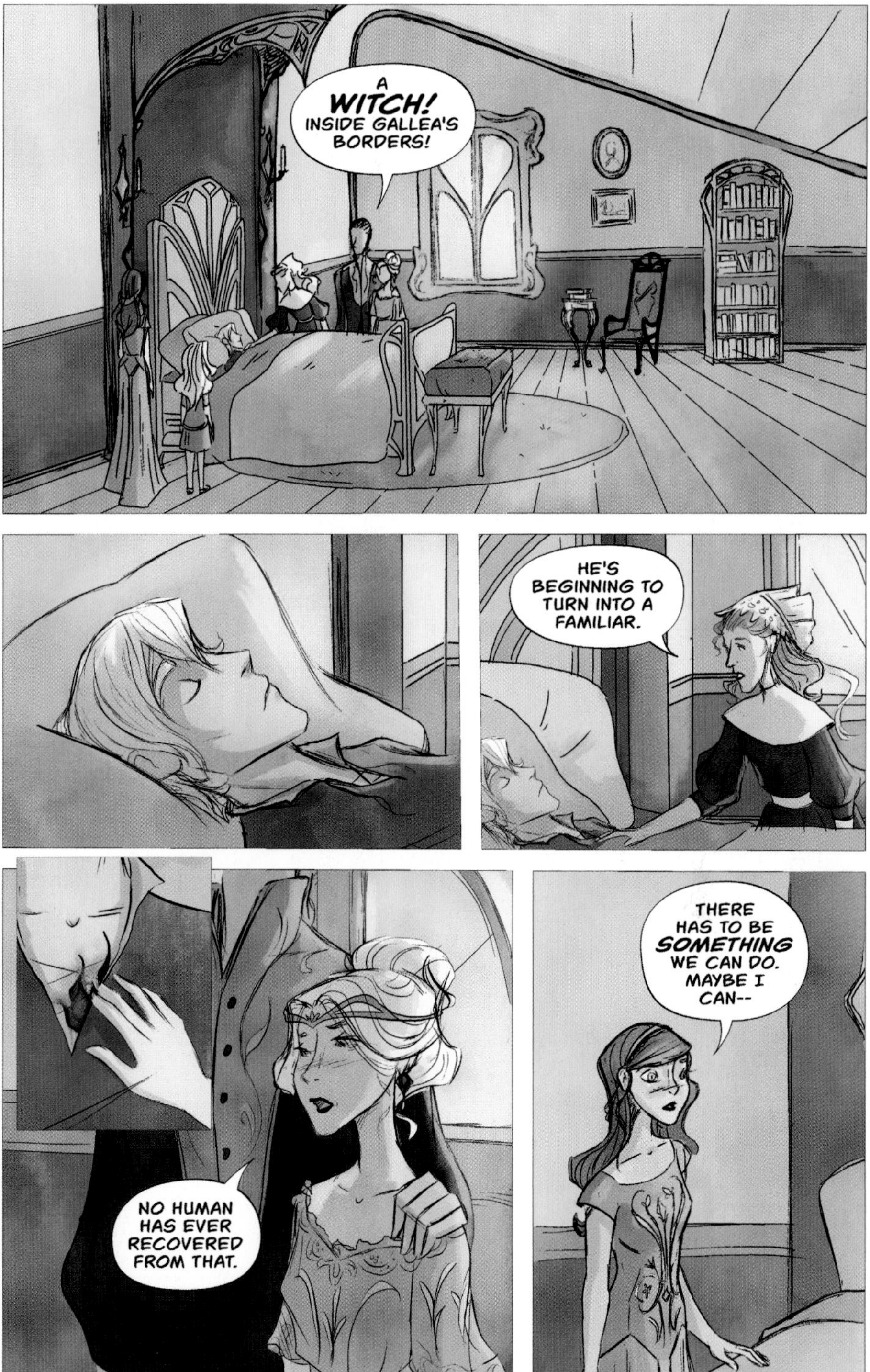
A WITCH! INSIDE GALLEA'S BORDERS!
HE'S BEGINNING TO TURN INTO A FAMILIAR.
NO HUMAN HAS EVER RECOVERED FROM THAT.
THERE HAS TO BE SOMETHING WE CAN DO. MAYBE I CAN--

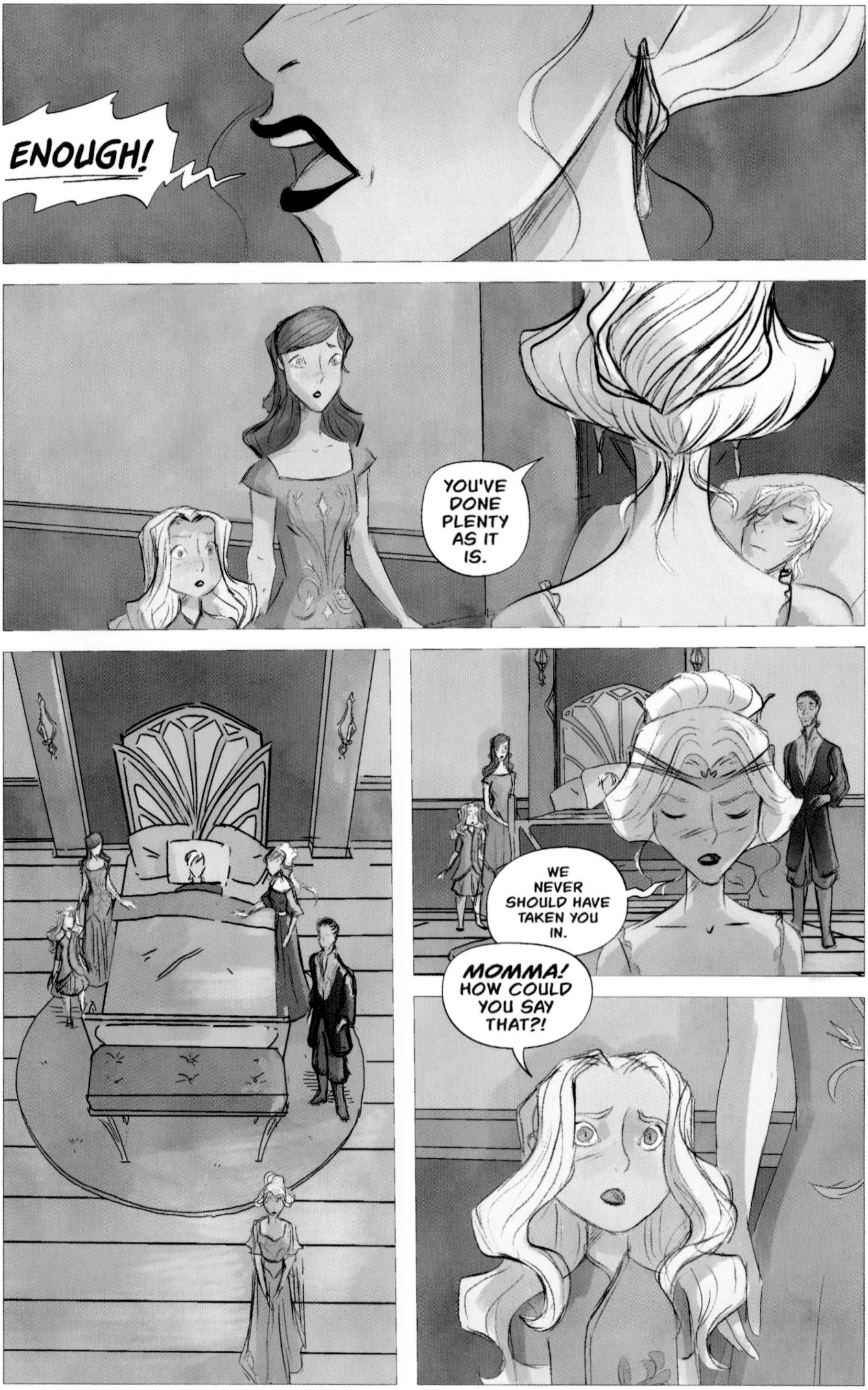
ENOUGH!
YOU'VE DONE PLENTY AS IT IS.
WE NEVER SHOULD HAVE TAKEN YOU IN.
MOMMA! HOW COULD YOU SAY THAT?!

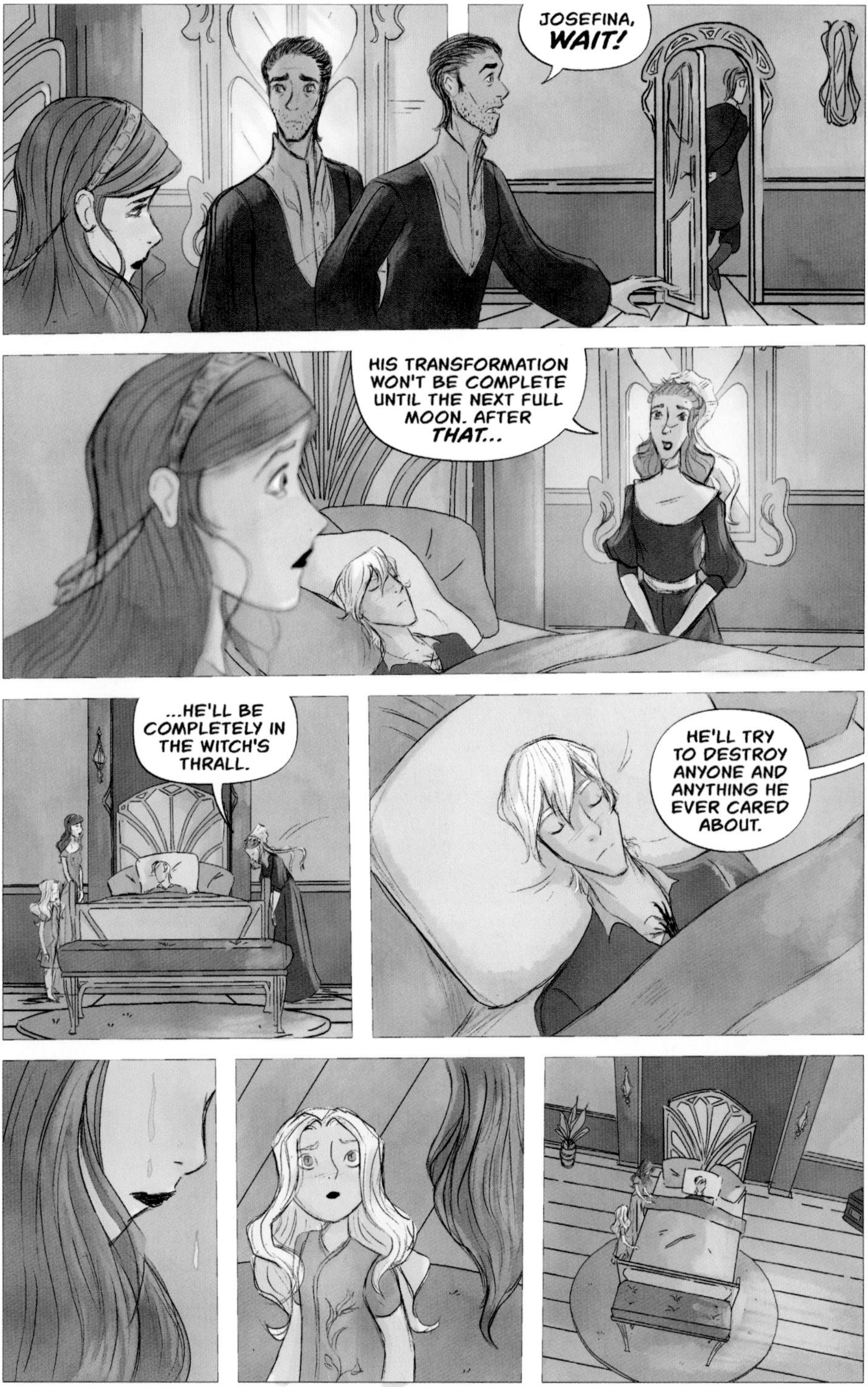
JOSEFINA, WAIT!
HIS TRANSFORMATION WON'T BE COMPLETE UNTIL THE NEXT FULL MOON. AFTER THAT...
...HE'LL BE COMPLETELY IN THE WITCH'S THRALL.
HE'LL TRY TO DESTROY ANYONE AND ANYTHING HE EVER CARED ABOUT.

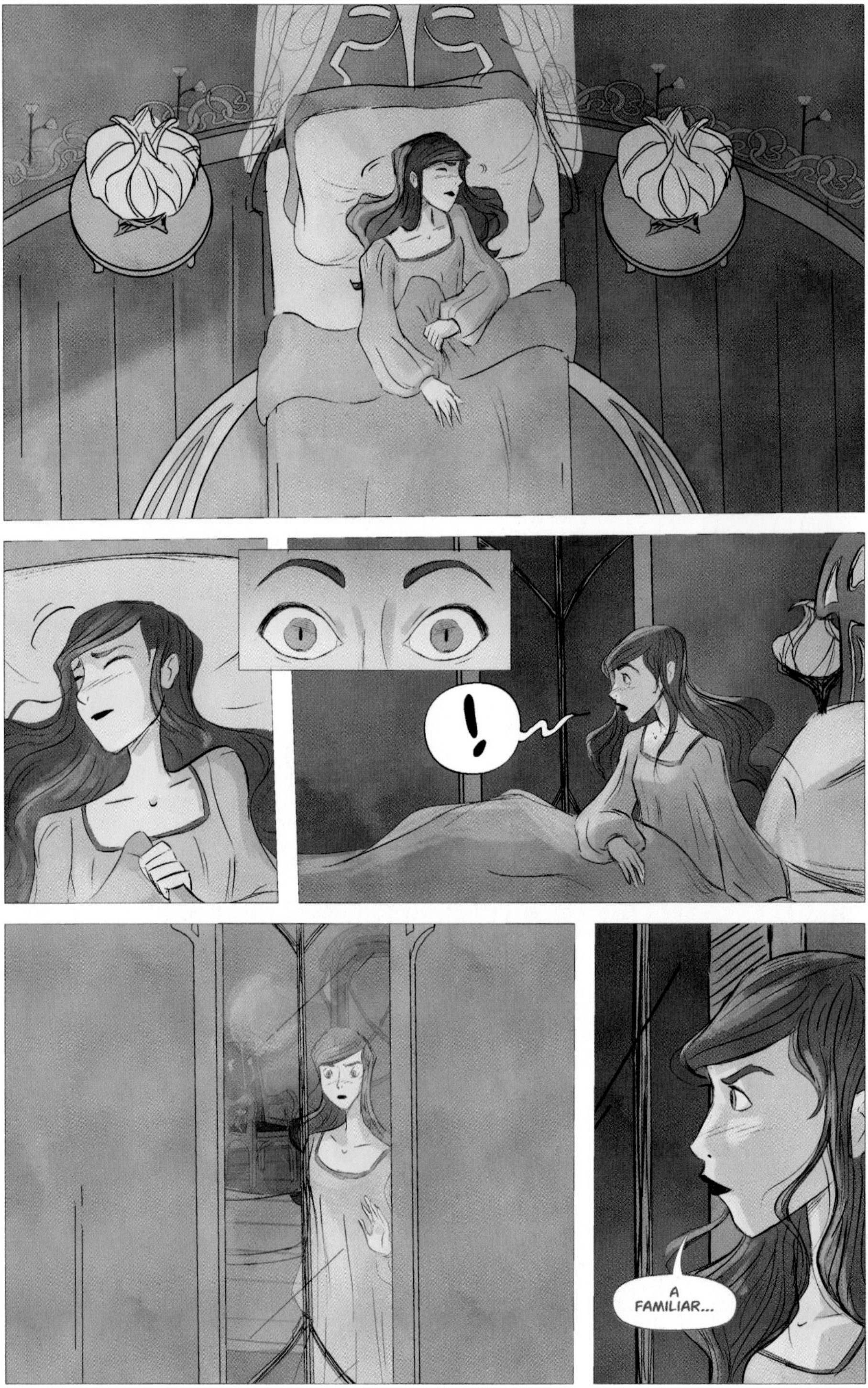
!
A FAMILIAR...

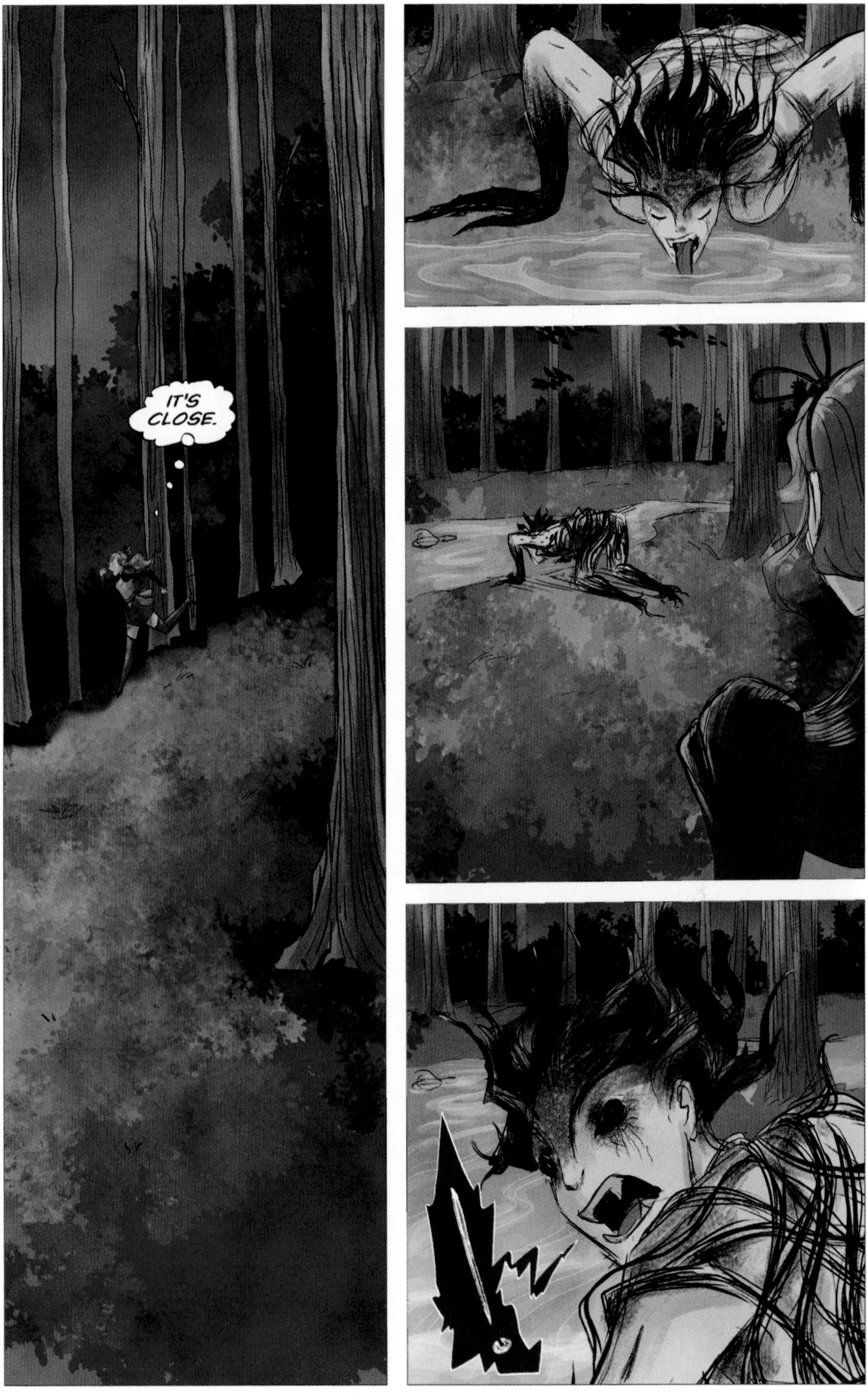
IT'S CLOSE.

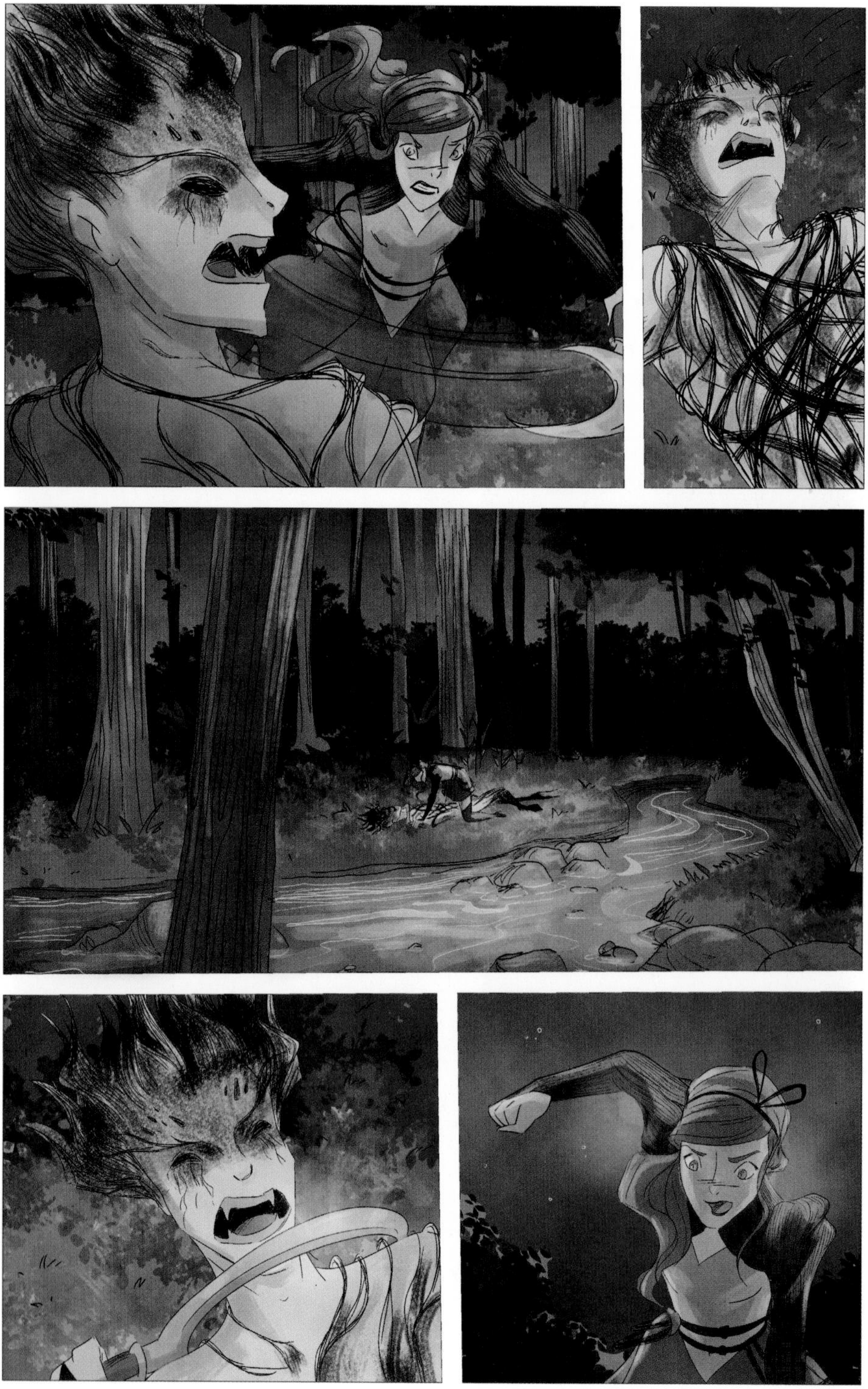

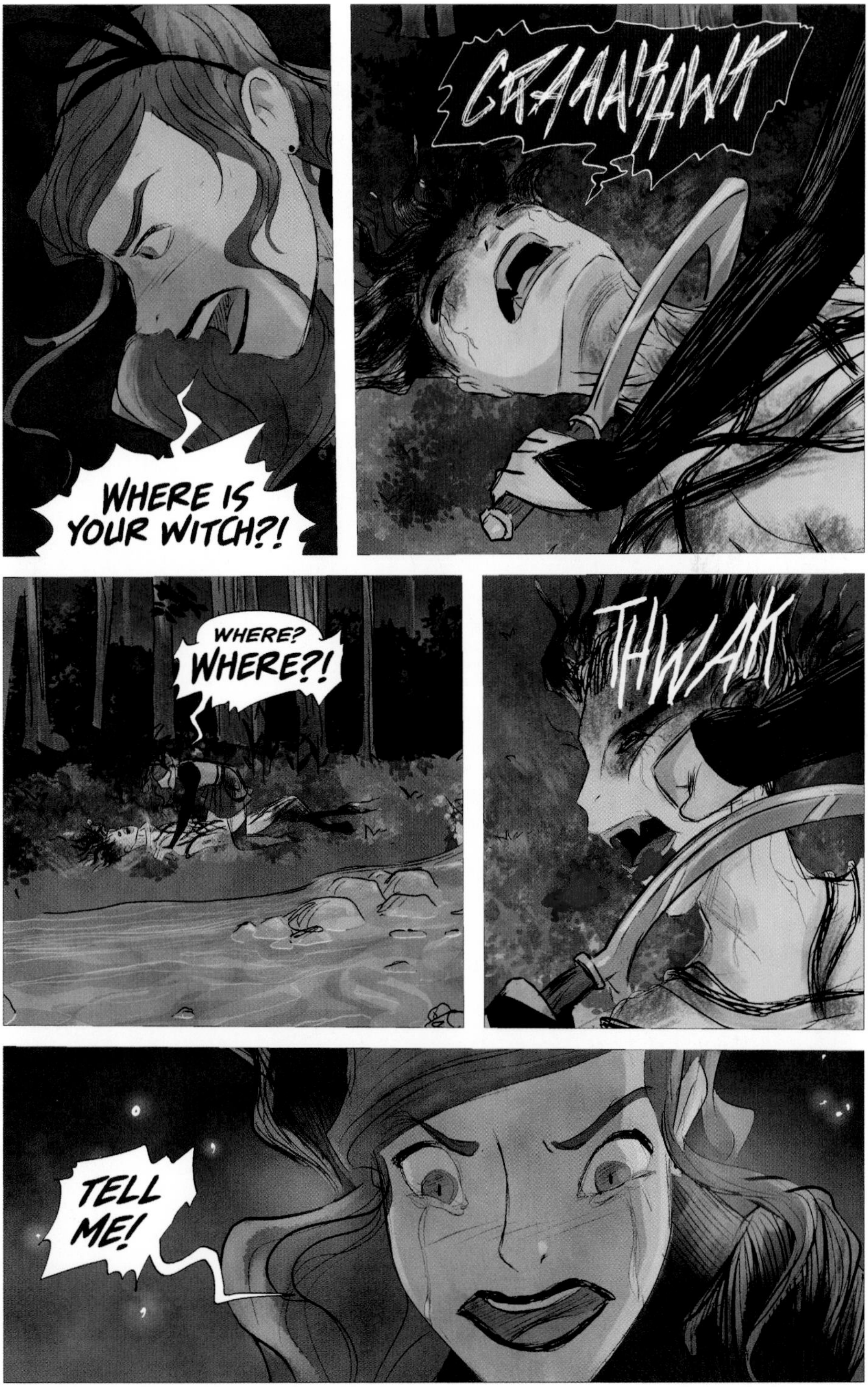
WHERE IS YOUR WITCH?!
GRAAAHHWK
WHERE? WHERE?!
THWAK
TELL ME!

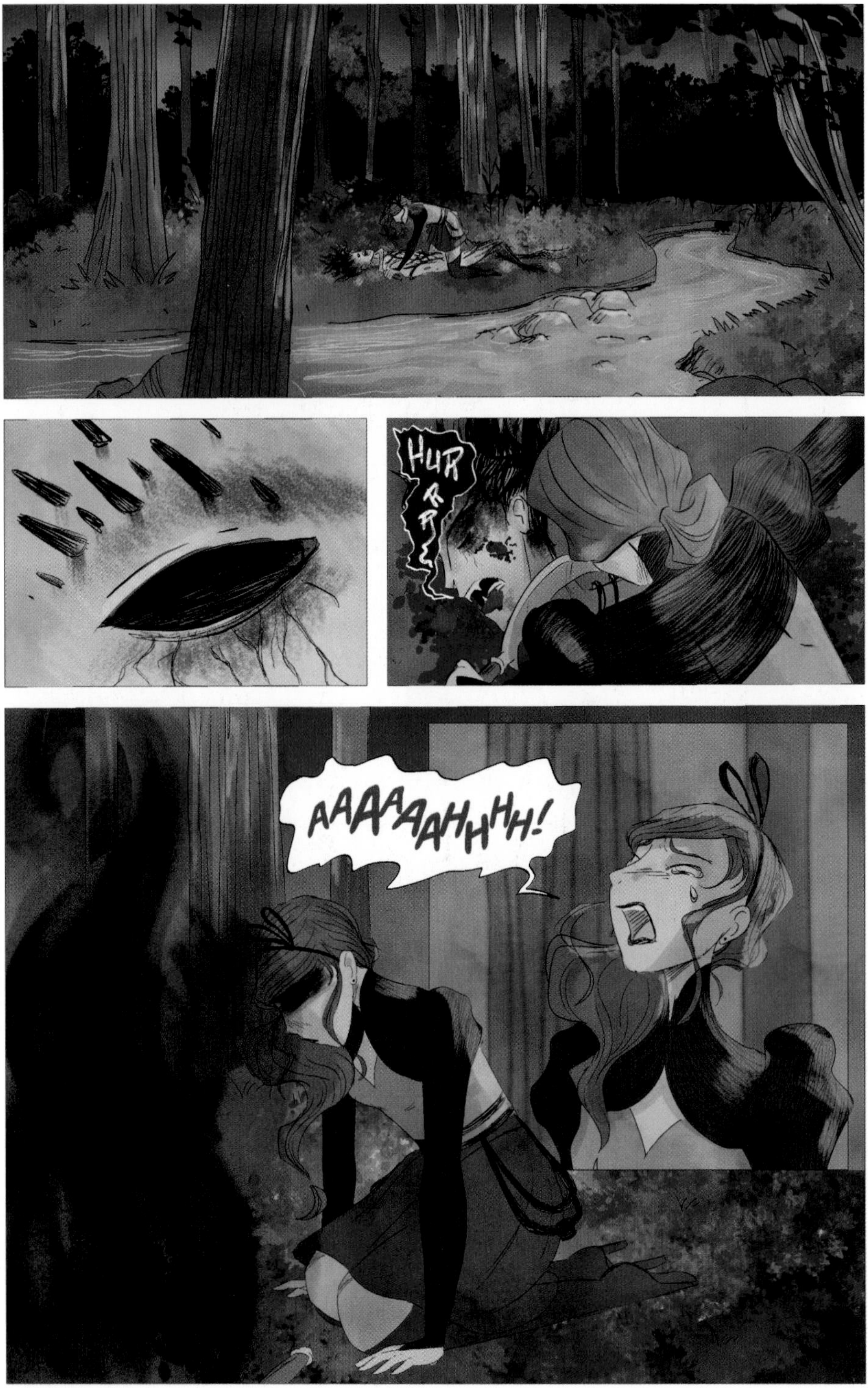
HURRR
AAAAAAHHHH!

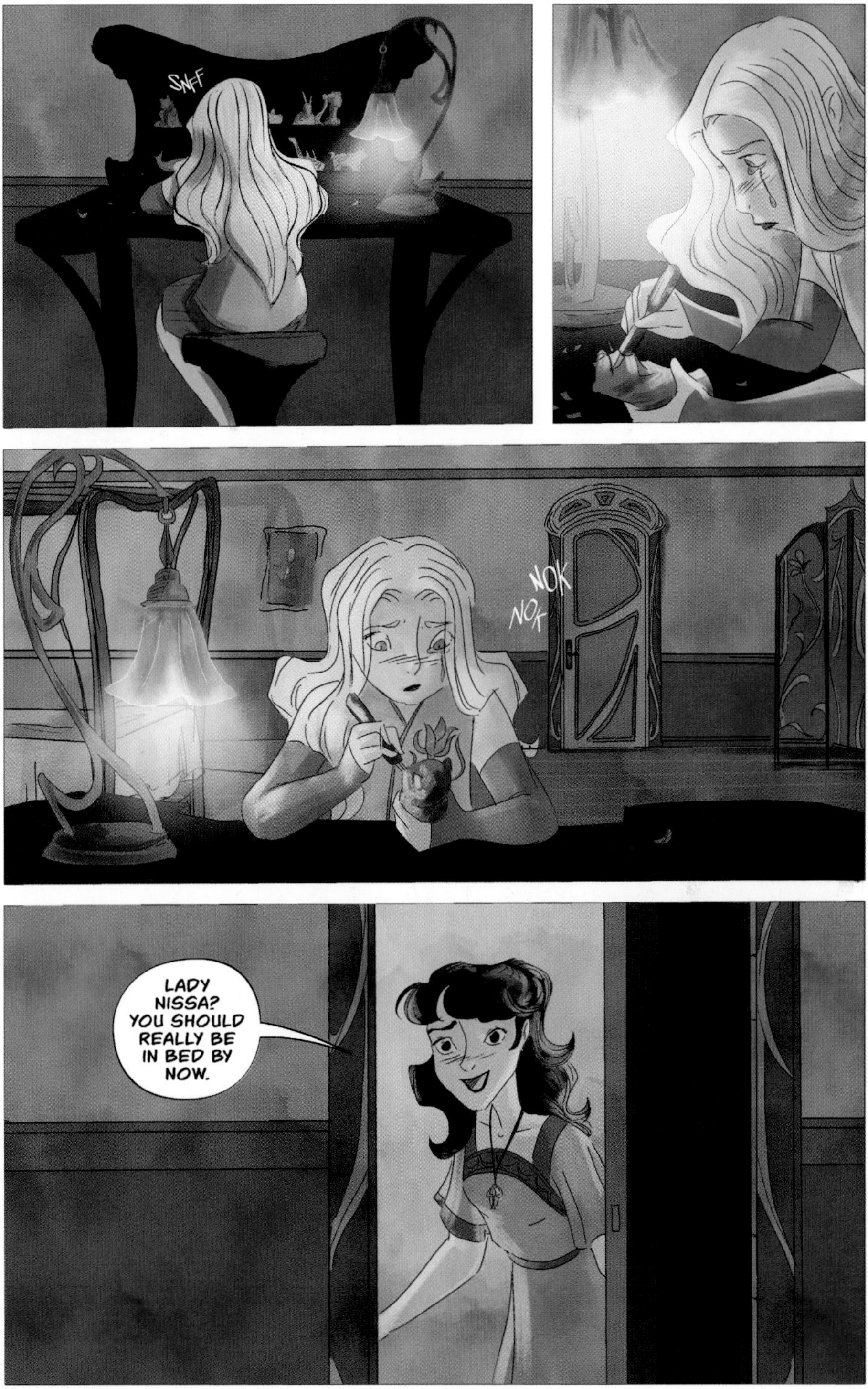
SNFF
NOK
NOK
LADY NISSA? YOU SHOULD REALLY BE IN BED BY NOW.

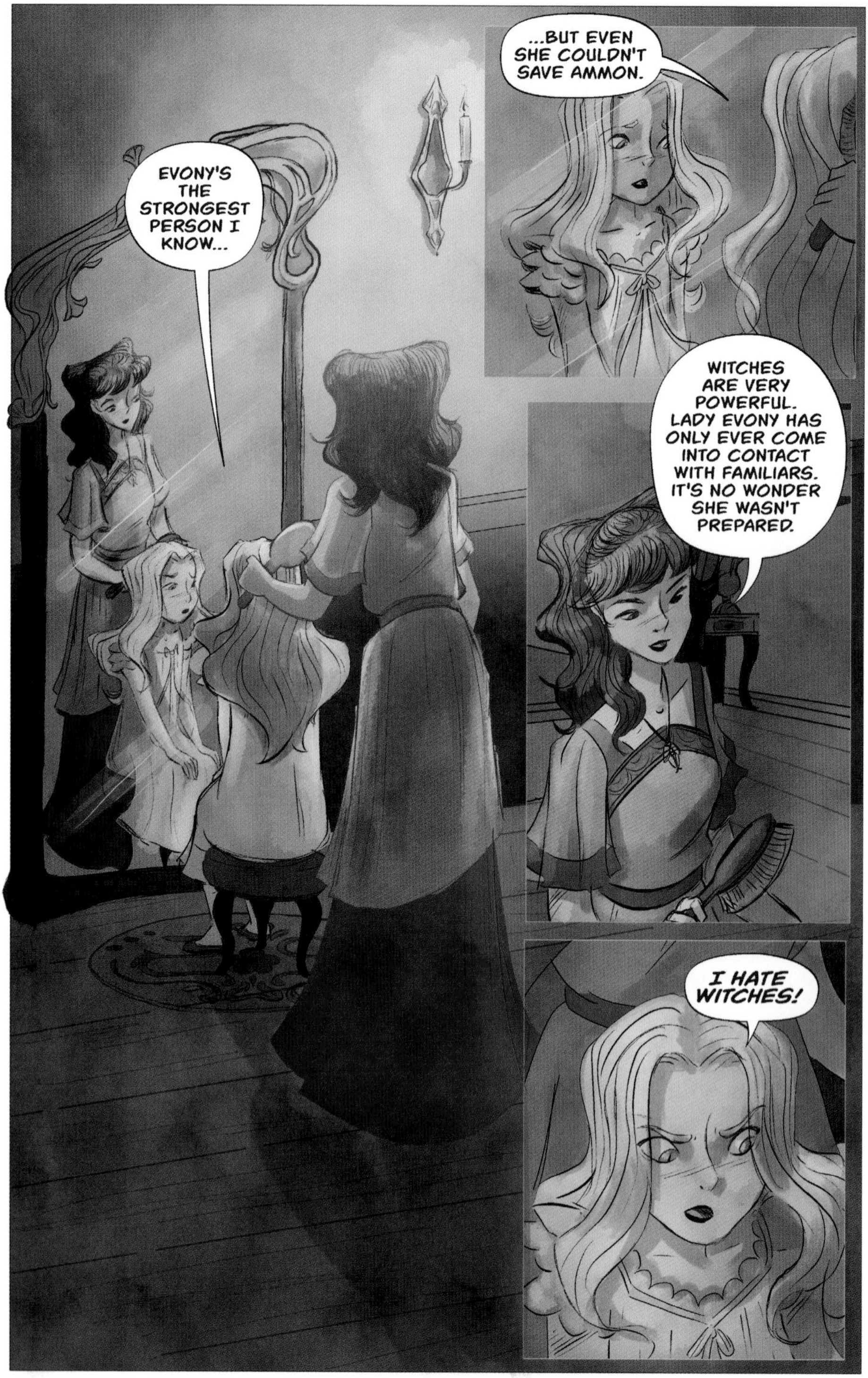
EVONY'S THE STRONGEST PERSON I KNOW...
...BUT EVEN SHE COULDN'T SAVE AMMON.
WITCHES ARE VERY POWERFUL. LADY EVONY HAS ONLY EVER COME INTO CONTACT WITH FAMILIARS. IT'S NO WONDER SHE WASN'T PREPARED.
I HATE WITCHES!

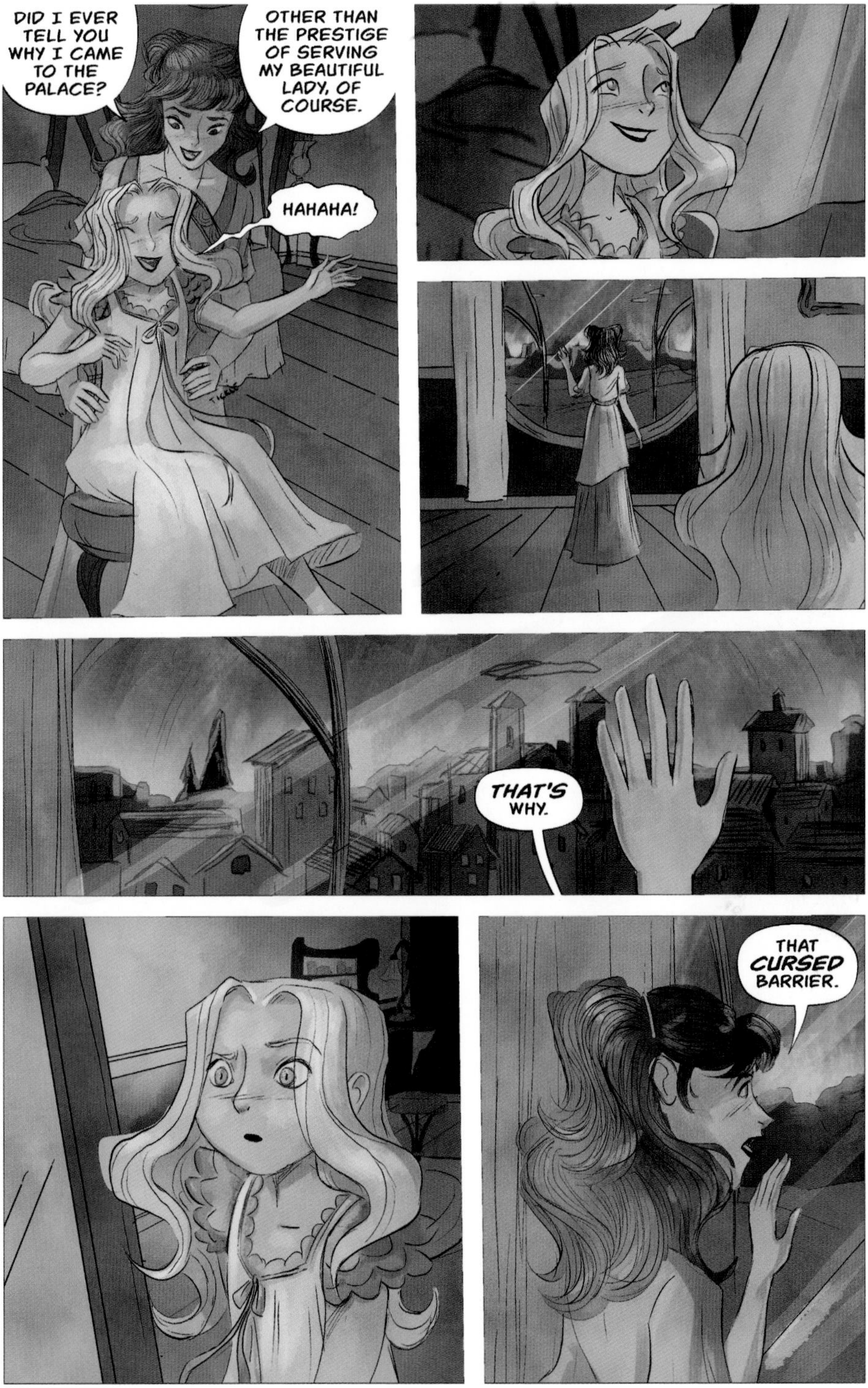
DID I EVER TELL YOU WHY I CAME TO THE PALACE?
OTHER THAN THE PRESTIGE OF SERVING MY BEAUTIFUL LADY, OF COURSE.
HAHAHA!
THAT'S WHY.
THAT CURSED BARRIER.

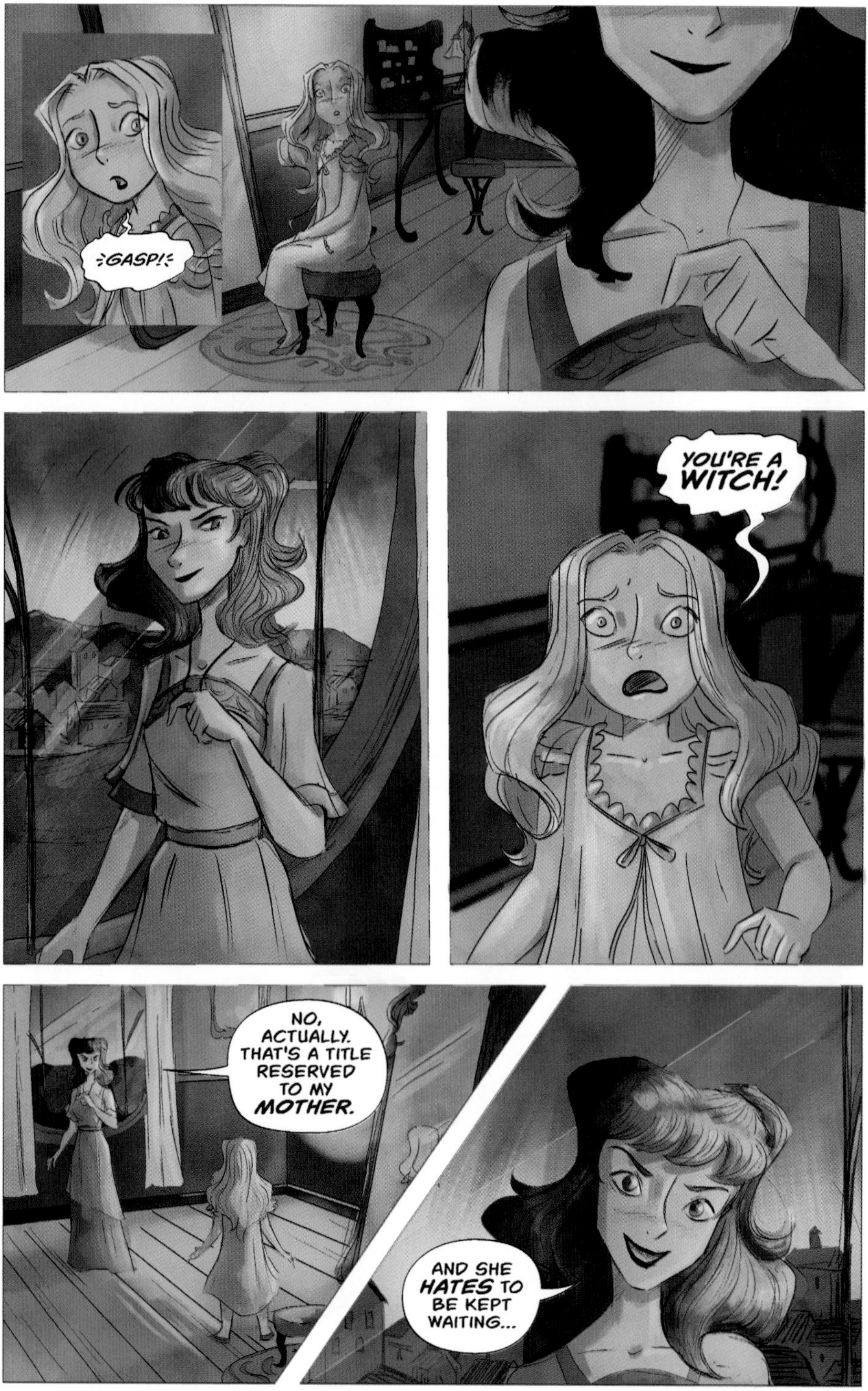
GASP!
YOU'RE A WITCH!
NO, ACTUALLY. THAT'S A TITLE RESERVED TO MY MOTHER.
AND SHE HATES TO BE KEPT WAITING...

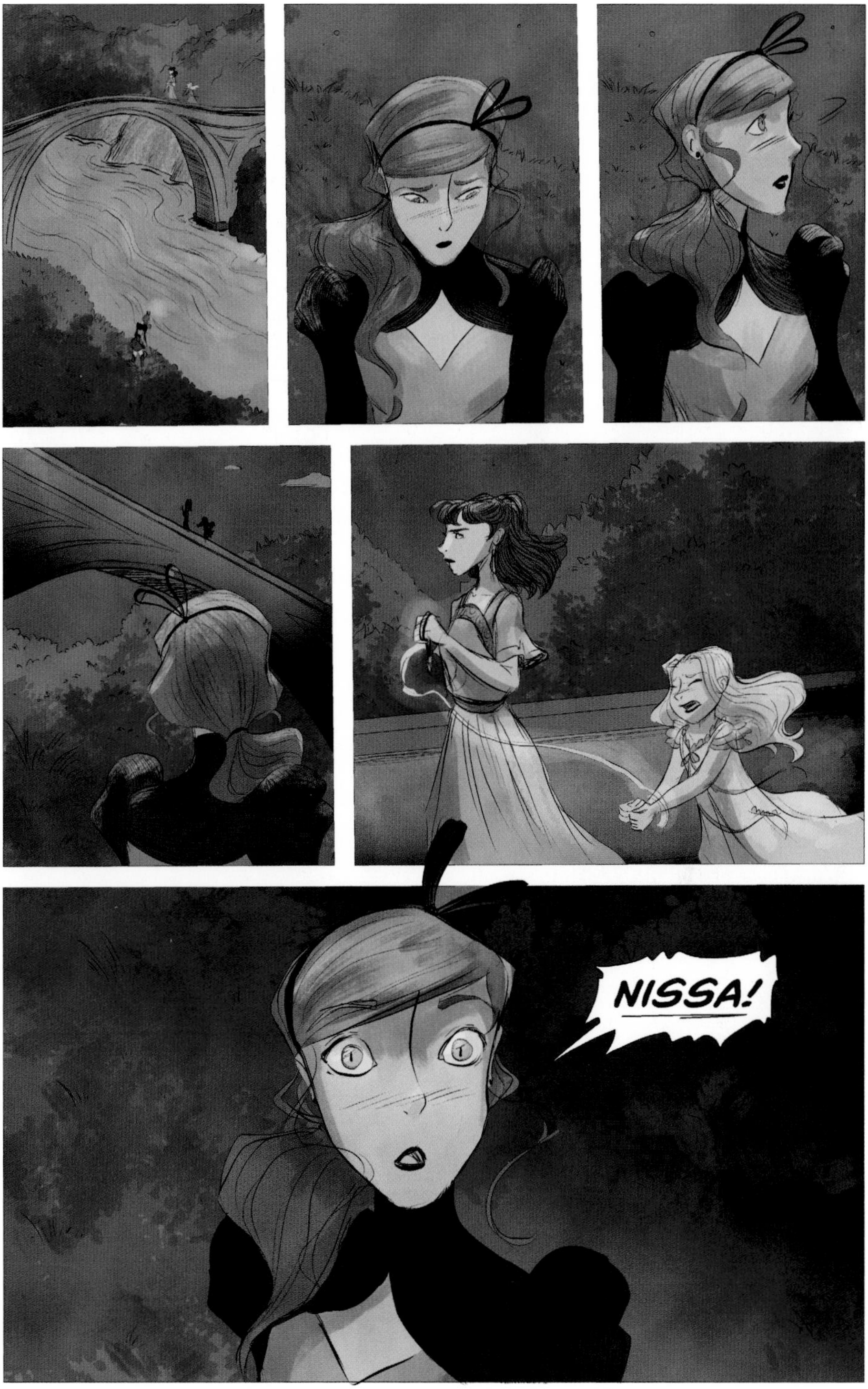
NISSA!

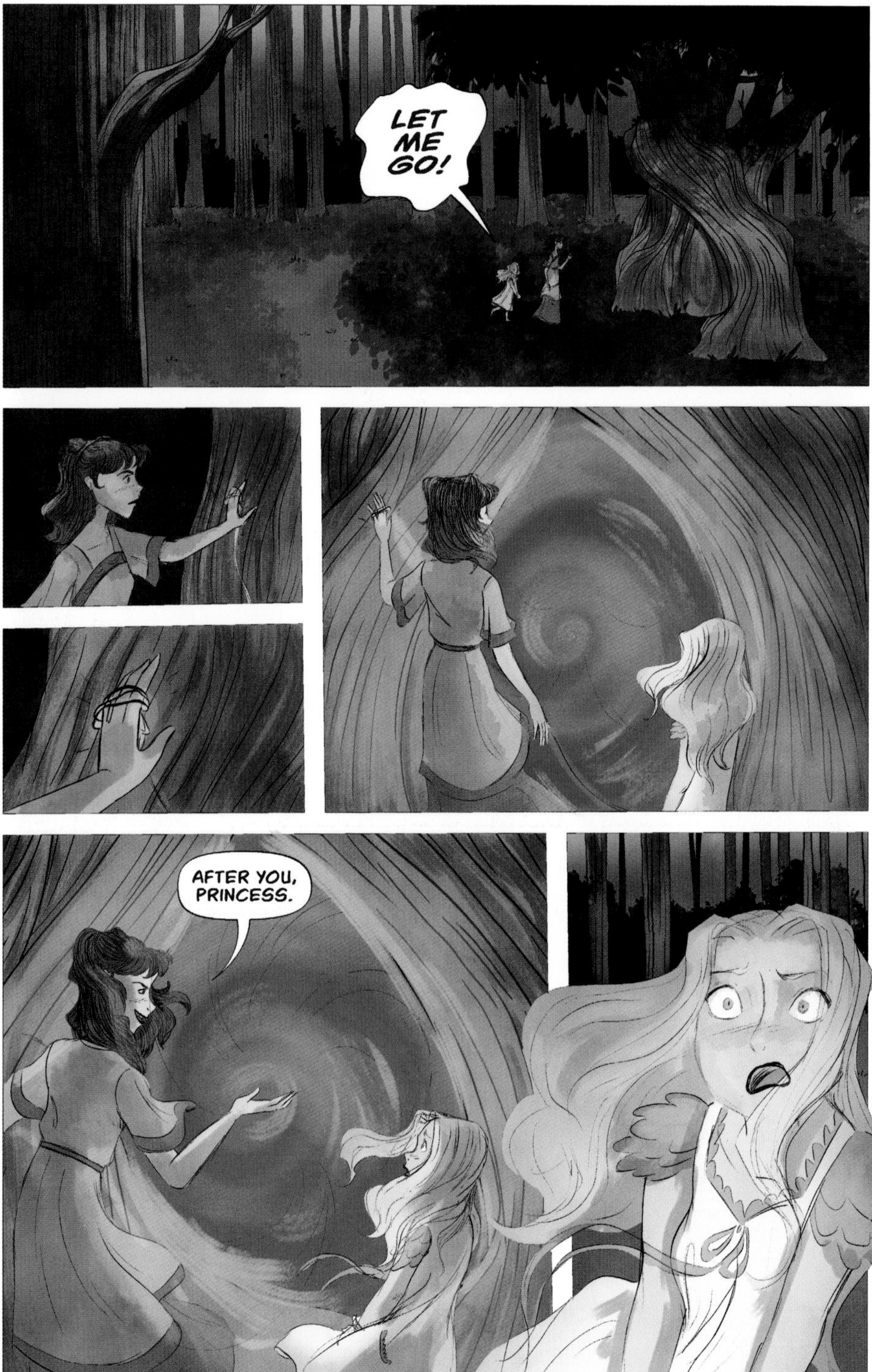
LET ME GO!
AFTER YOU, PRINCESS.

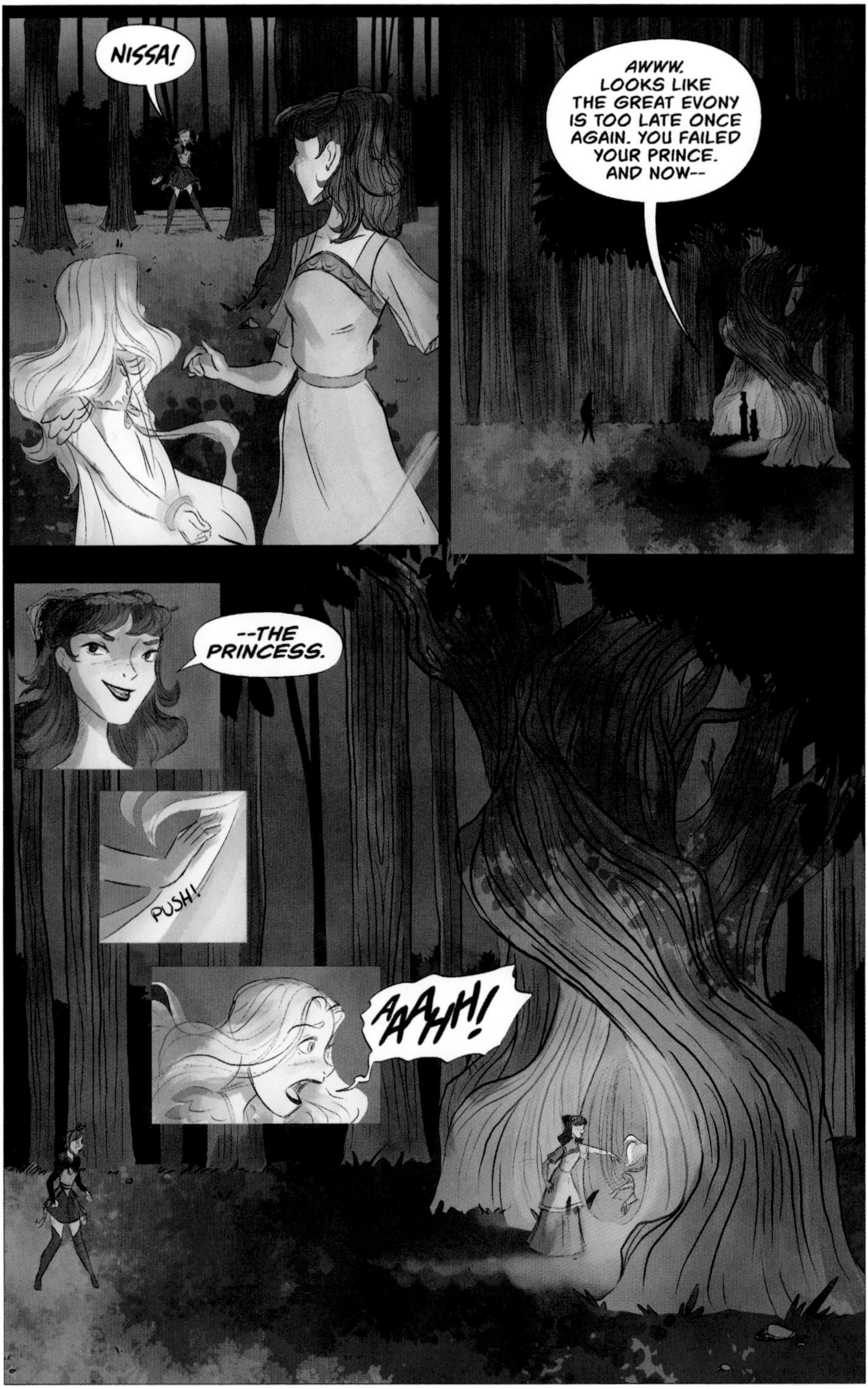
NISSA!
AWWW. LOOKS LIKE THE GREAT EVONY IS TOO LATE ONCE AGAIN. YOU FAILED YOUR PRINCE. AND NOW--
--THE PRINCESS.
PUSH!
AAAHH!

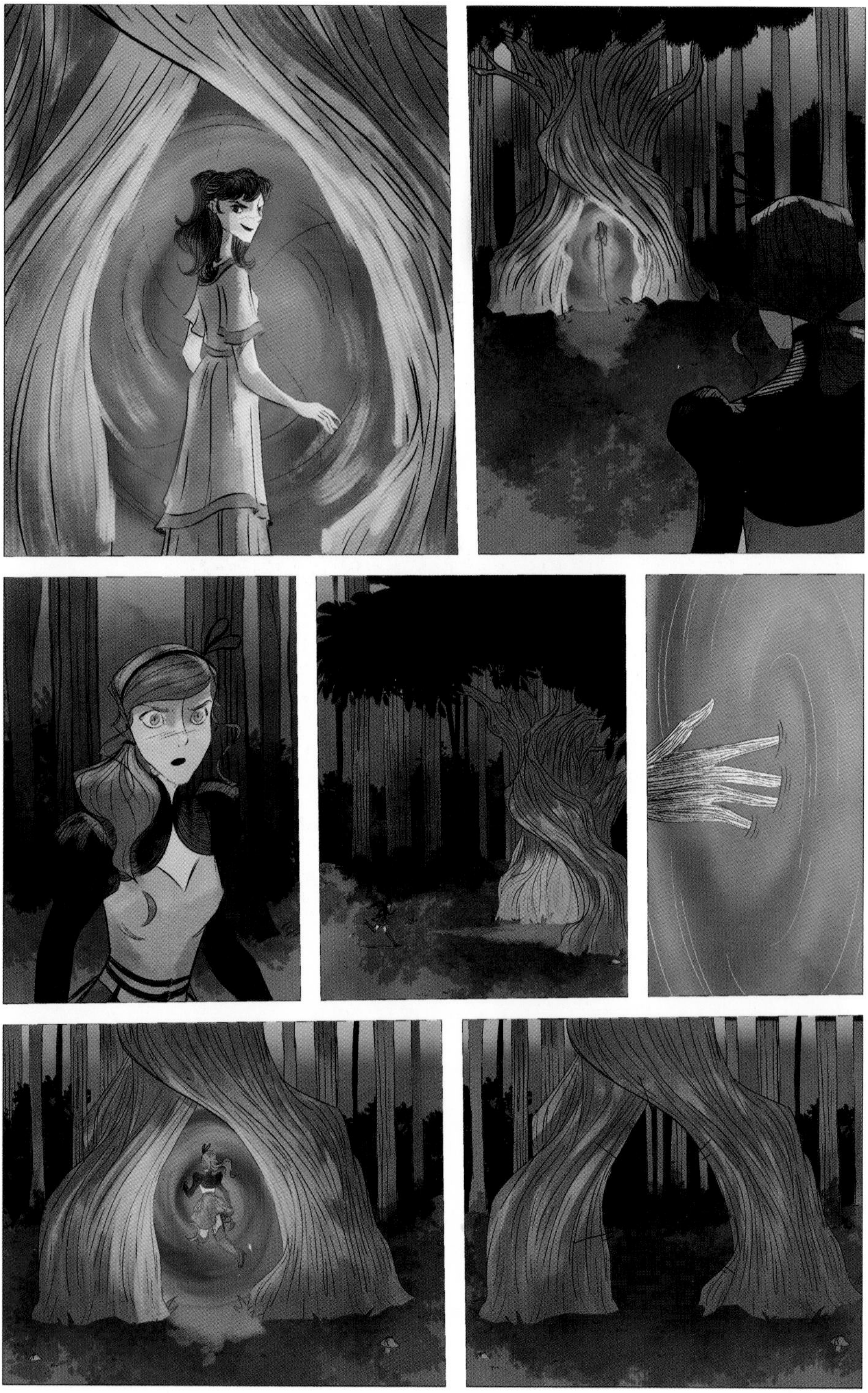

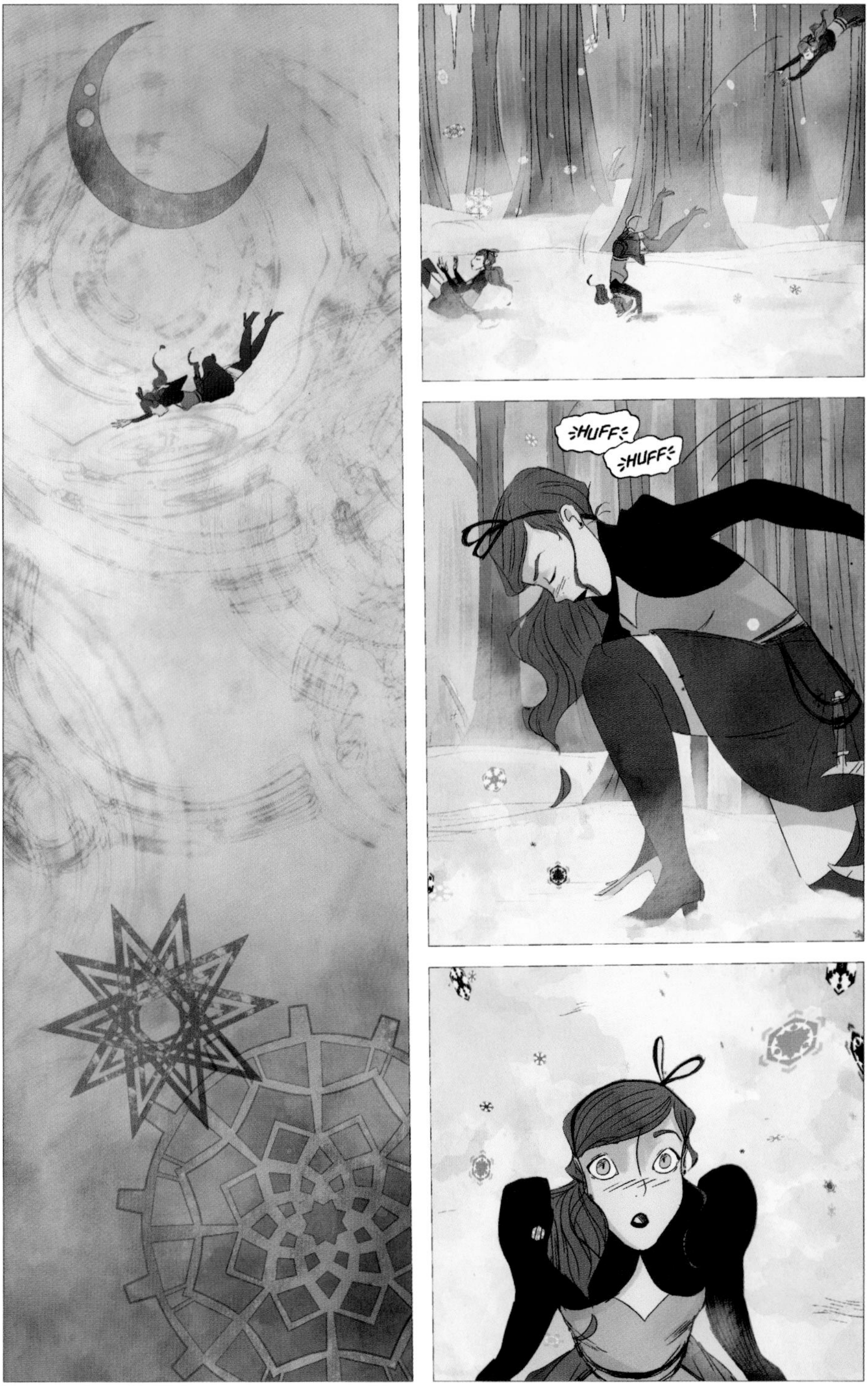
HUFF
HUFF

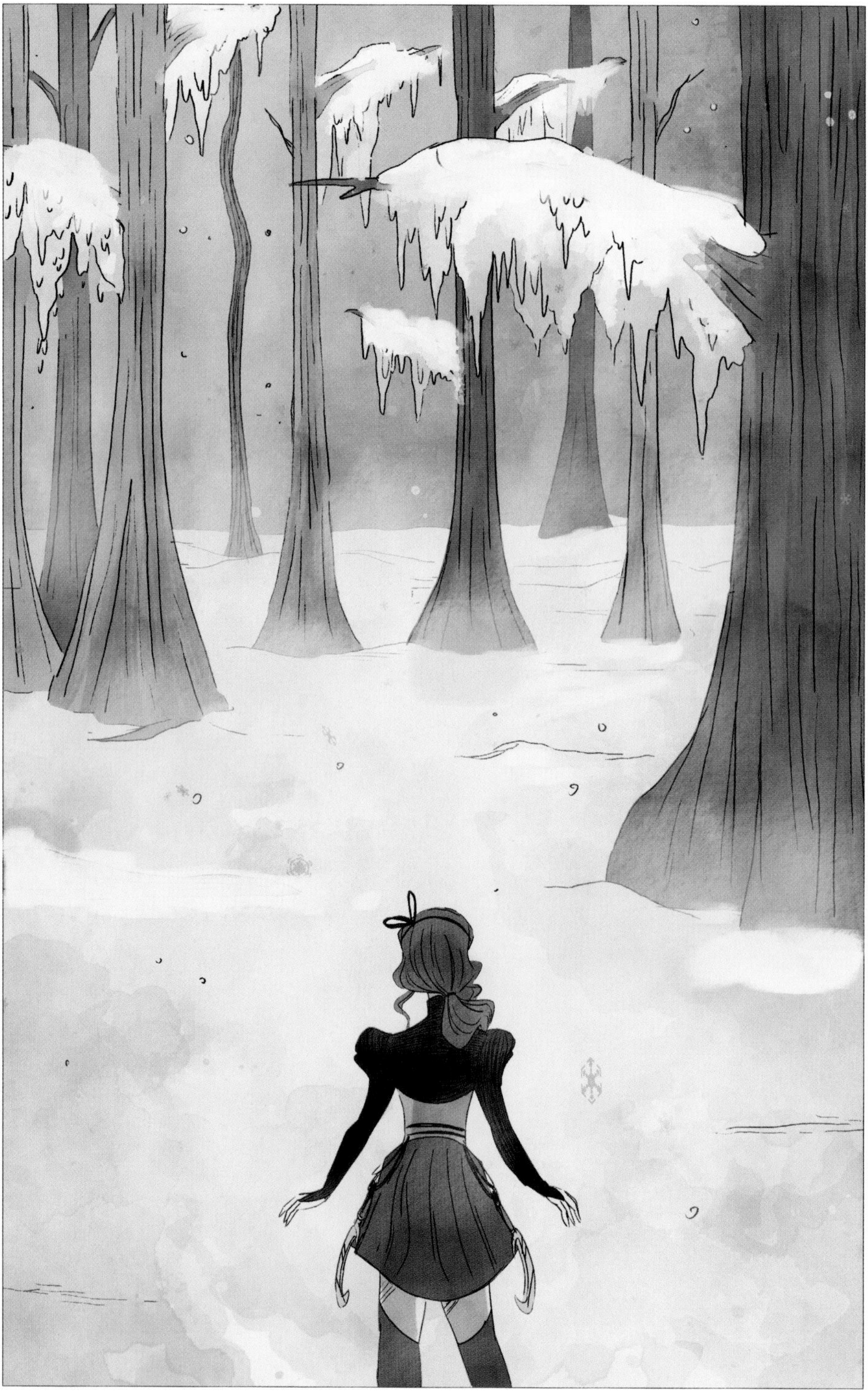

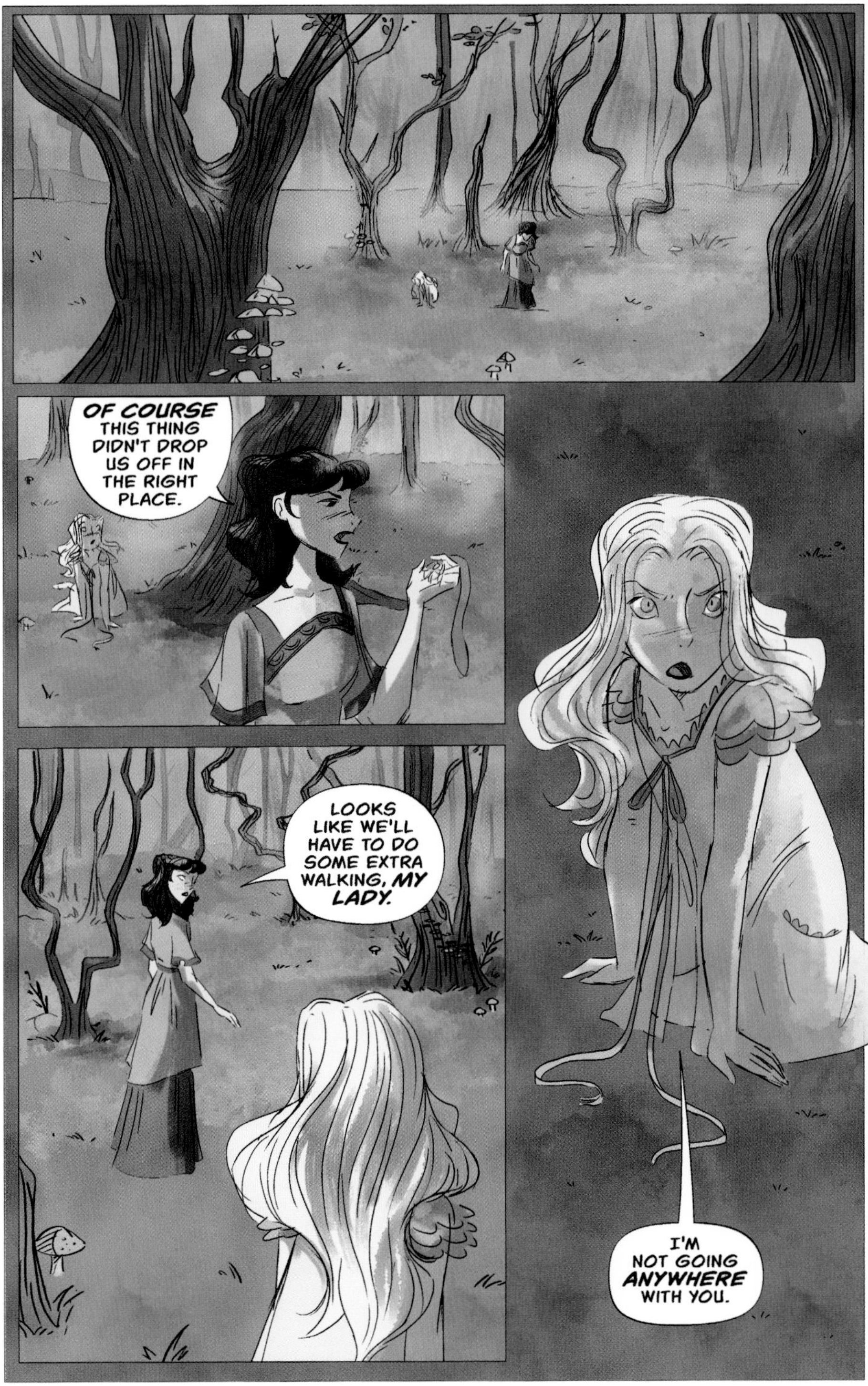
OF COURSE THIS THING DIDN'T DROP US OFF IN THE RIGHT PLACE.
LOOKS LIKE WE'LL HAVE TO DO SOME EXTRA WALKING, MY LADY.
I'M NOT GOING ANYWHERE WITH YOU.

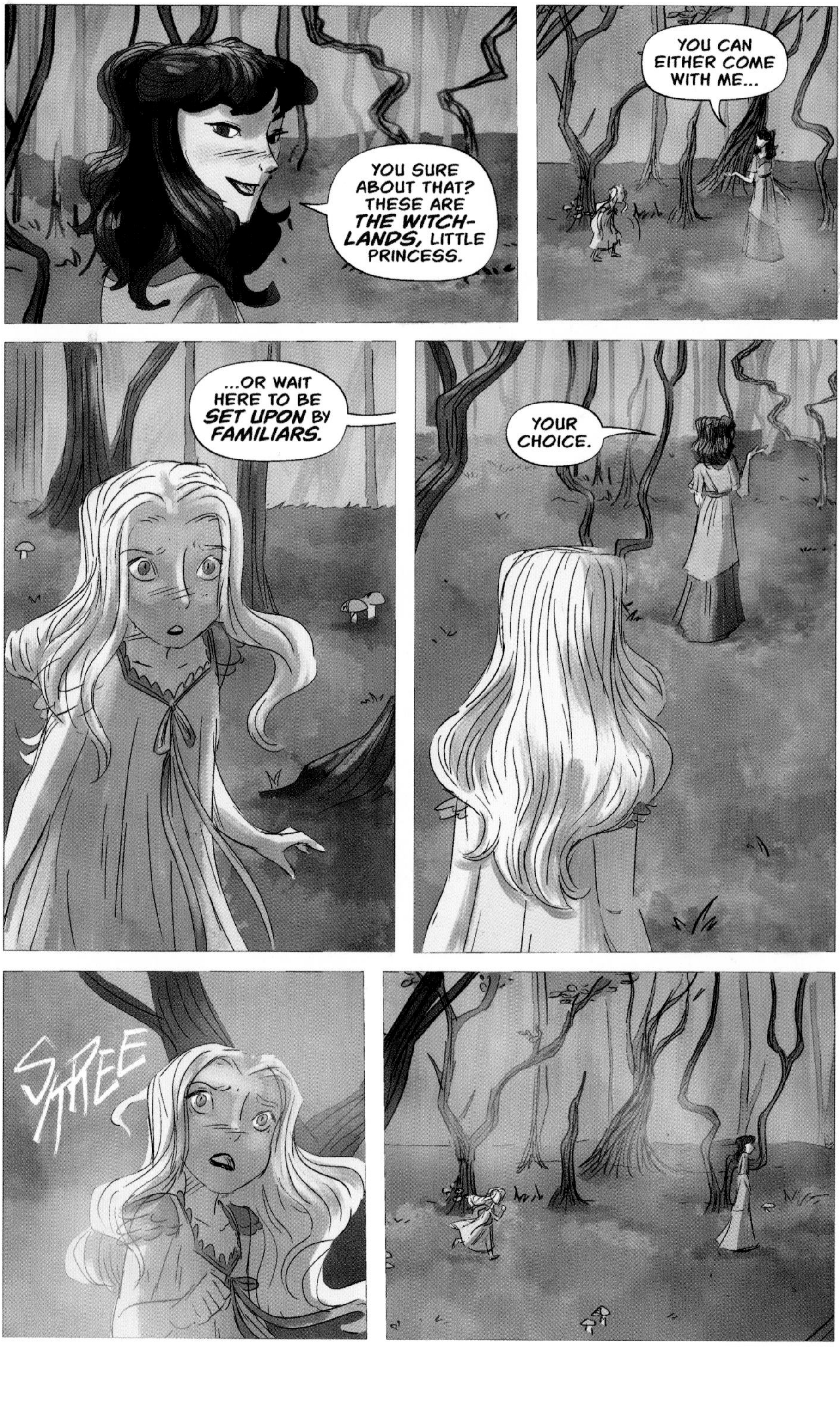
YOU SURE ABOUT THAT? THESE ARE THE WITCH-LANDS, LITTLE PRINCESS.
YOU CAN EITHER COME WITH ME...
...OR WAIT HERE TO BE SET UPON BY FAMILIARS.
YOUR CHOICE.
SKREE

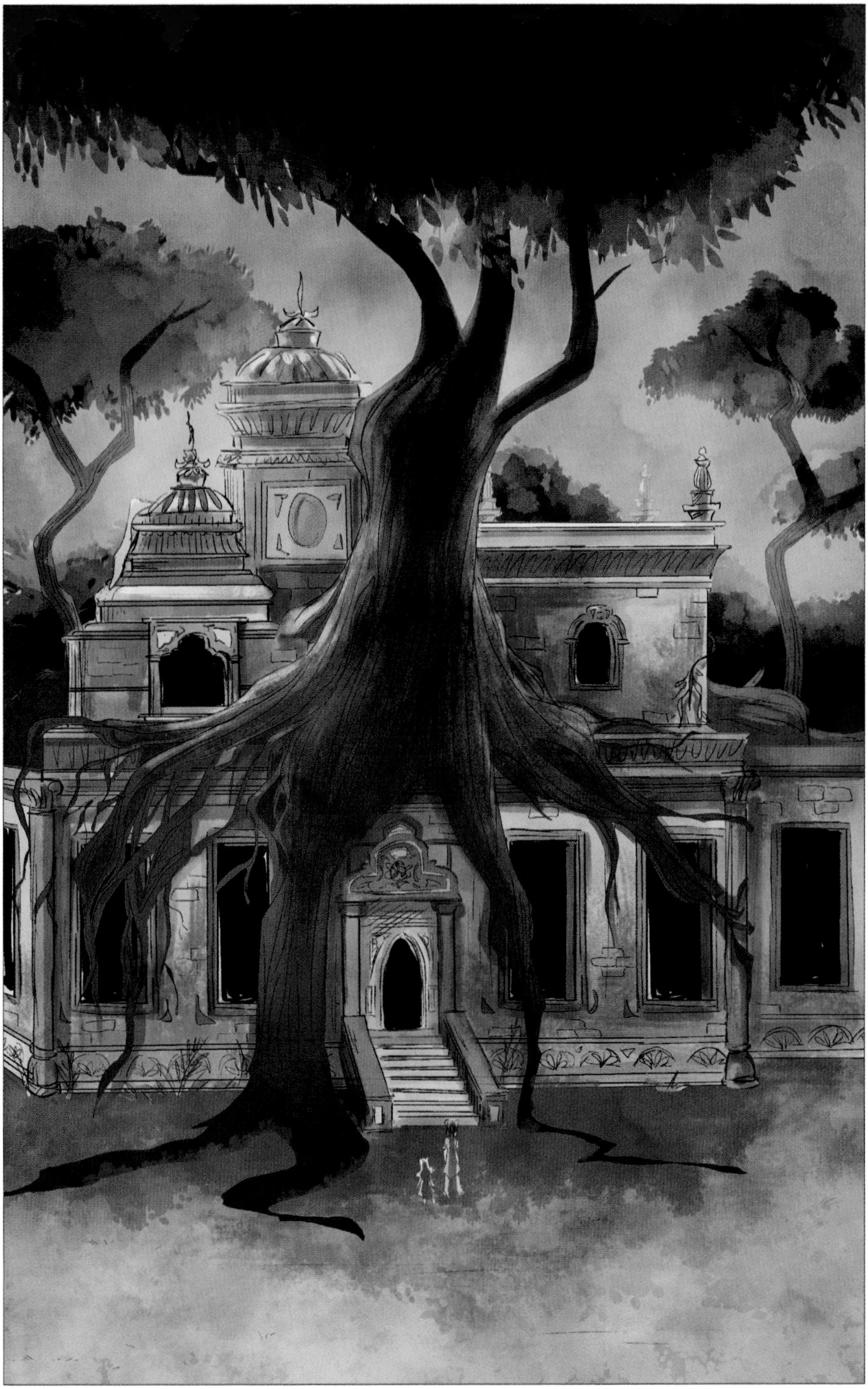

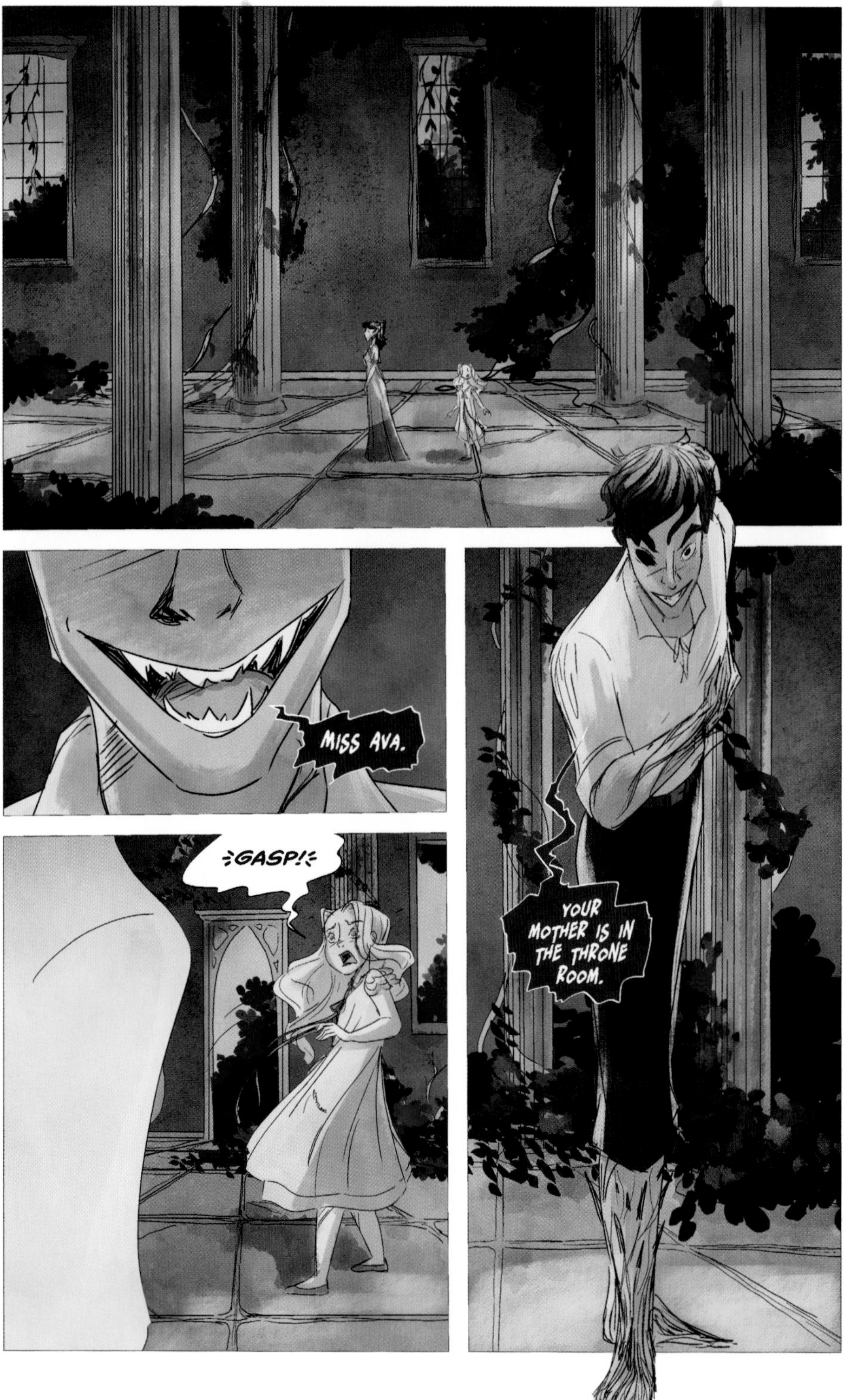
MISS AVA.
YOUR MOTHER IS IN THE THRONE ROOM.
GASP!

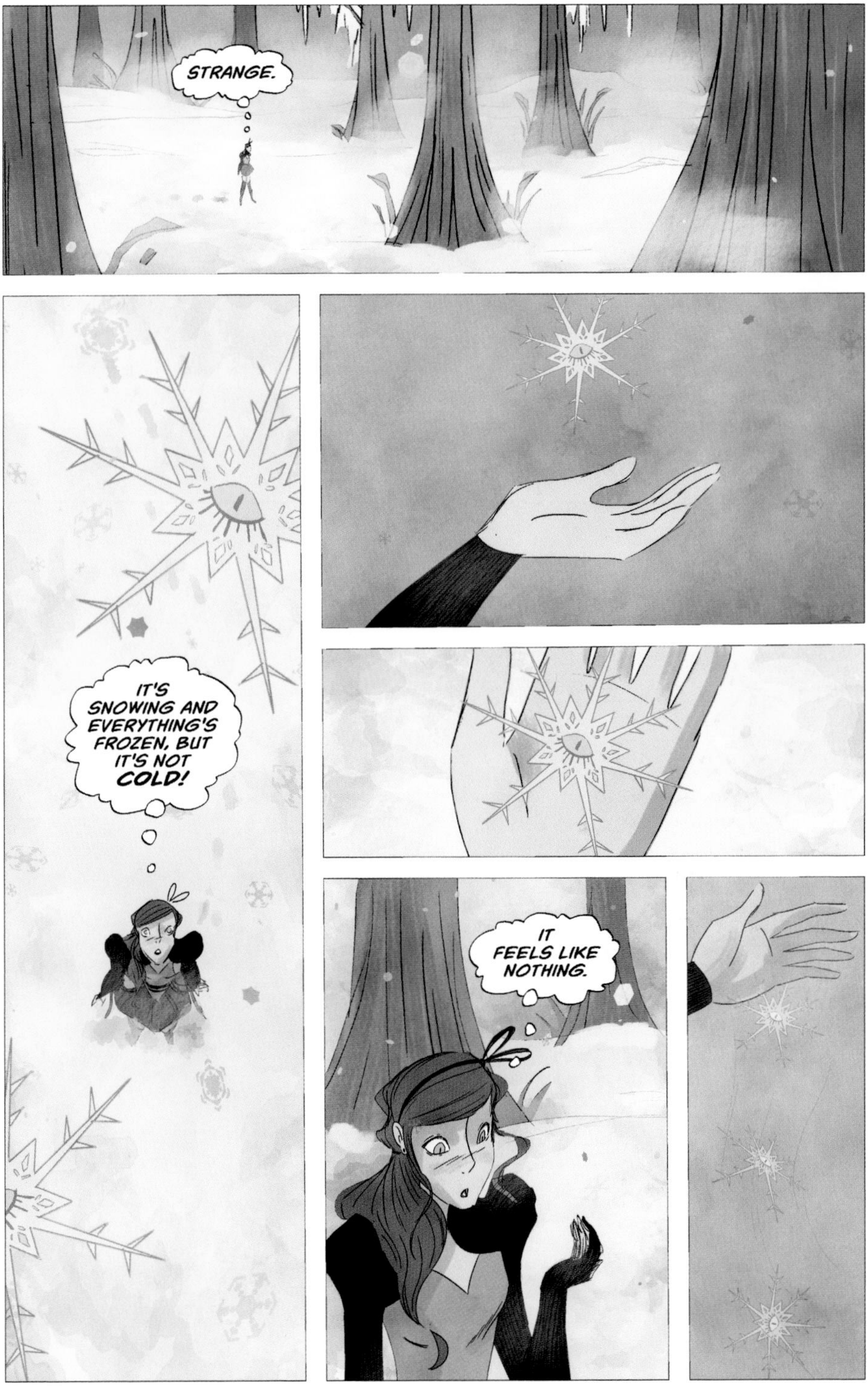
STRANGE.
IT'S SNOWING AND EVERYTHING'S FROZEN, BUT IT'S NOT **COLD!**
IT FEELS LIKE NOTHING.

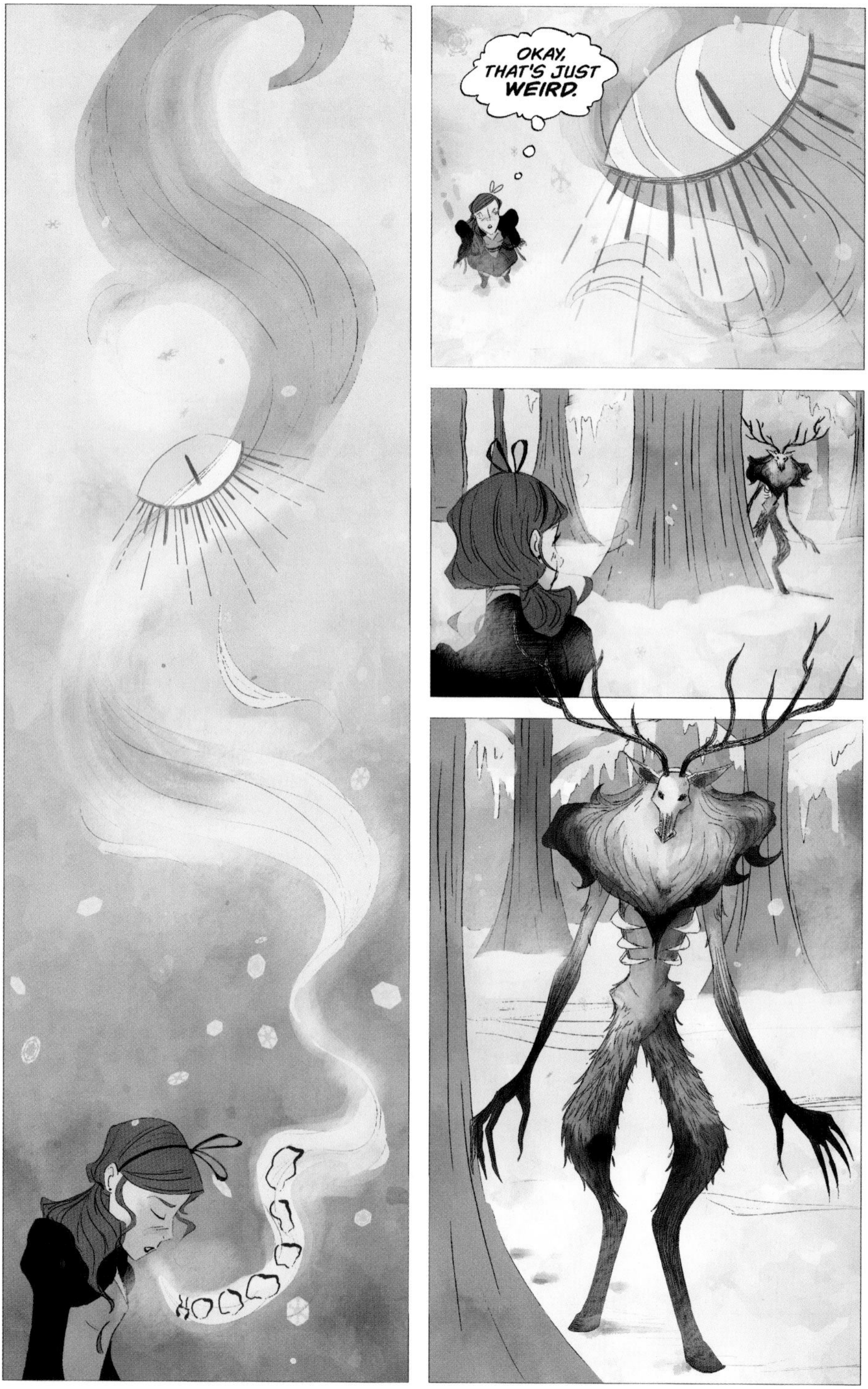
OKAY, THAT'S JUST WEIRD.

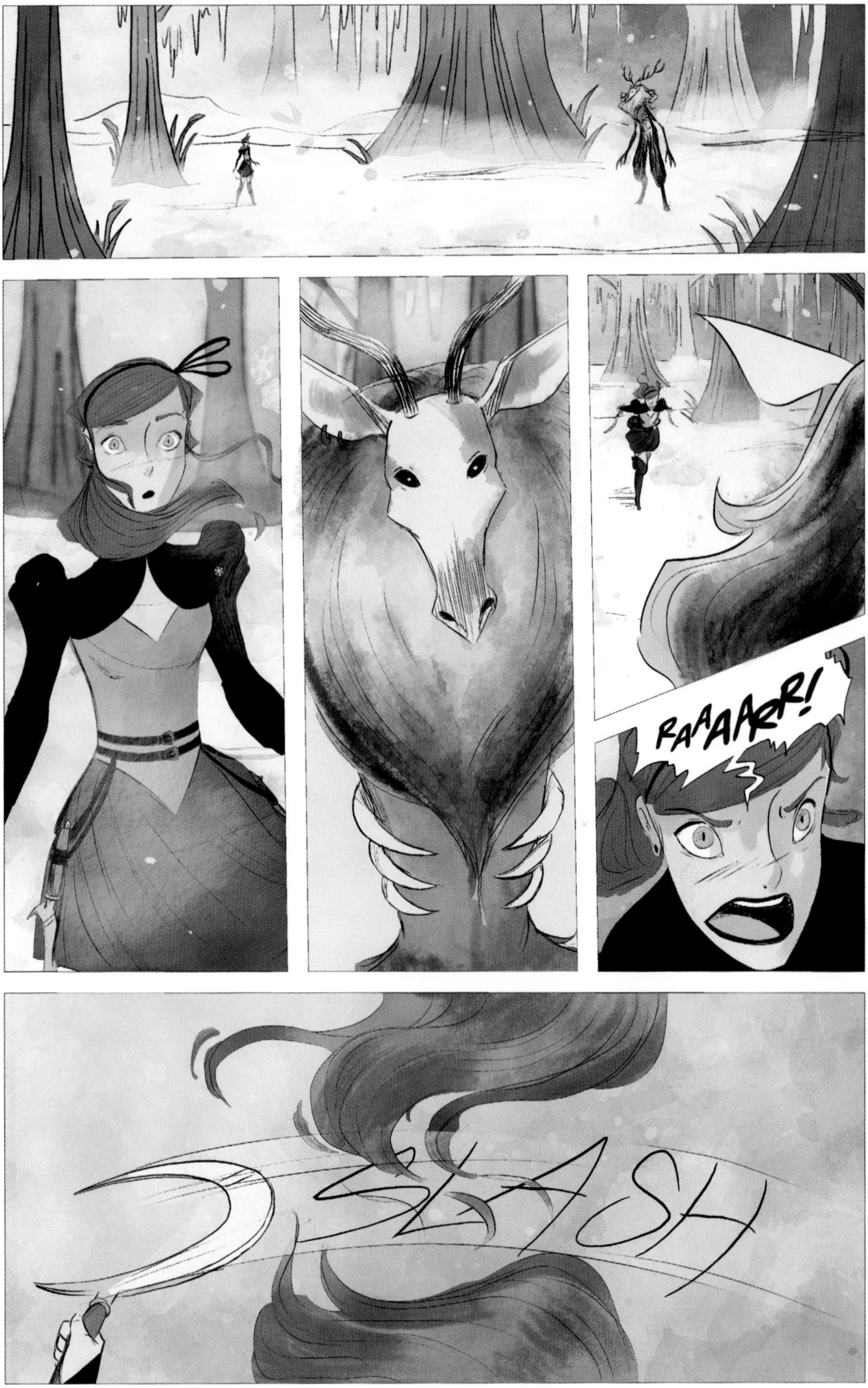
RAAAARR!
SLASH

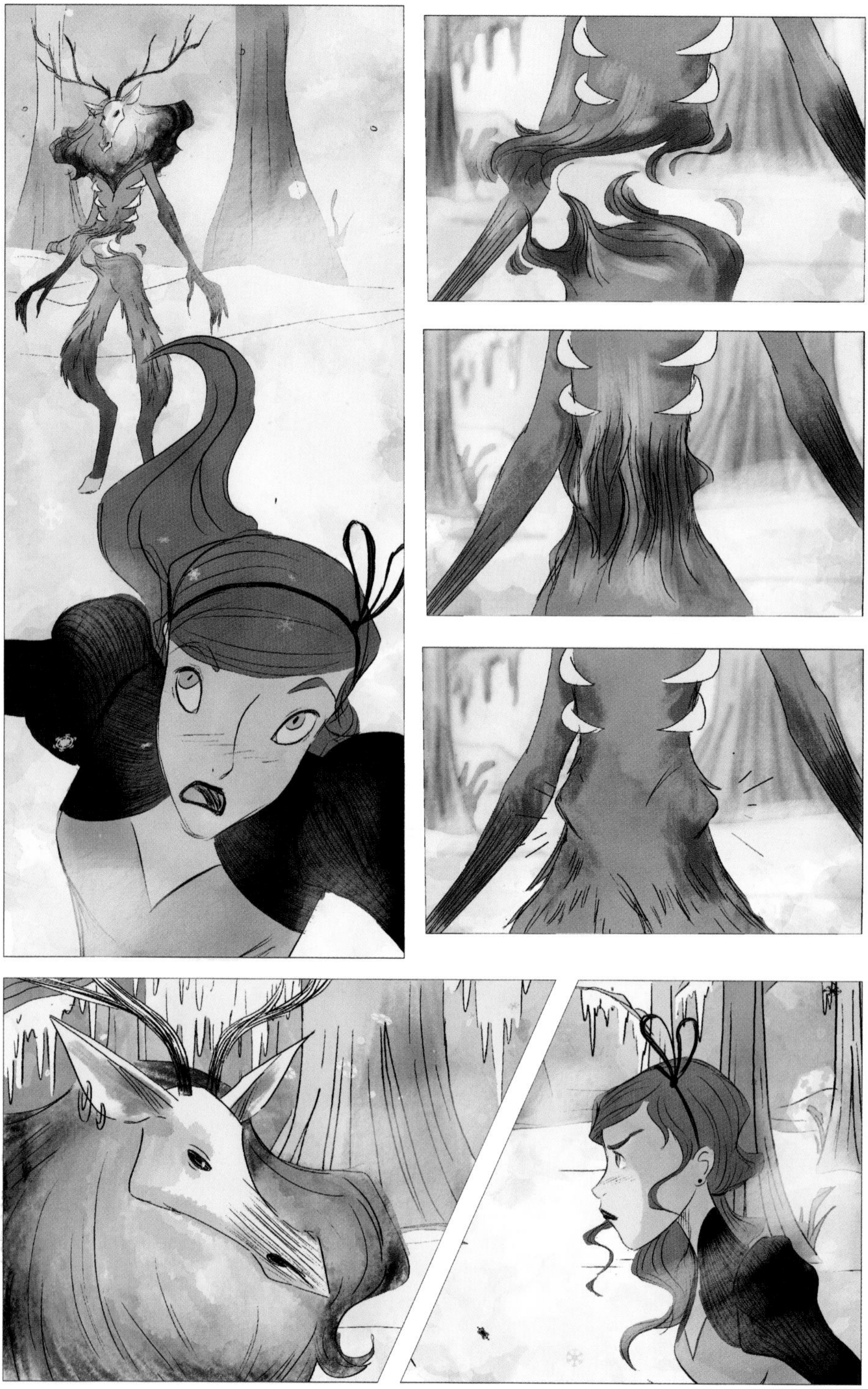

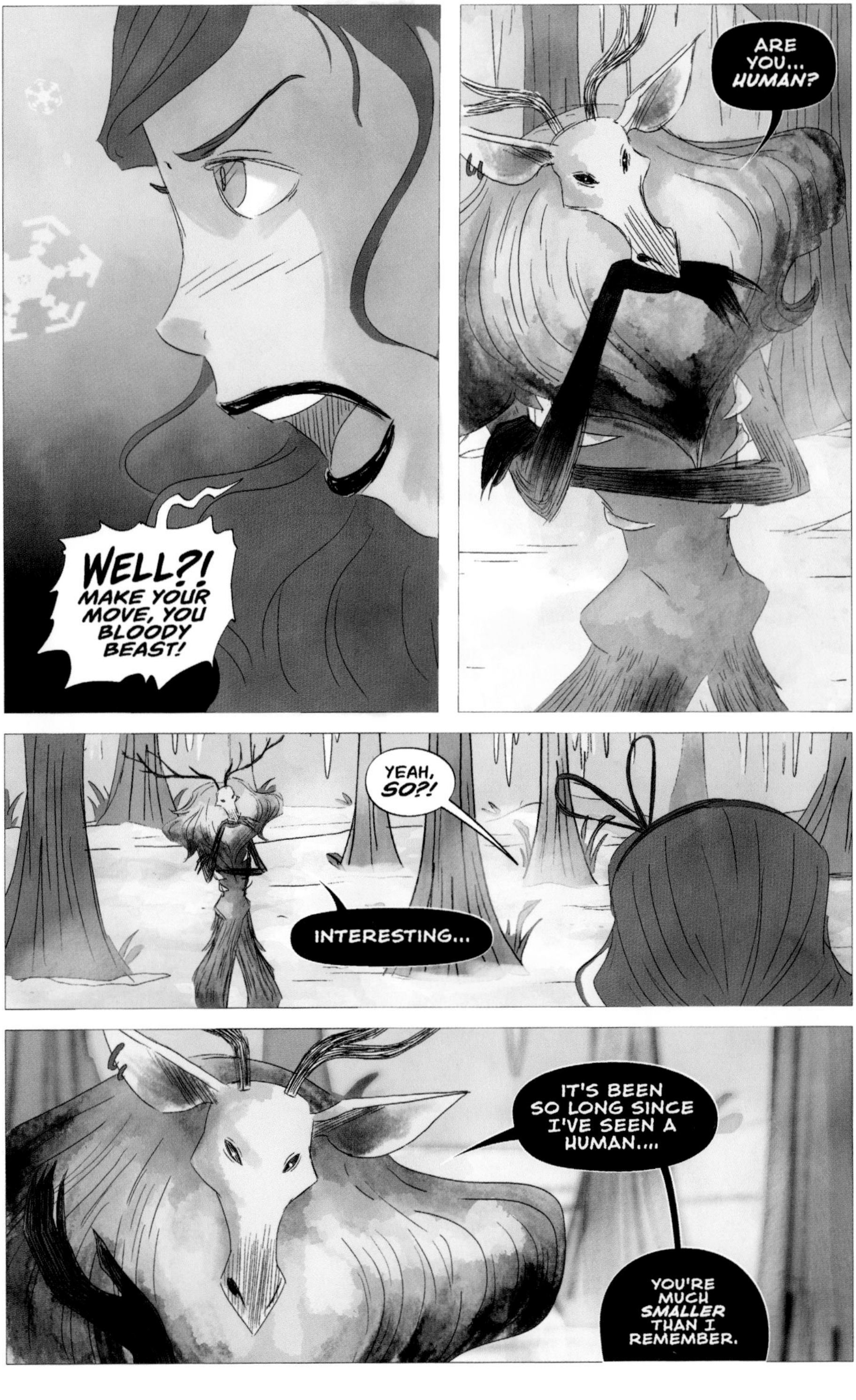
WELL?! MAKE YOUR MOVE, YOU BLOODY BEAST!
ARE YOU... HUMAN?
YEAH, SO?!
INTERESTING...
IT'S BEEN SO LONG SINCE I'VE SEEN A HUMAN....
YOU'RE MUCH SMALLER THAN I REMEMBER.

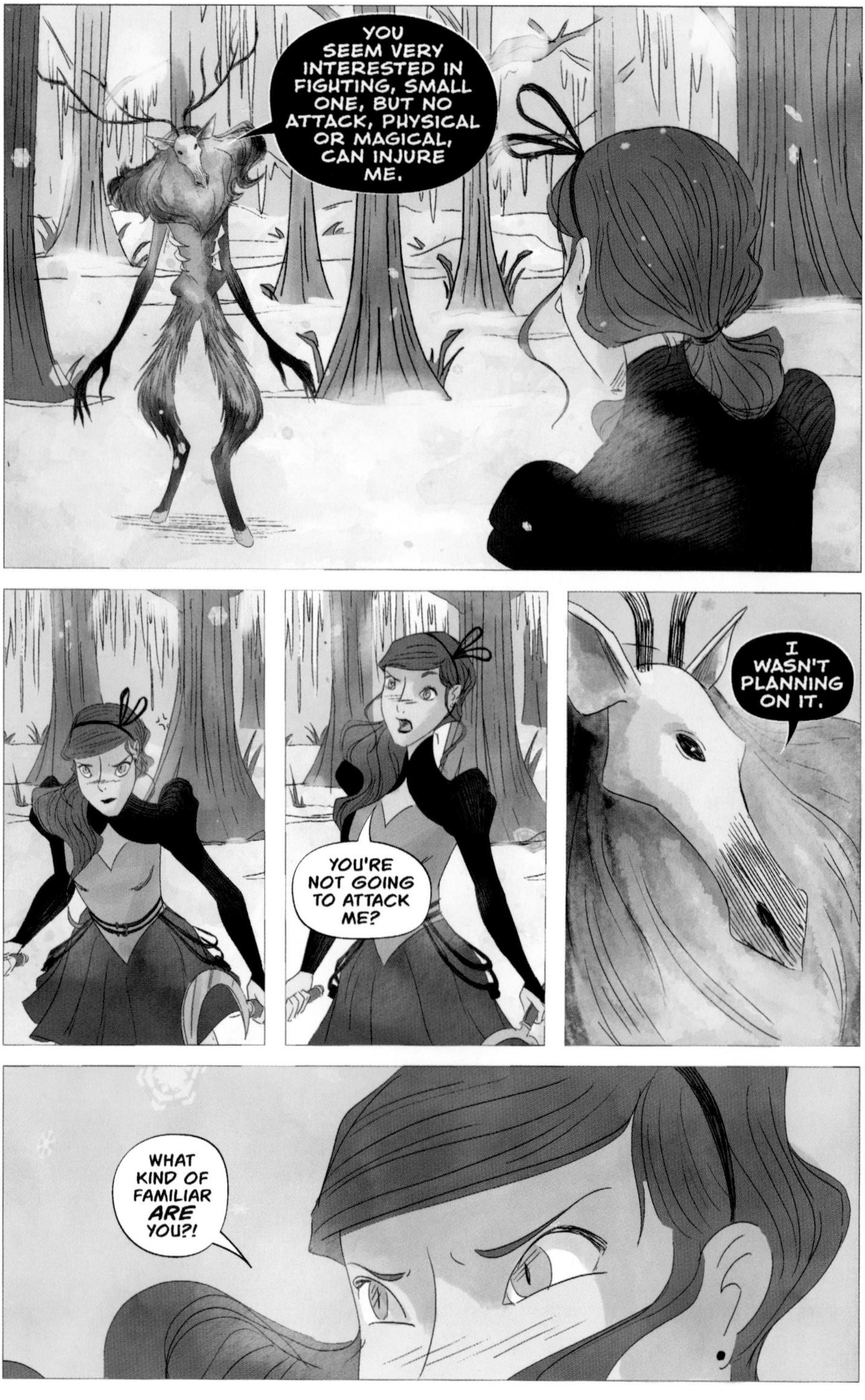
YOU SEEM VERY INTERESTED IN FIGHTING, SMALL ONE, BUT NO ATTACK, PHYSICAL OR MAGICAL, CAN INJURE ME.
YOU'RE NOT GOING TO ATTACK ME?
I WASN'T PLANNING ON IT.
WHAT KIND OF FAMILIAR ARE YOU?!

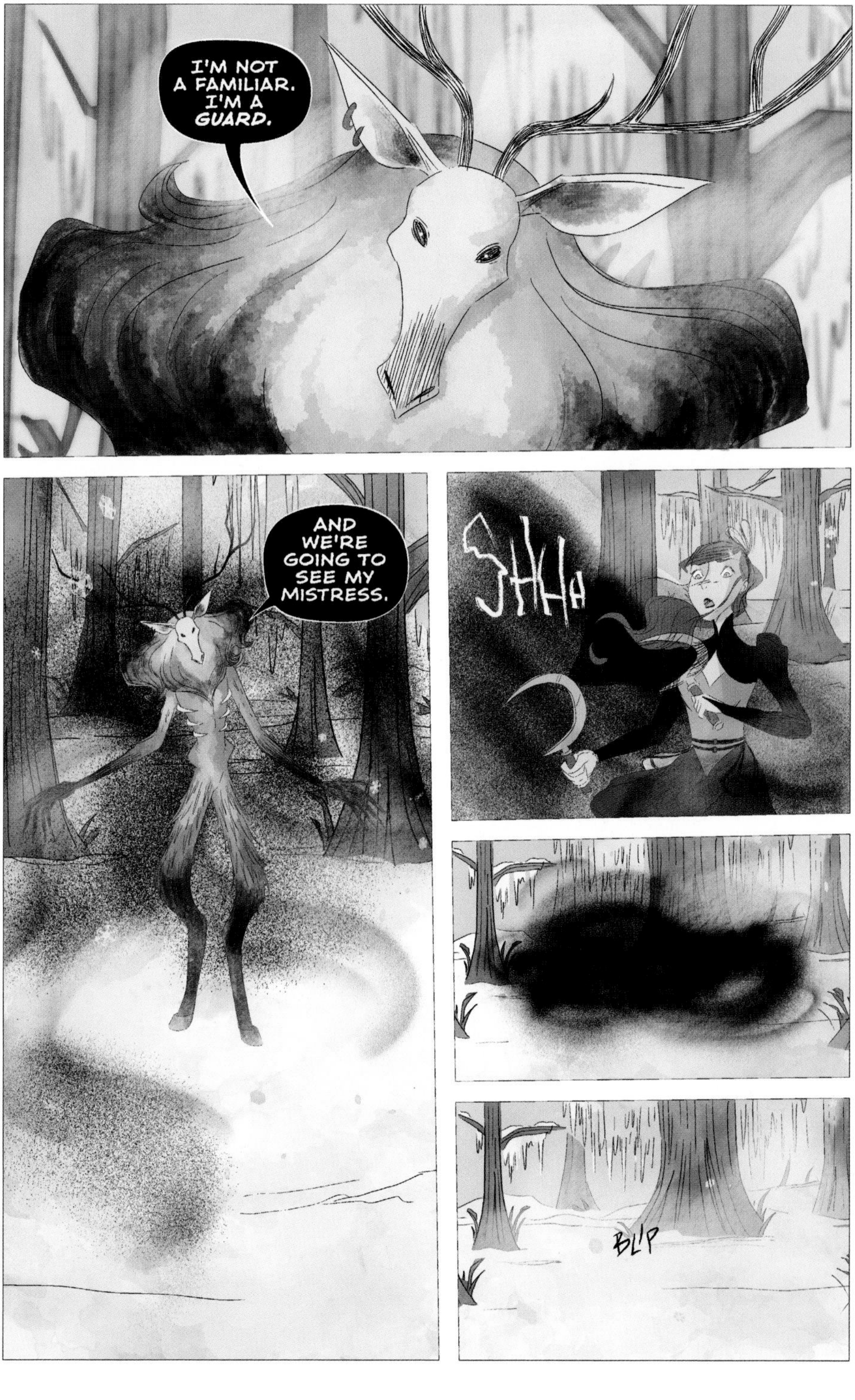
I'M NOT A FAMILIAR. I'M A GUARD.
AND WE'RE GOING TO SEE MY MISTRESS.
SHHA
BLIP

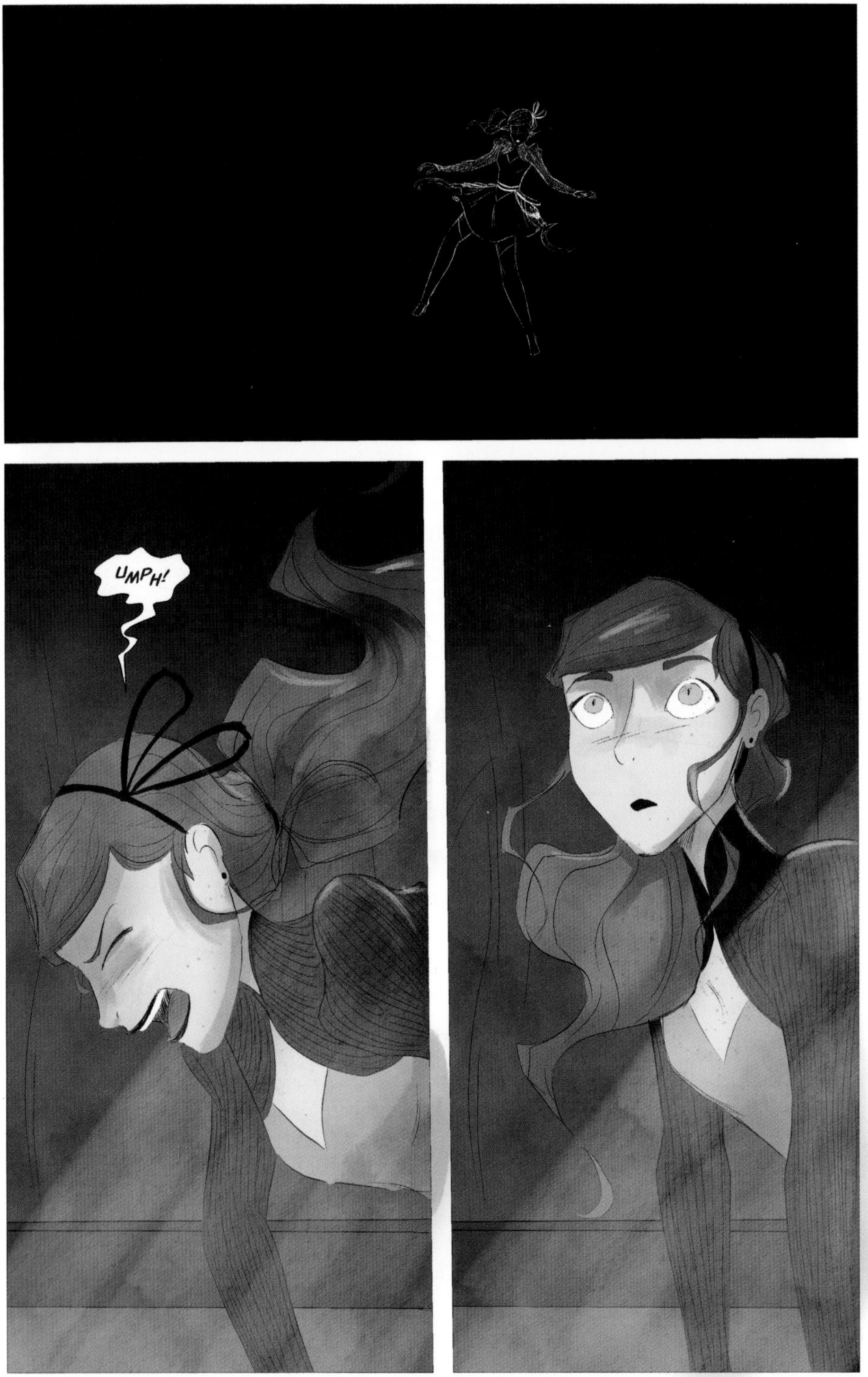
UMPH!

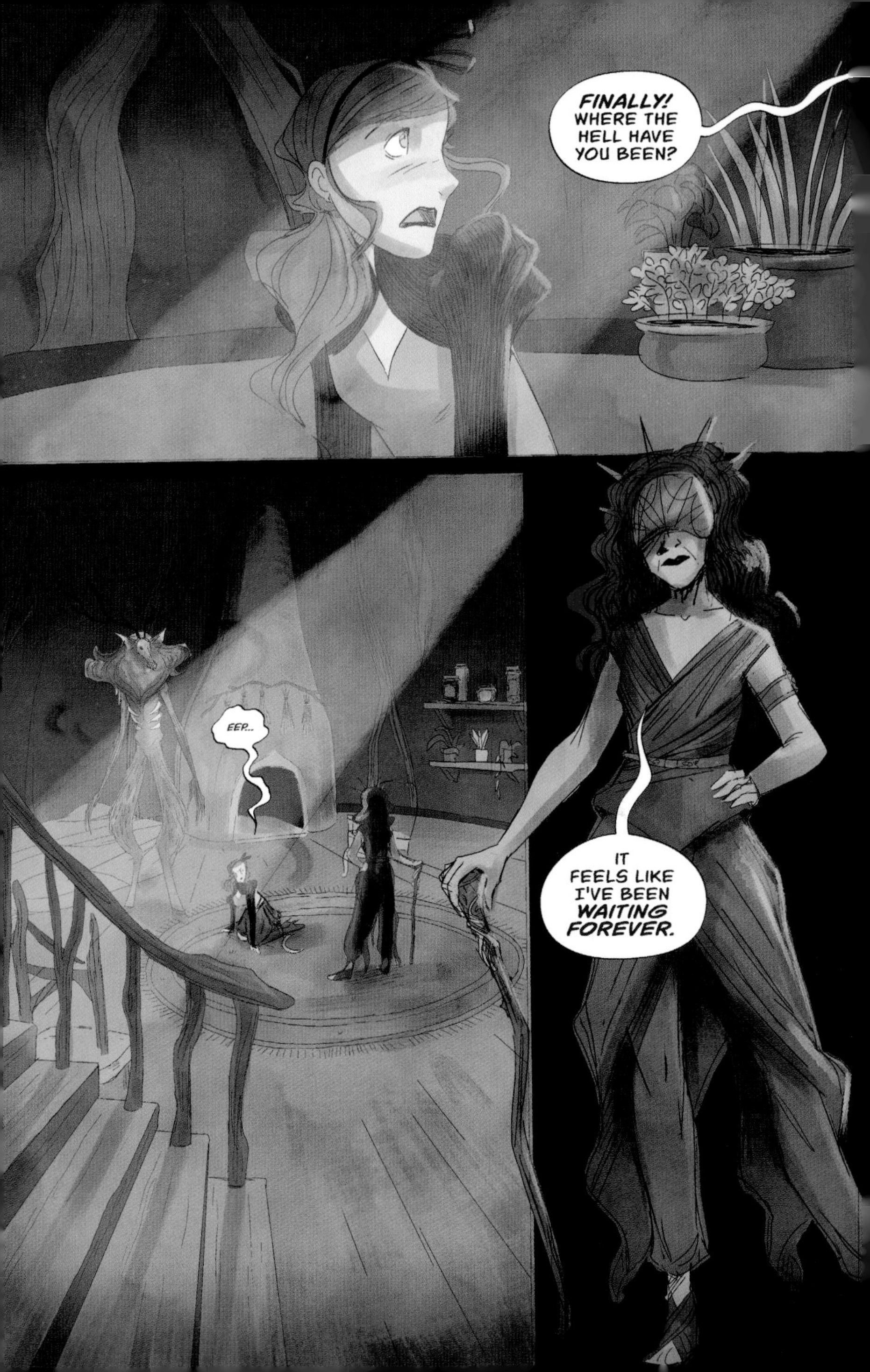
FINALLY! WHERE THE HELL HAVE YOU BEEN?
EEP...
IT FEELS LIKE I'VE BEEN WAITING FOREVER.

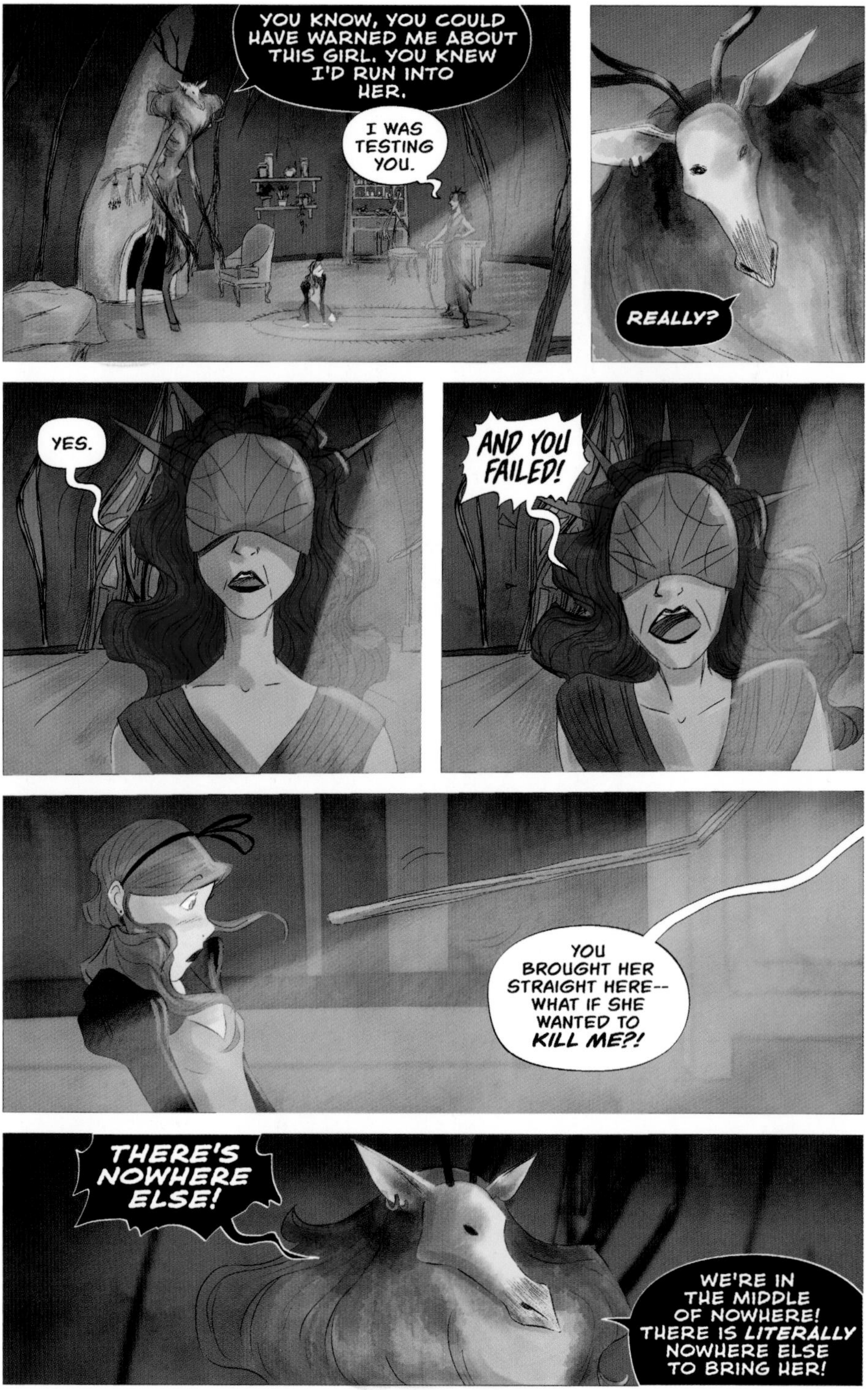
YOU KNOW, YOU COULD HAVE WARNED ME ABOUT THIS GIRL. YOU KNEW I'D RUN INTO HER.
I WAS TESTING YOU.
REALLY?
YES.
AND YOU FAILED!
YOU BROUGHT HER STRAIGHT HERE-- WHAT IF SHE WANTED TO KILL ME?!
THERE'S NOWHERE ELSE!
WE'RE IN THE MIDDLE OF NOWHERE! THERE IS LITERALLY NOWHERE ELSE TO BRING HER!

WOULD YOU BE HAPPIER IF I JUST LET HER WANDER THE LANDSCAPE?

HMPH...

UGH, MY HEAD...

≈SIGH≈ IT'S ALMOST ANNOYING, BEING THIS RIGHT ALL THE TIME.

IF YOU TWO AREN'T GOING TO KILL ME, CAN YOU AT LEAST TELL ME WHAT'S GOING ON?

SWIG

AND WHAT *FUN* WOULD *THAT* BE?

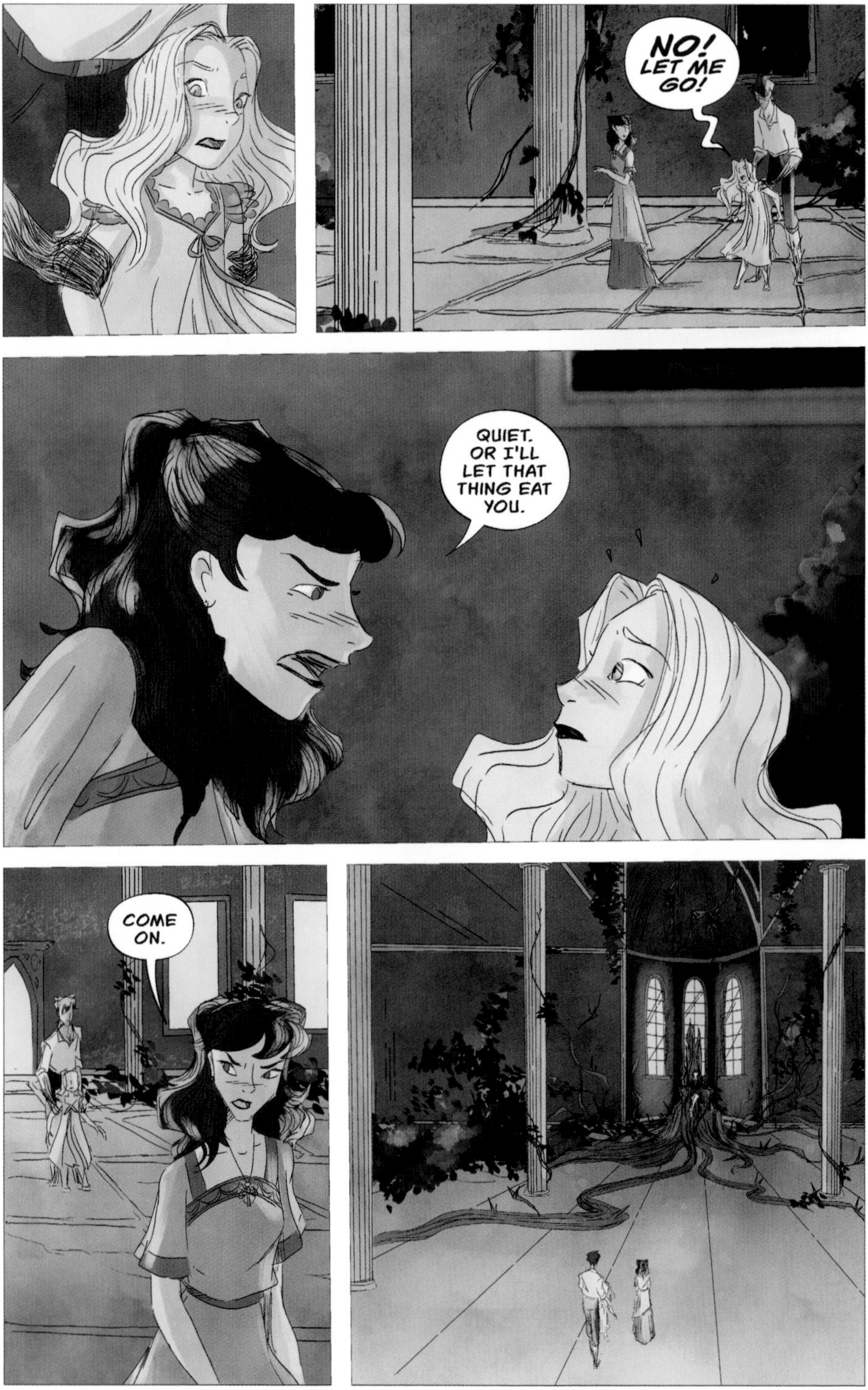
NO! LET ME GO!
QUIET. OR I'LL LET THAT THING EAT YOU.
COME ON.

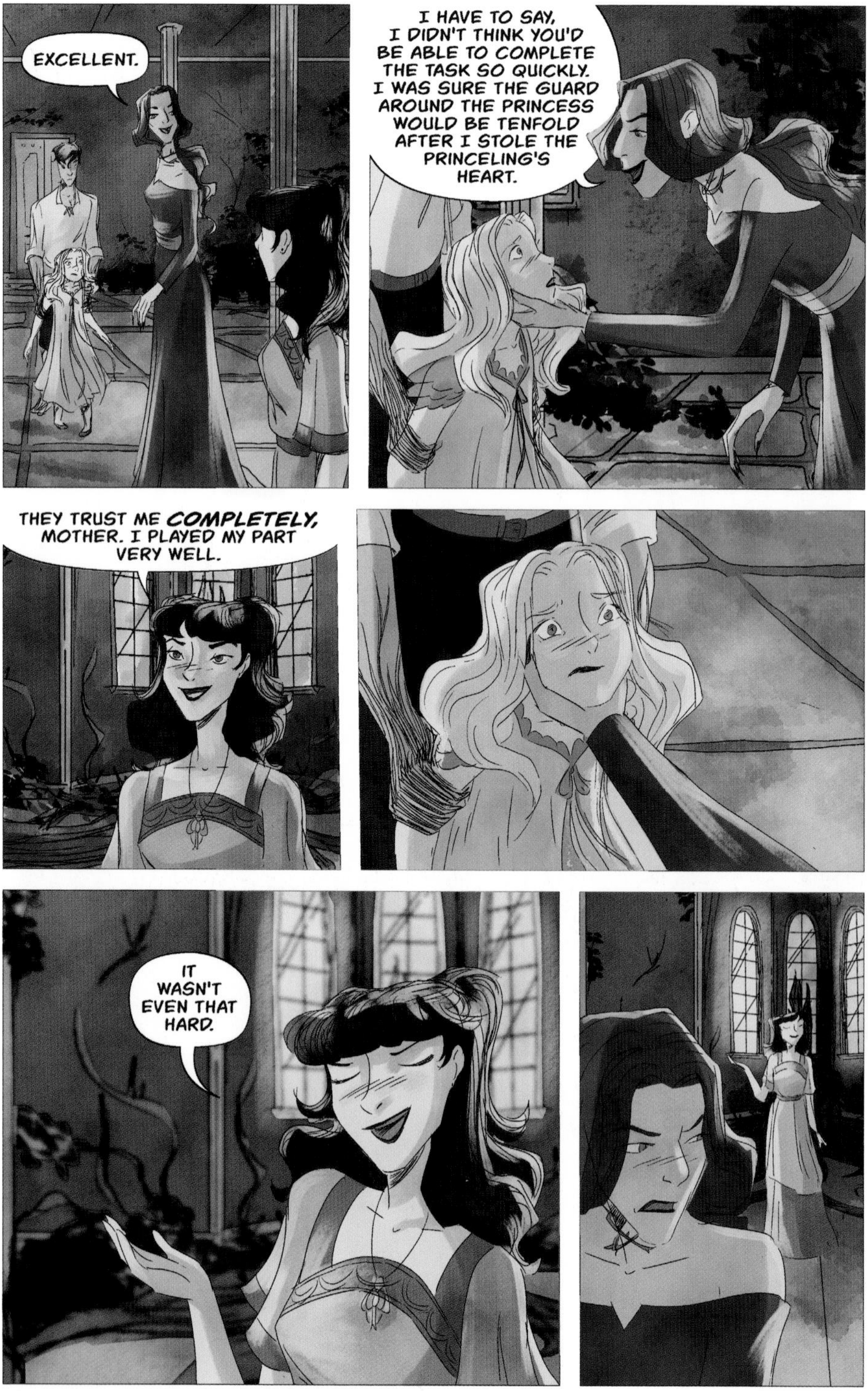
EXCELLENT.
I HAVE TO SAY, I DIDN'T THINK YOU'D BE ABLE TO COMPLETE THE TASK SO QUICKLY. I WAS SURE THE GUARD AROUND THE PRINCESS WOULD BE TENFOLD AFTER I STOLE THE PRINCELING'S HEART.
THEY TRUST ME COMPLETELY, MOTHER. I PLAYED MY PART VERY WELL.
IT WASN'T EVEN THAT HARD.

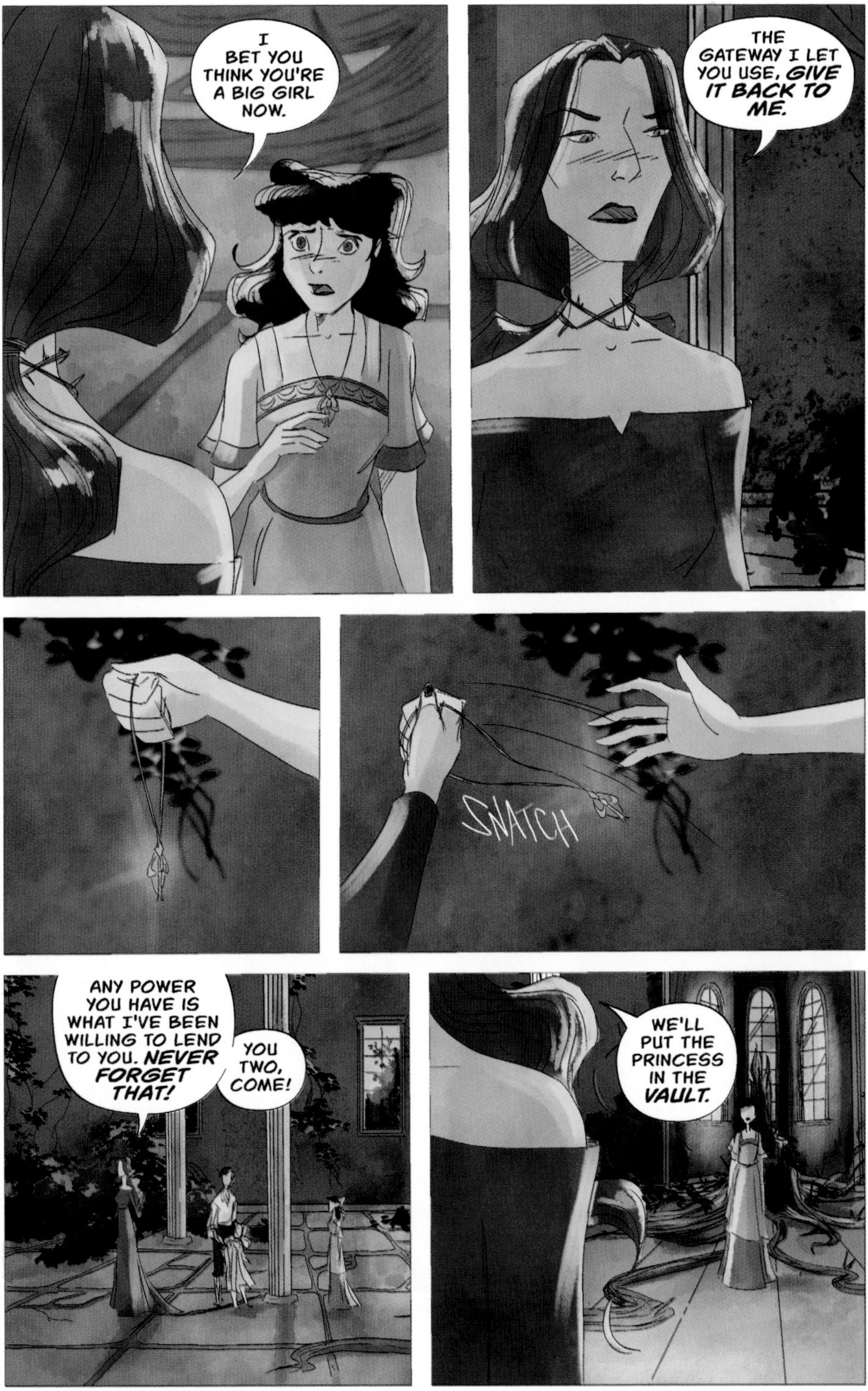
I BET YOU THINK YOU'RE A BIG GIRL NOW.
THE GATEWAY I LET YOU USE, GIVE IT BACK TO ME.
SNATCH
ANY POWER YOU HAVE IS WHAT I'VE BEEN WILLING TO LEND TO YOU. NEVER FORGET THAT!
YOU TWO, COME!
WE'LL PUT THE PRINCESS IN THE VAULT.

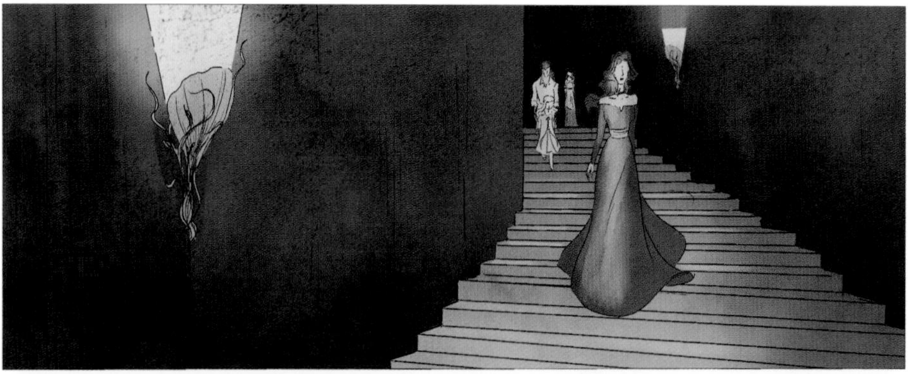
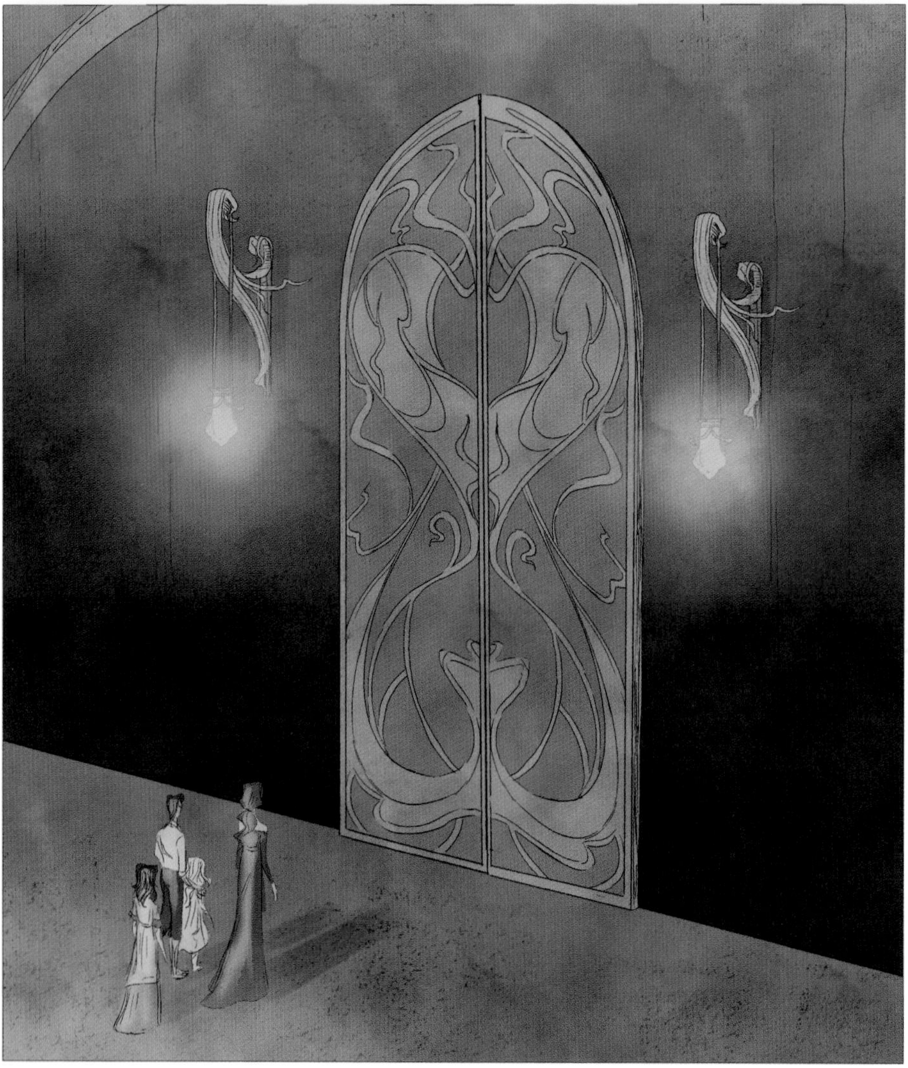

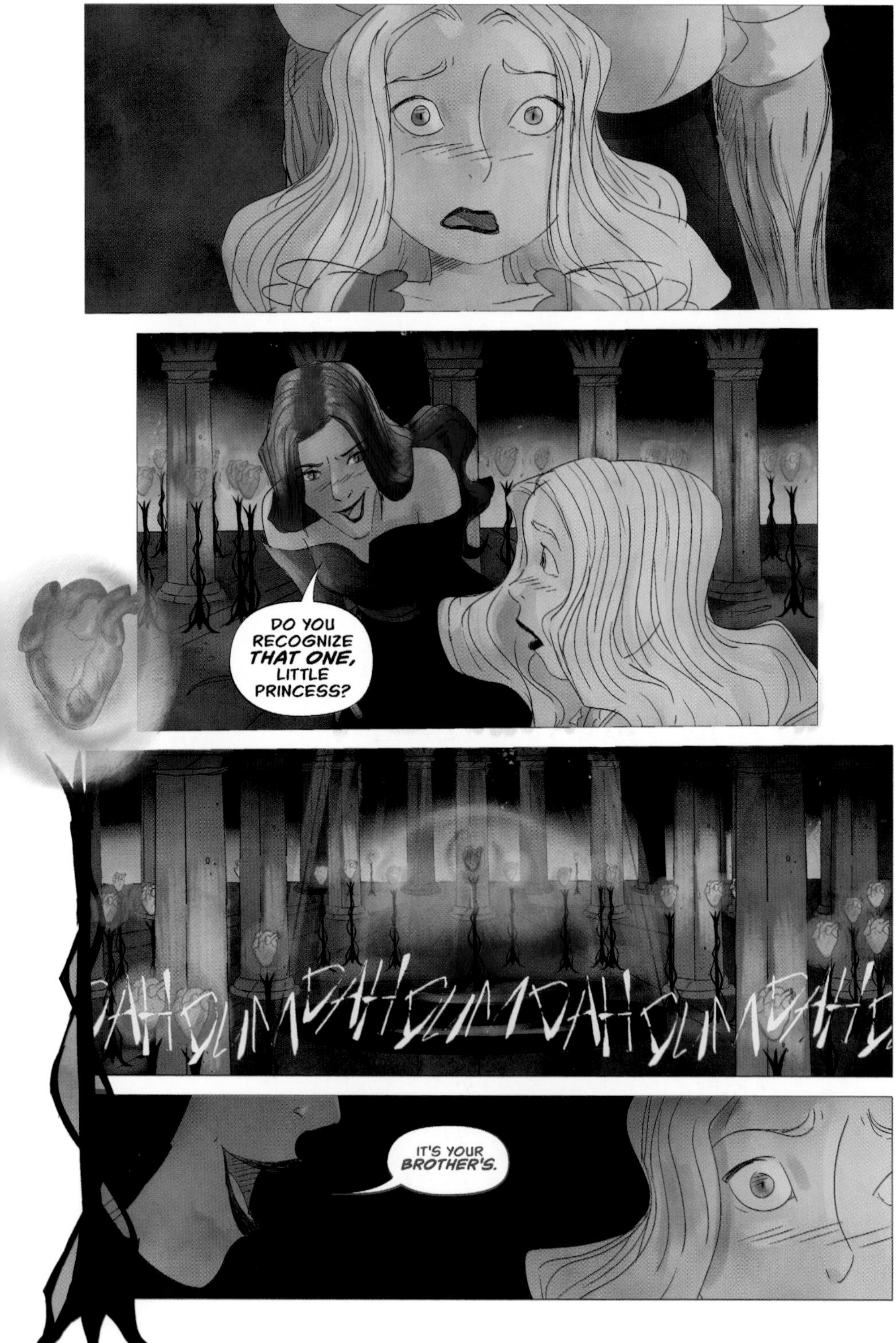
DO YOU RECOGNIZE *THAT ONE,* LITTLE PRINCESS?
IT'S YOUR *BROTHER'S.*

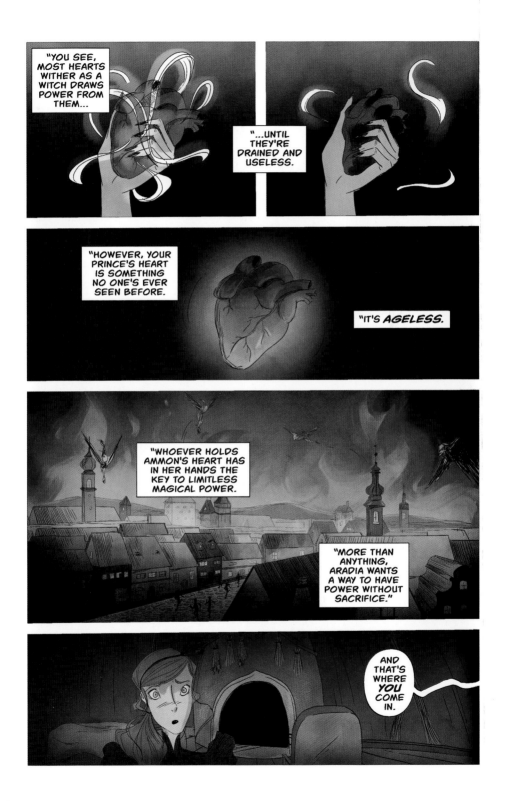

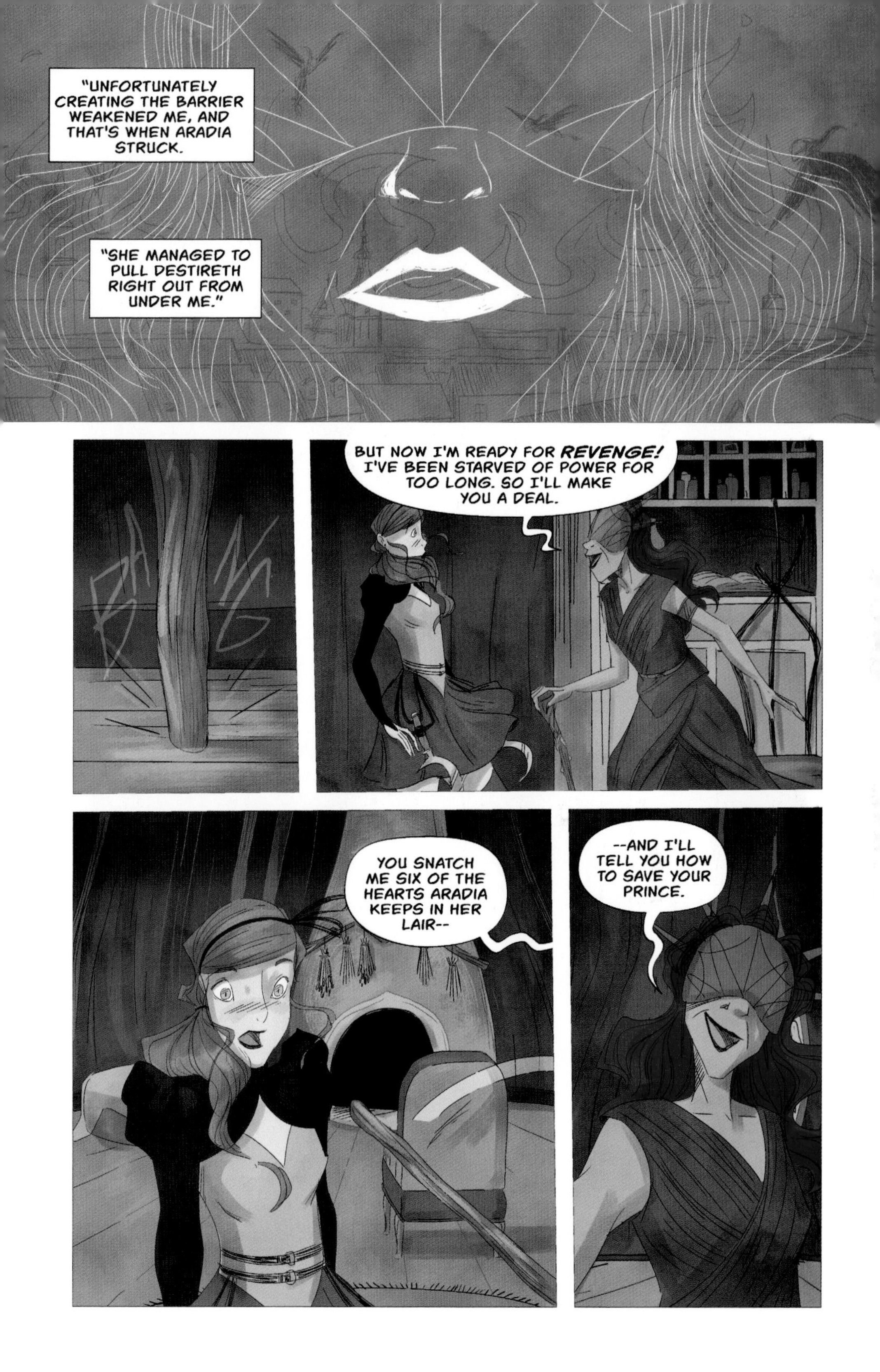
"UNFORTUNATELY CREATING THE BARRIER WEAKENED ME, AND THAT'S WHEN ARADIA STRUCK.
"SHE MANAGED TO PULL DESTIRETH RIGHT OUT FROM UNDER ME."
BANG
BUT NOW I'M READY FOR *REVENGE!* I'VE BEEN STARVED OF POWER FOR TOO LONG. SO I'LL MAKE YOU A DEAL.
YOU SNATCH ME SIX OF THE HEARTS ARADIA KEEPS IN HER LAIR--
--AND I'LL TELL YOU HOW TO SAVE YOUR PRINCE.

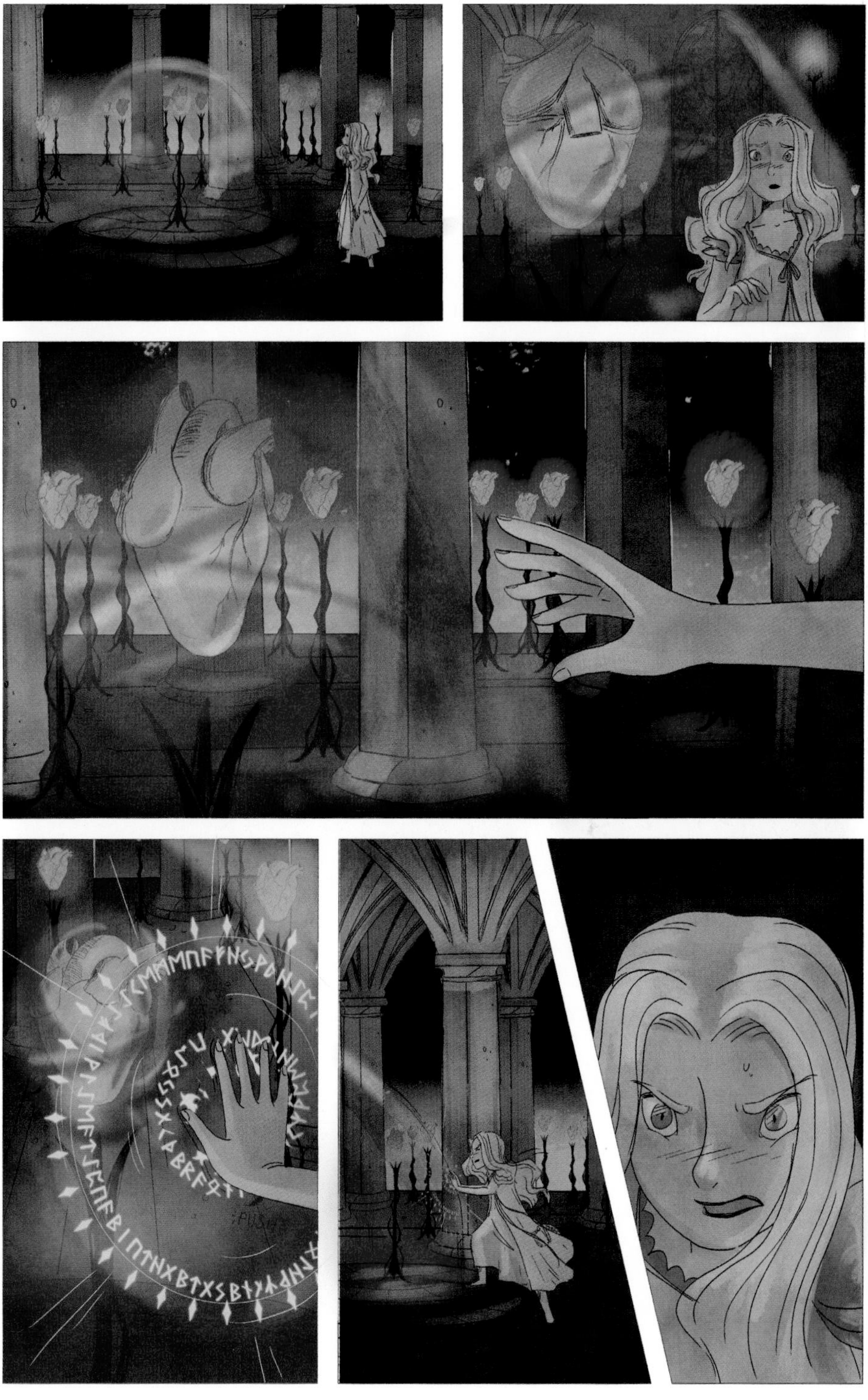
PUSH

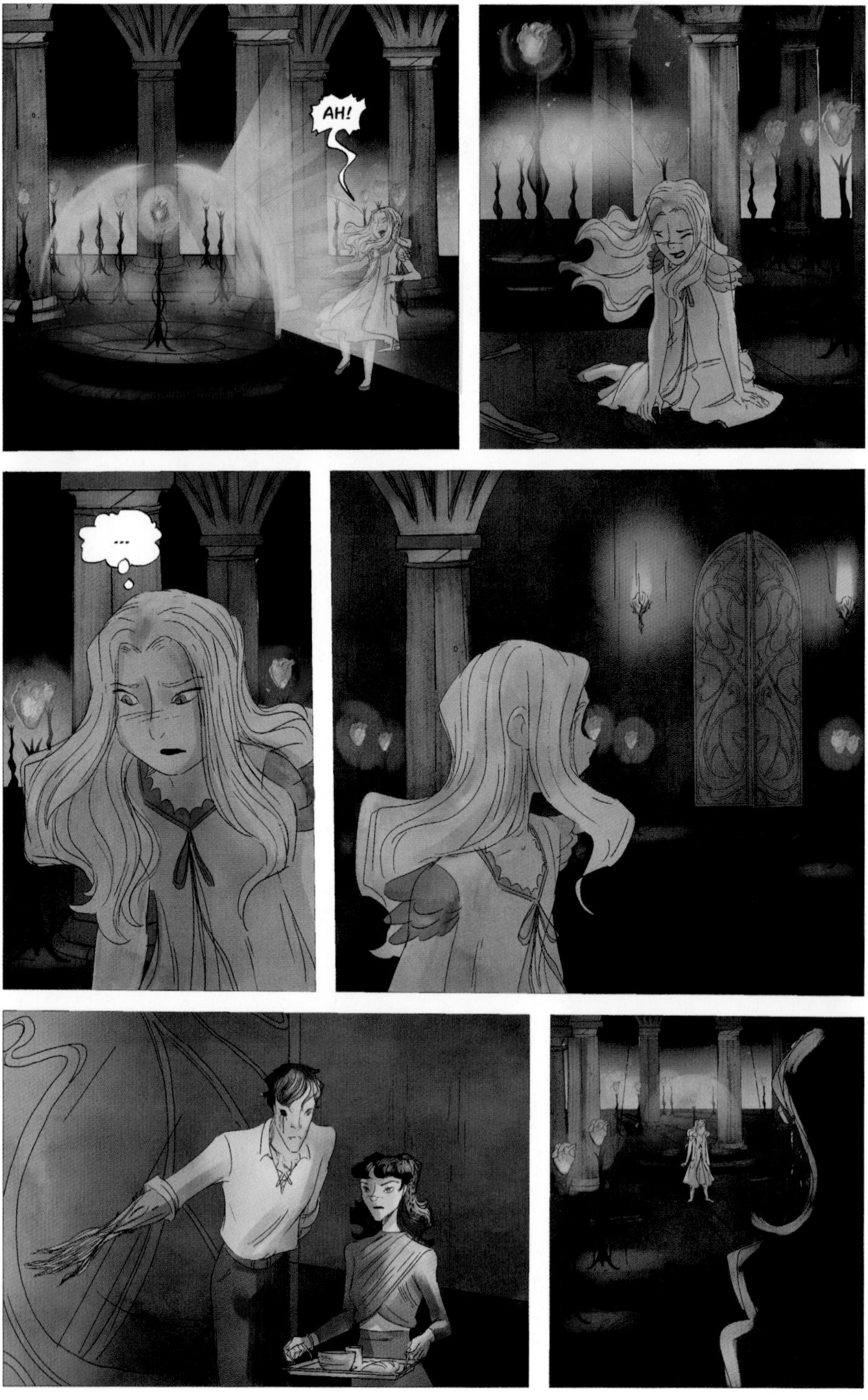
AH!
...

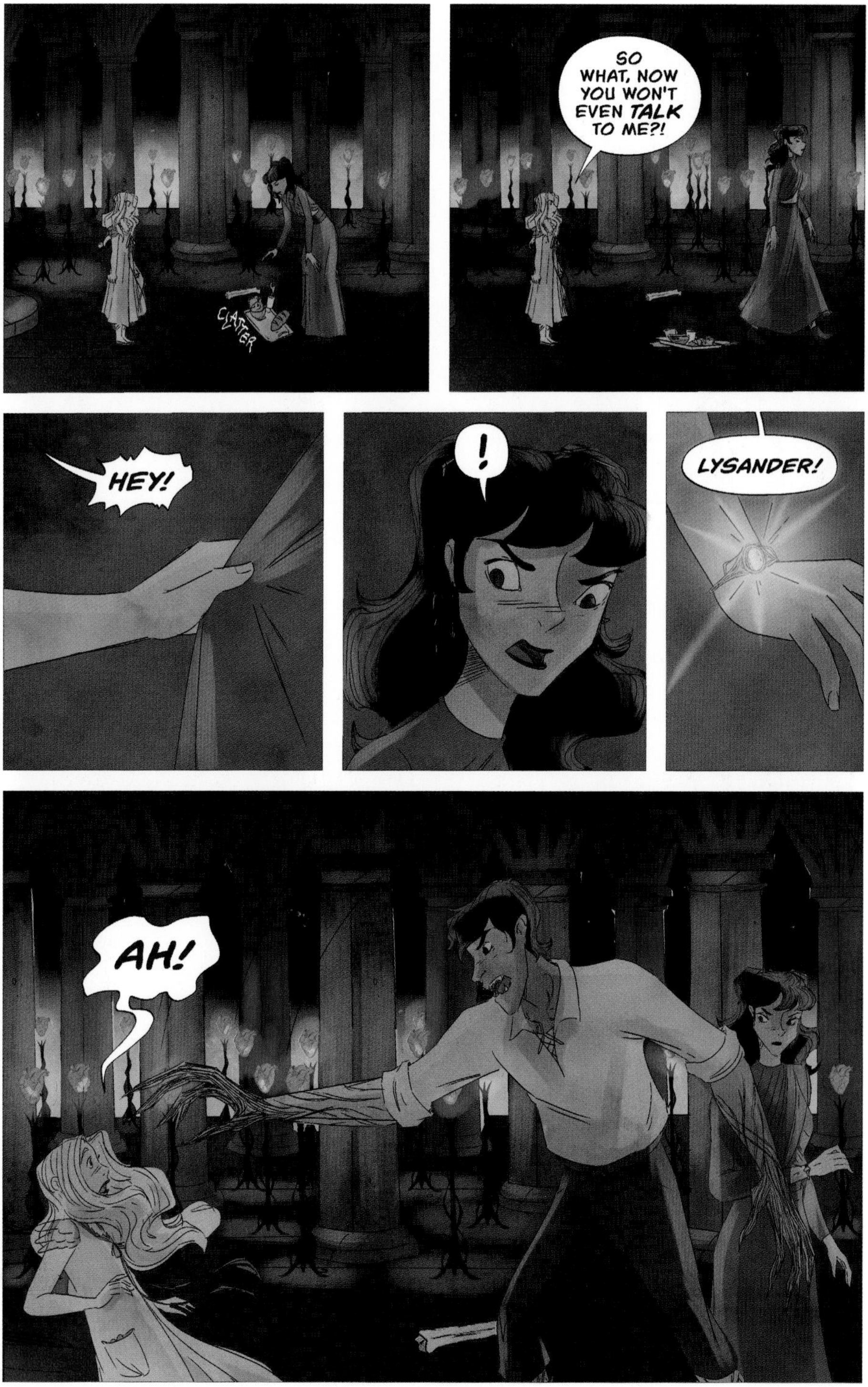
CLATTER
SO WHAT, NOW YOU WON'T EVEN TALK TO ME?!
HEY!
!
LYSANDER!
AH!

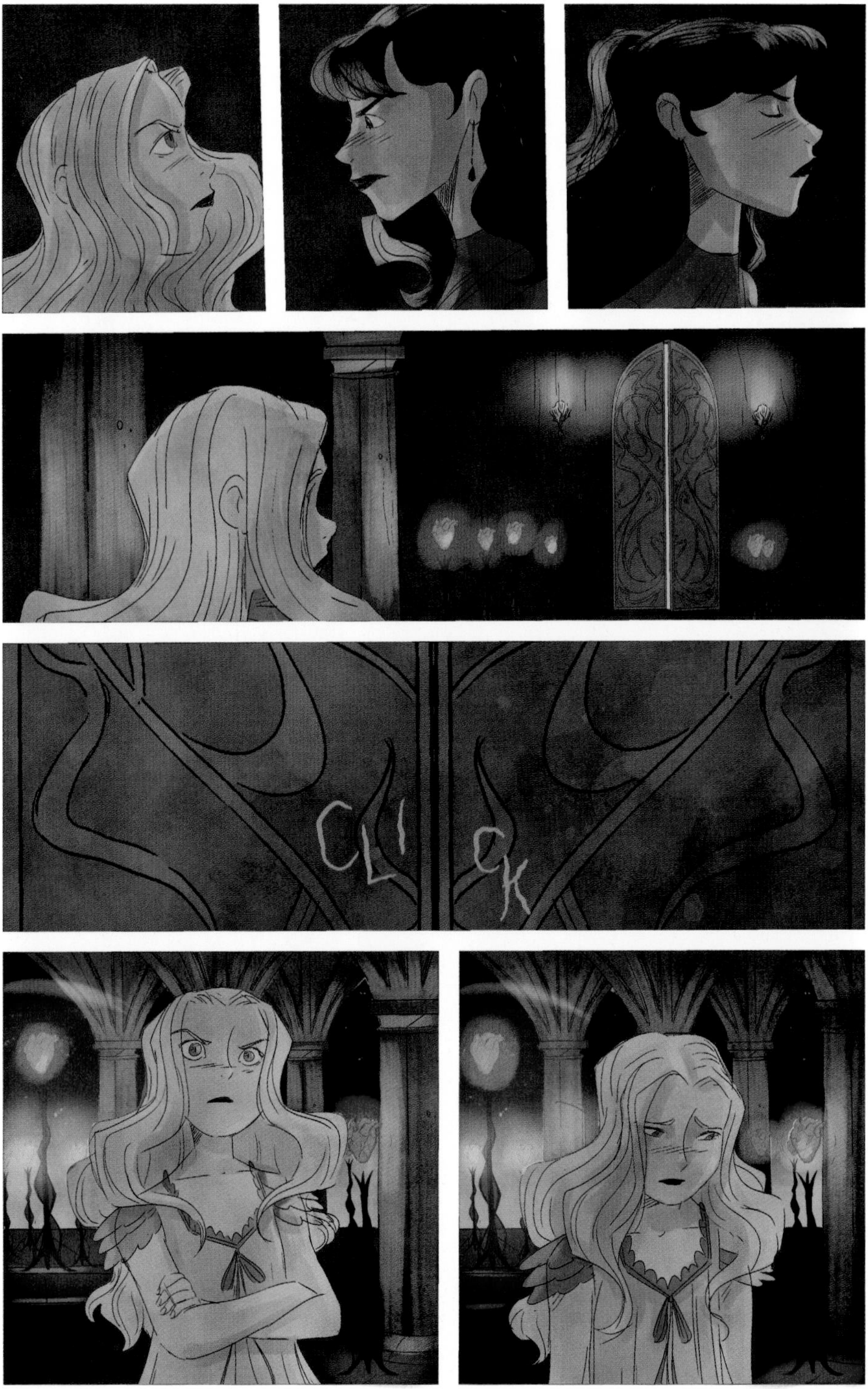
CLICK

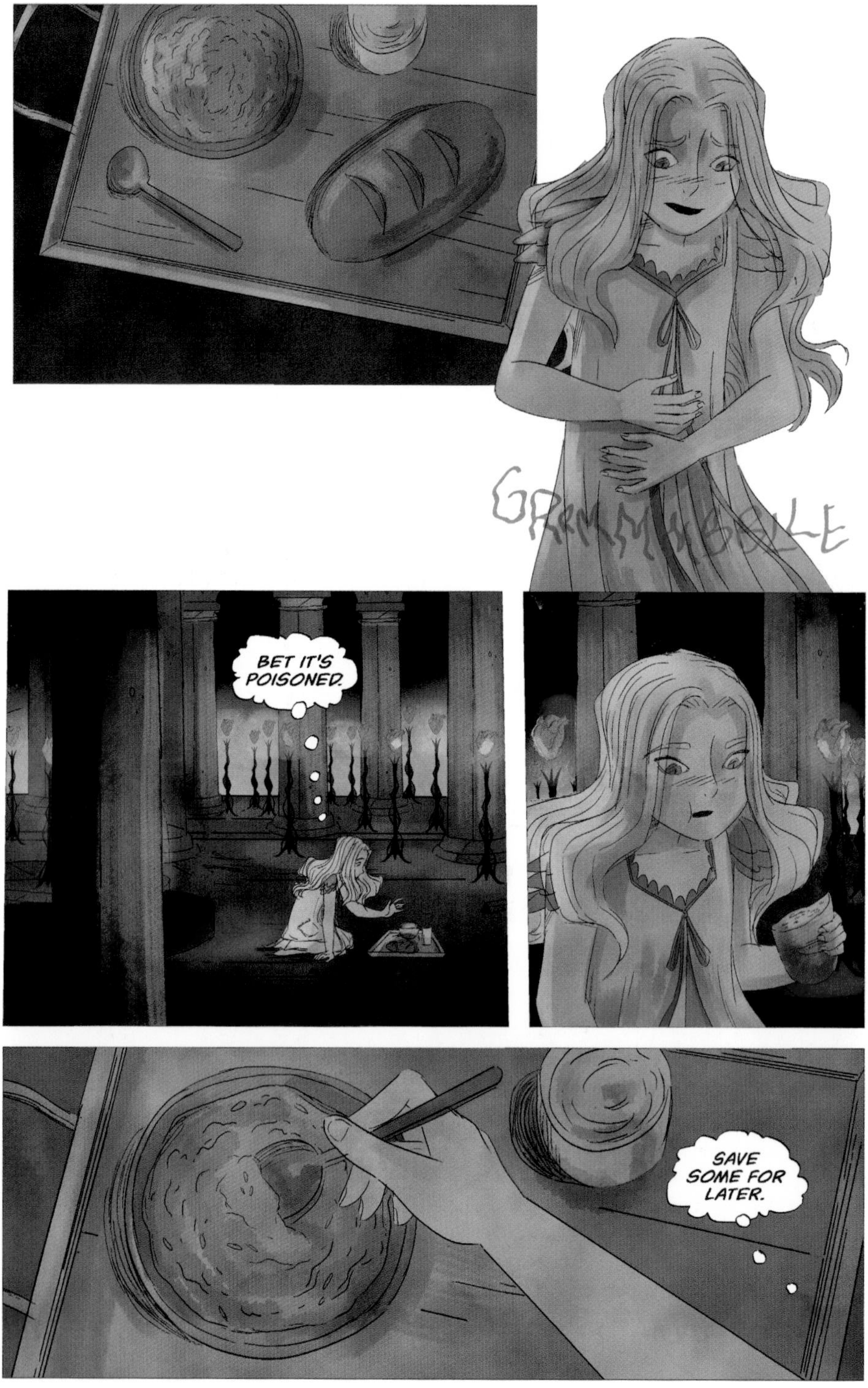
GRRMMMBBLLE
BET IT'S POISONED.
SAVE SOME FOR LATER.

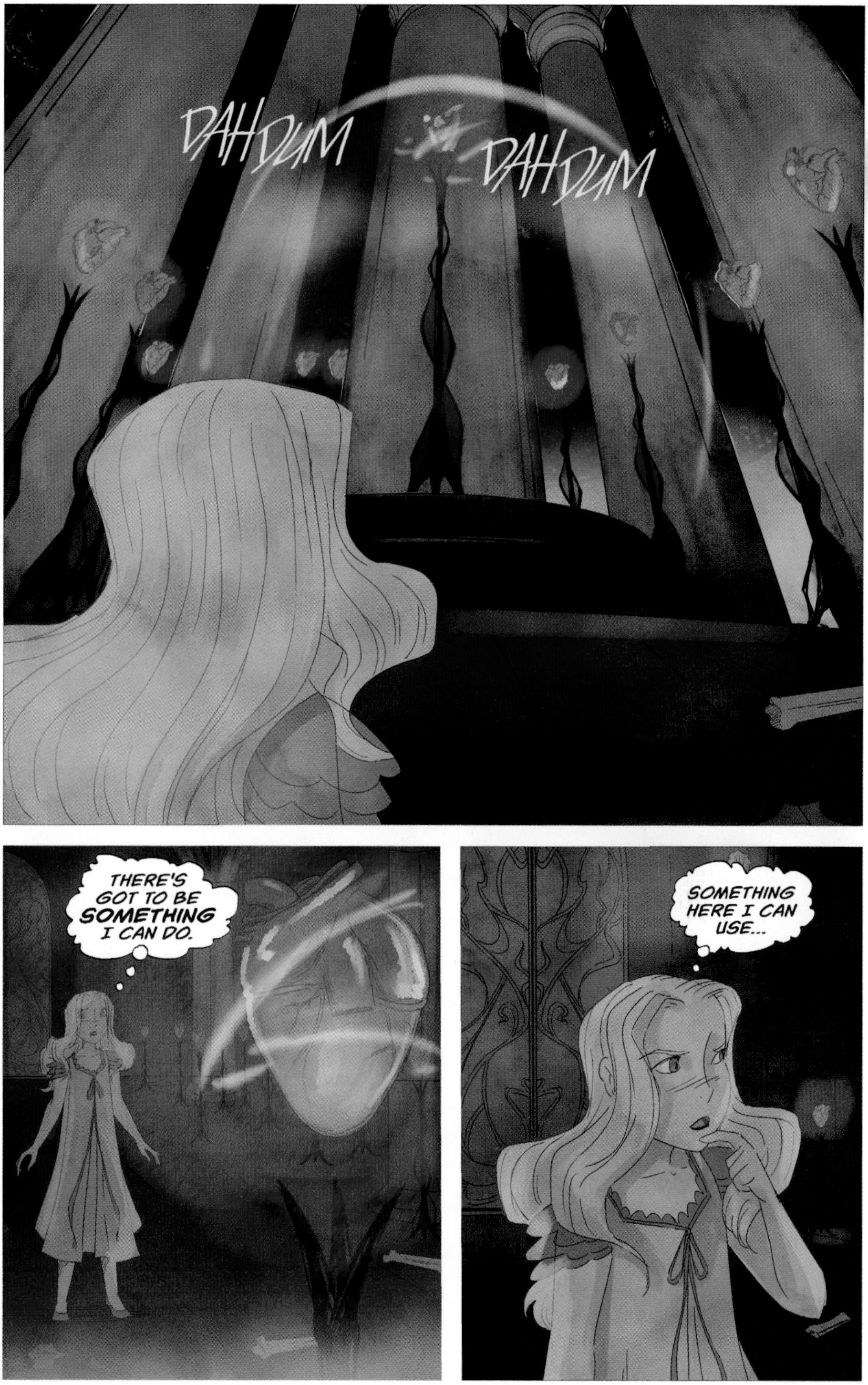
DAH DUM
DAH DUM
THERE'S GOT TO BE **SOMETHING** I CAN DO.
SOMETHING HERE I CAN USE...

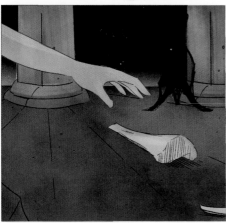

THOSE STANDS MIGHT MAKE GOOD CARVING TOOLS.

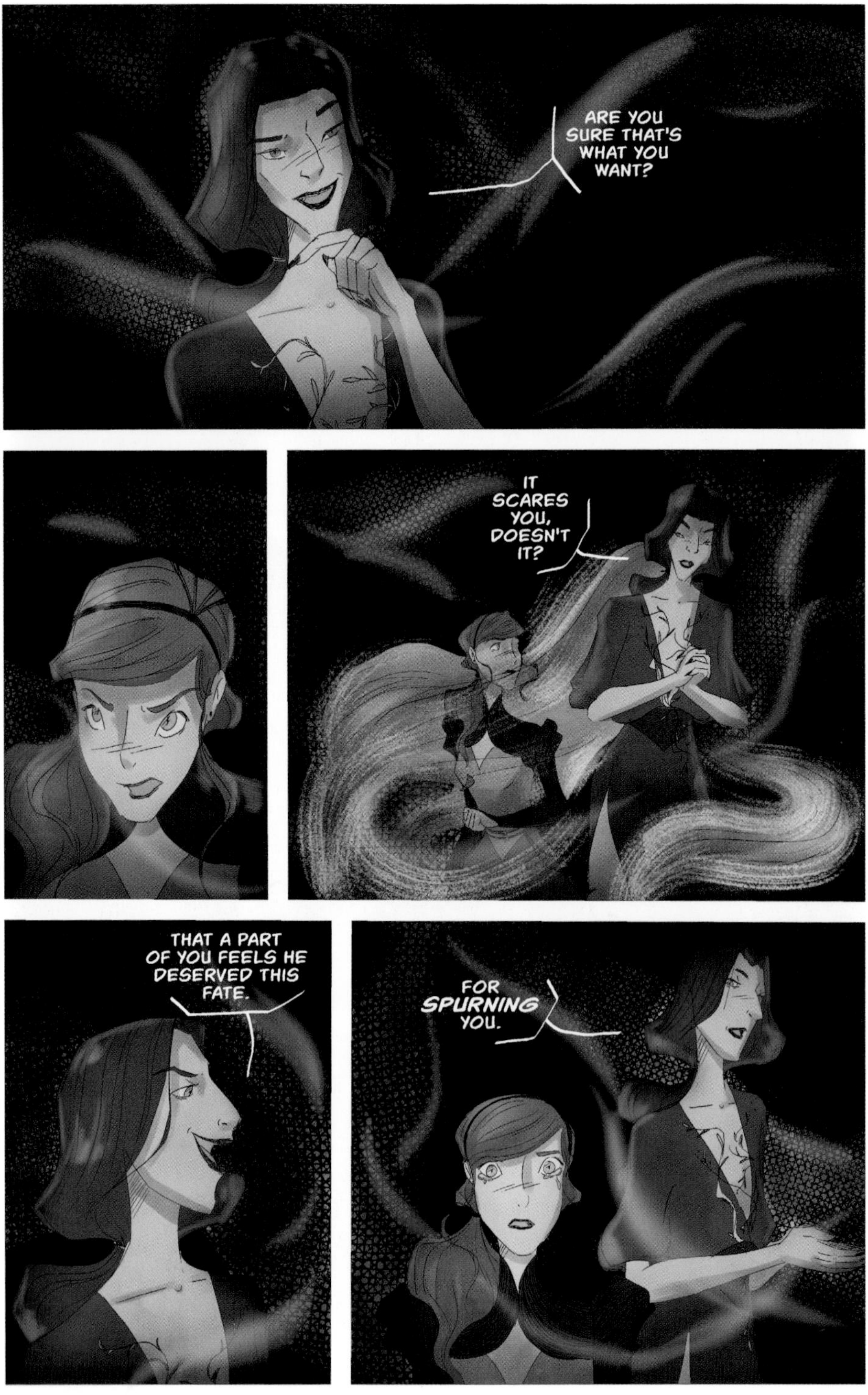
ARE YOU SURE THAT'S WHAT YOU WANT?
IT SCARES YOU, DOESN'T IT?
THAT A PART OF YOU FEELS HE DESERVED THIS FATE.
FOR *SPURNING* YOU.

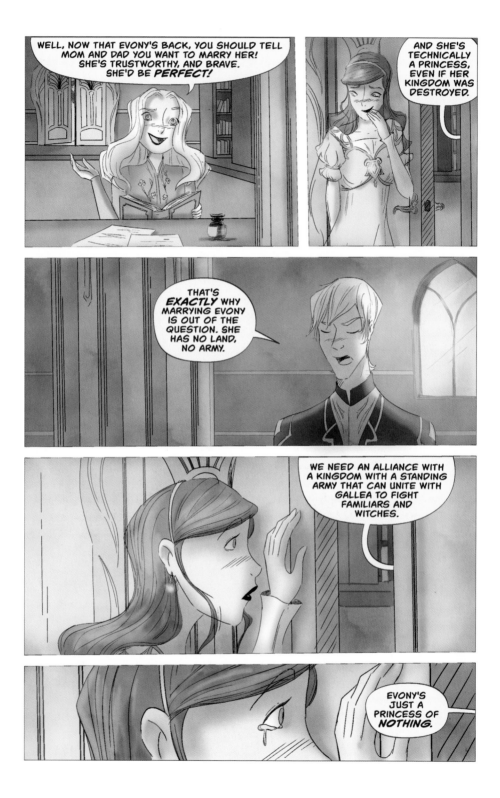

LEAVE ME ALONE!

I HATE YOU!

I HATE YOU!

ZIIIP

≈SIGH≈ THAT'S SO MUCH BETTER. I COULDN'T EVEN HEAR MYSELF THINK.

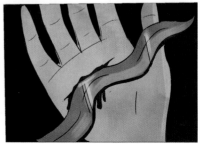

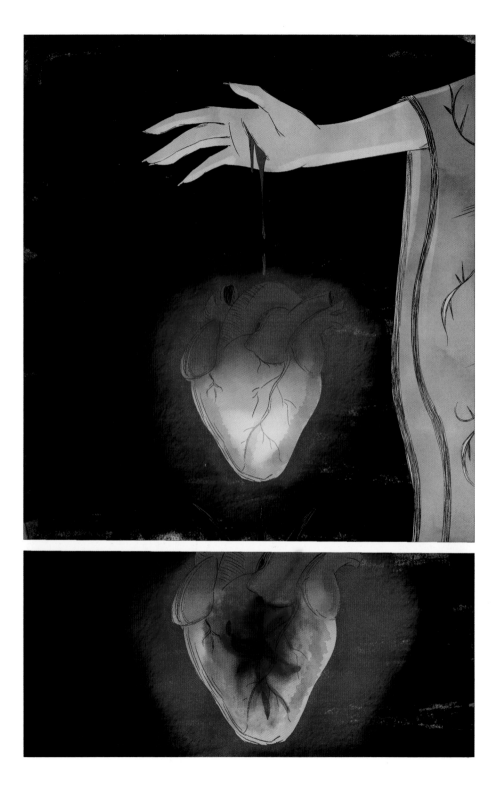

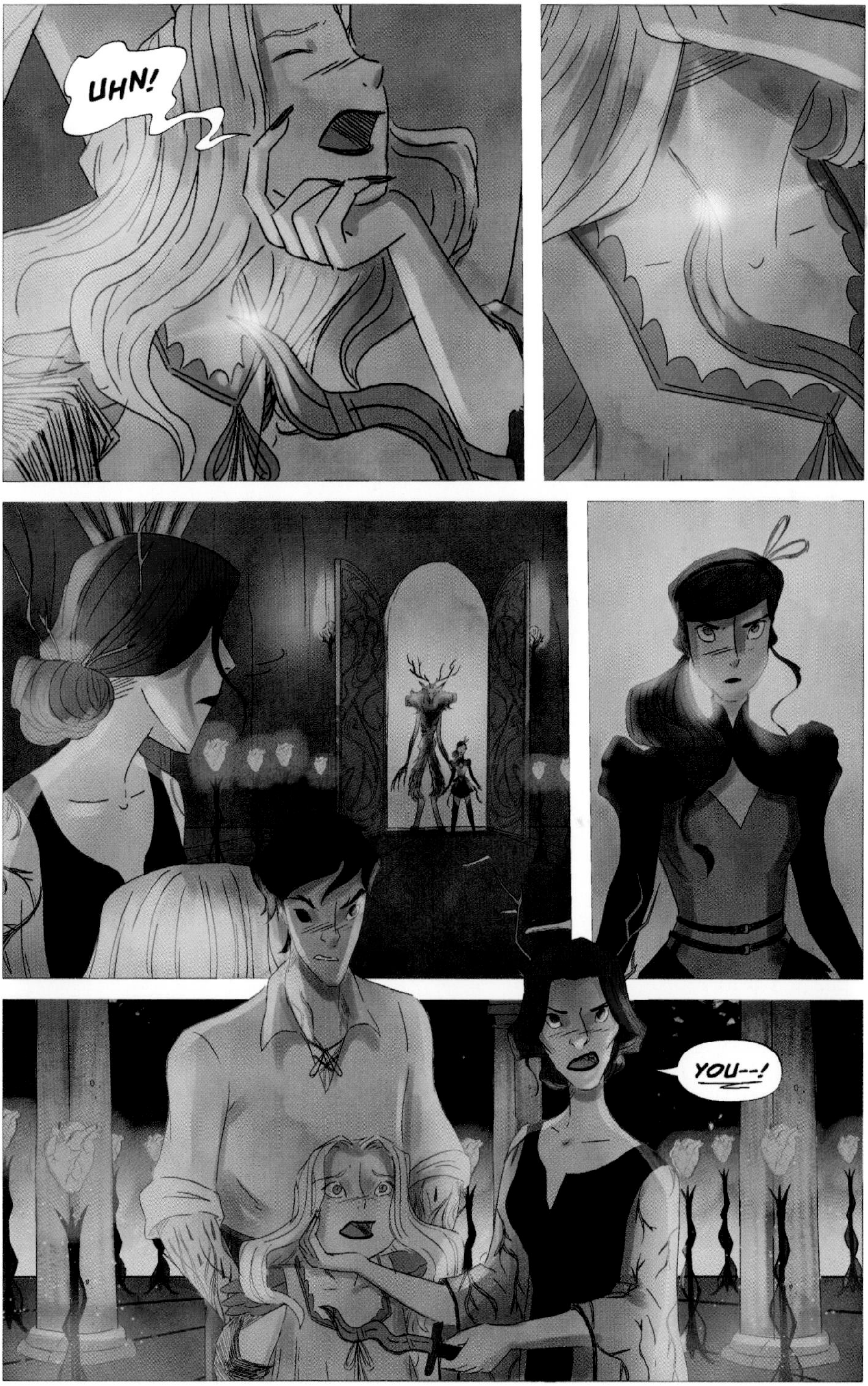
UHN!
YOU--!

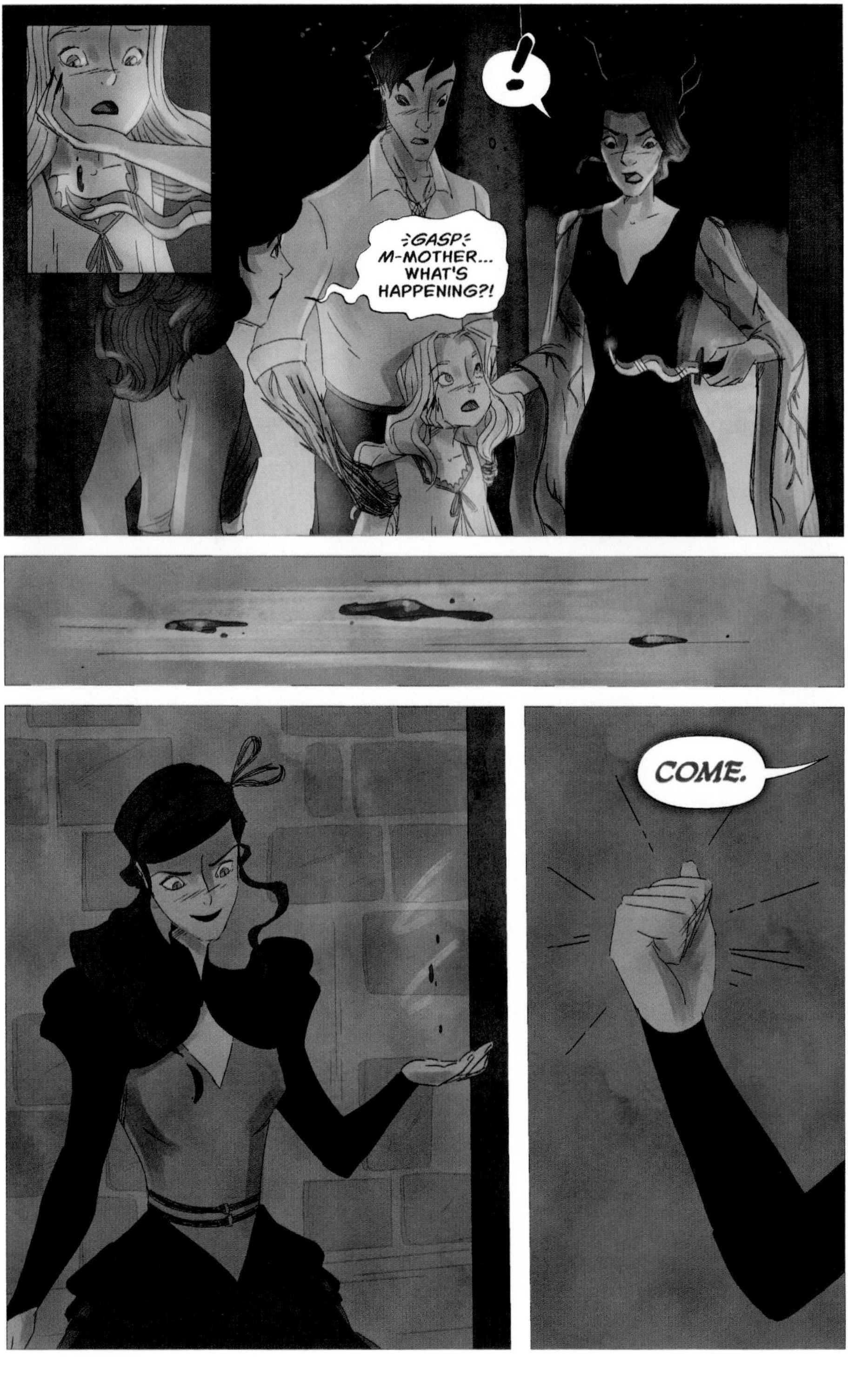
!
GASP
M-MOTHER...
WHAT'S
HAPPENING?!
COME.

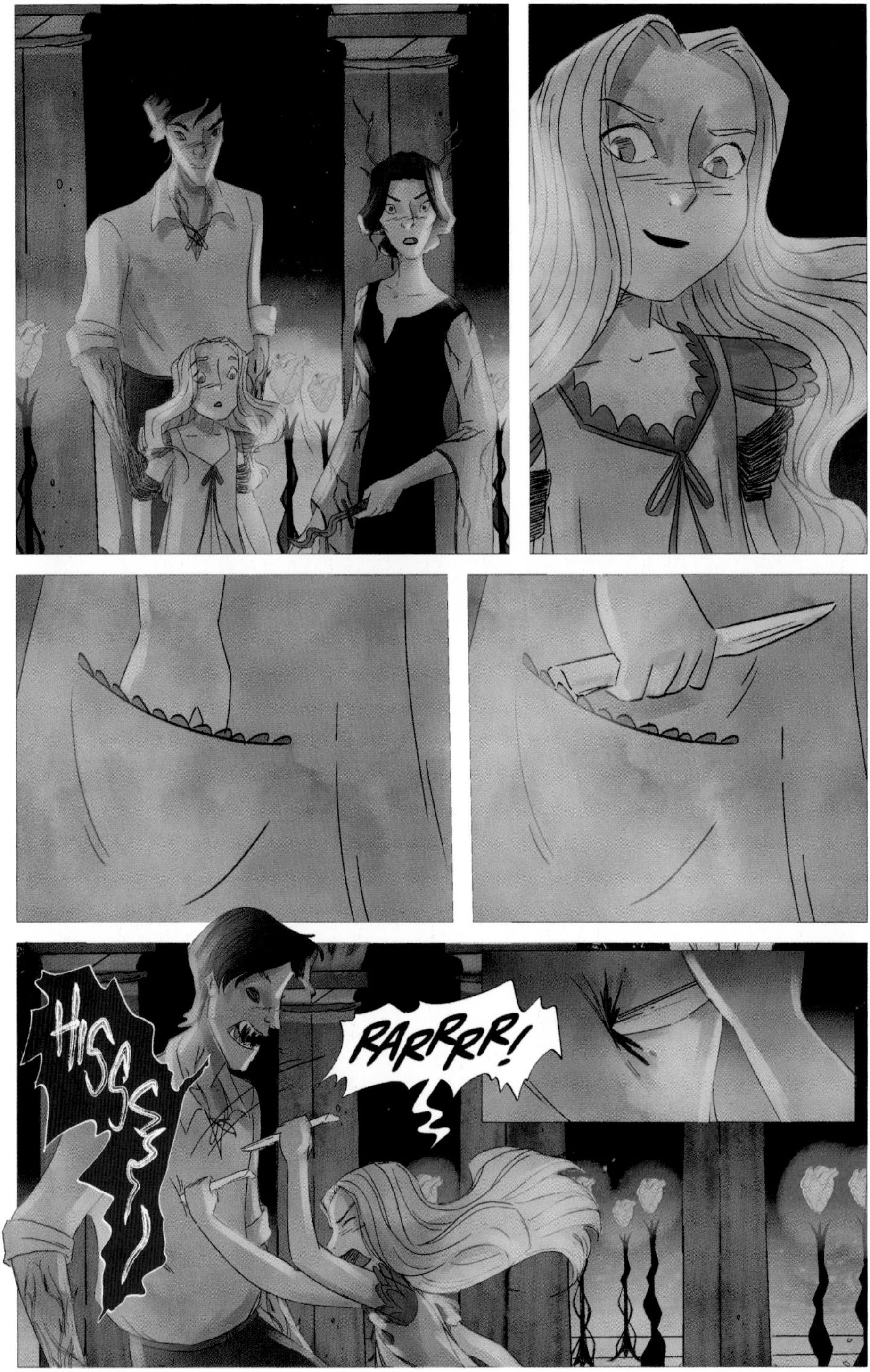
HISSSS!
RARRRR!

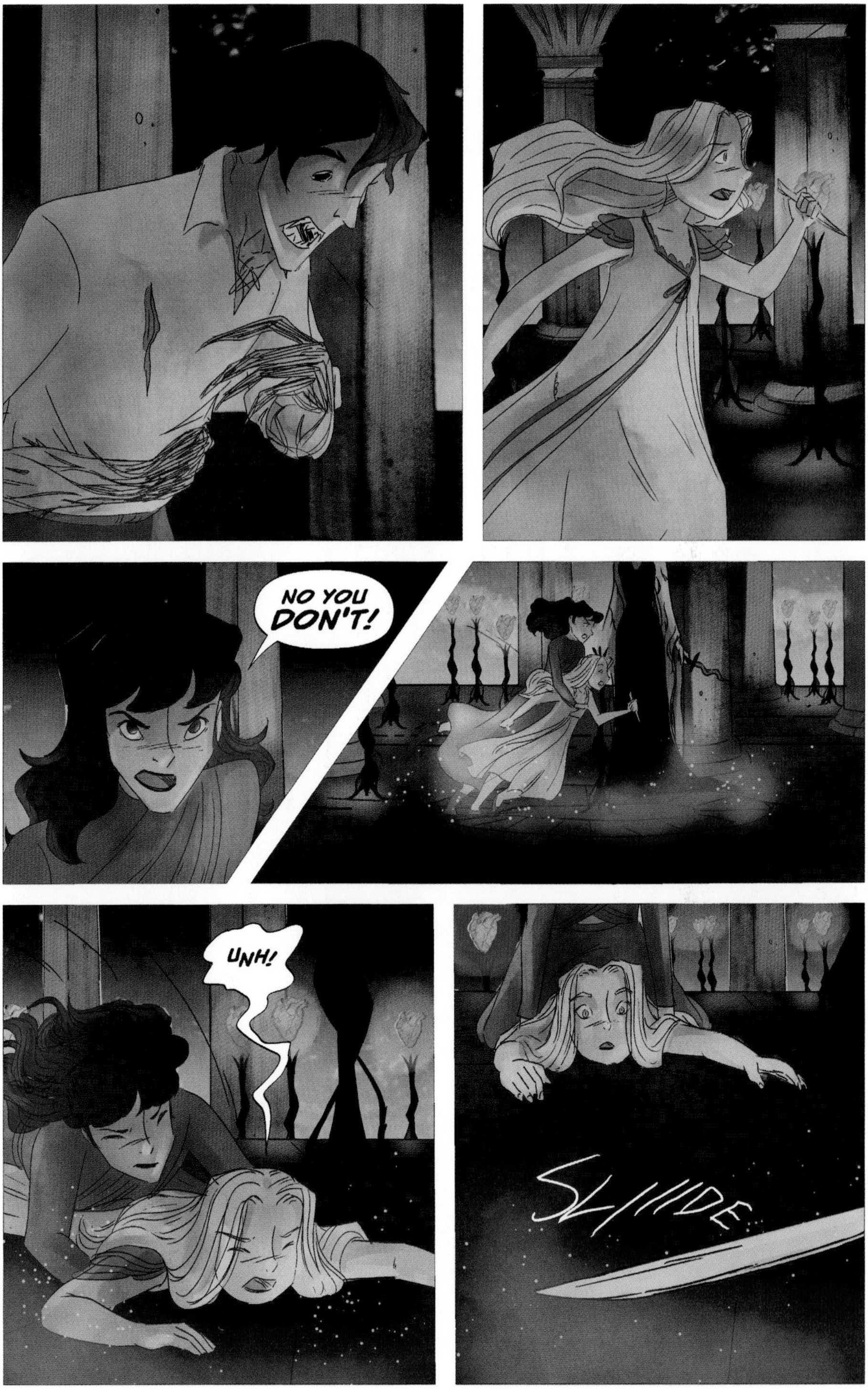
NO YOU DON'T!
UNH!
SLIIIDE

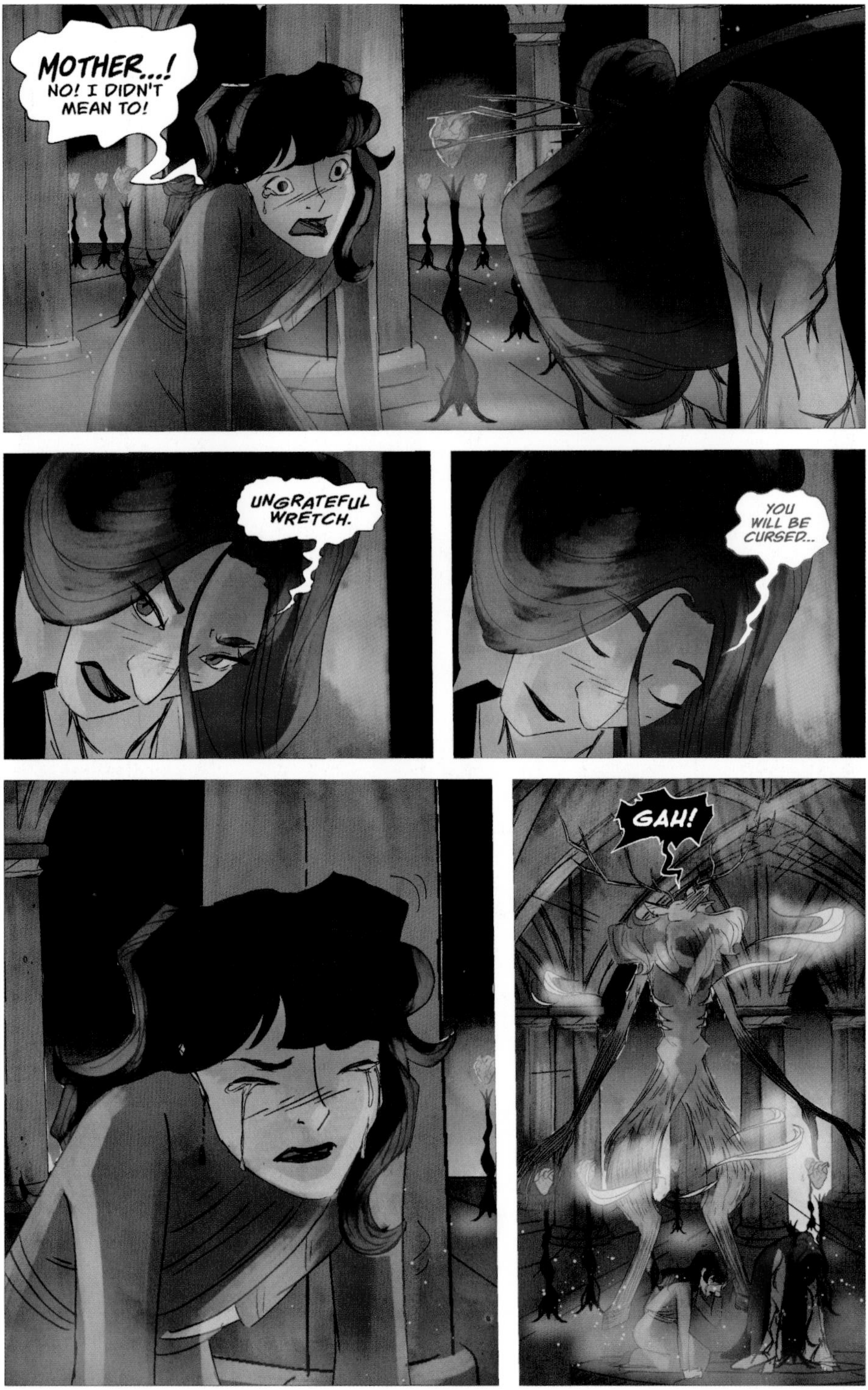
MOTHER...! NO! I DIDN'T MEAN TO!
UNGRATEFUL WRETCH.
YOU WILL BE CURSED...
GAH!

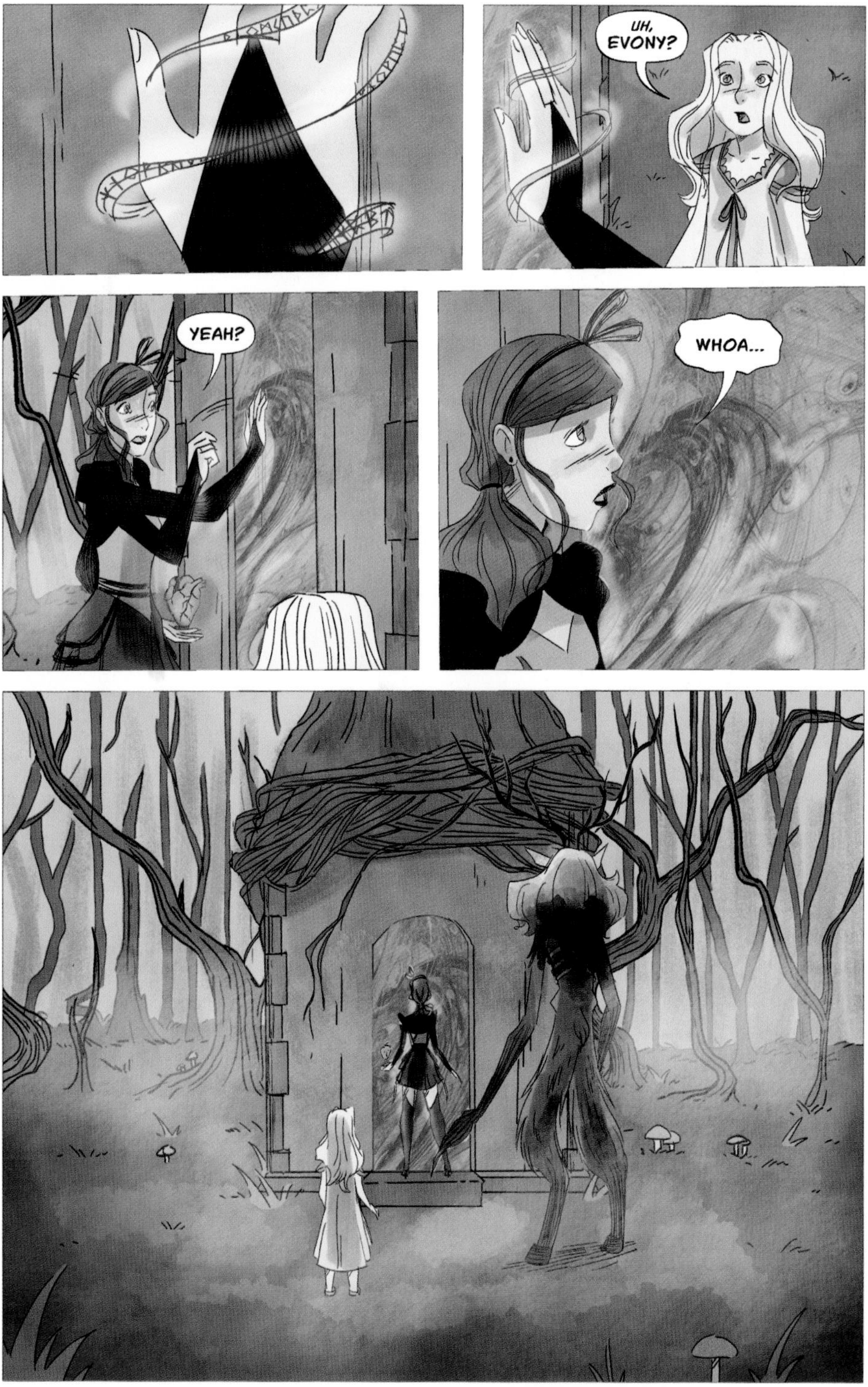
UH, EVONY?
YEAH?
WHOA...

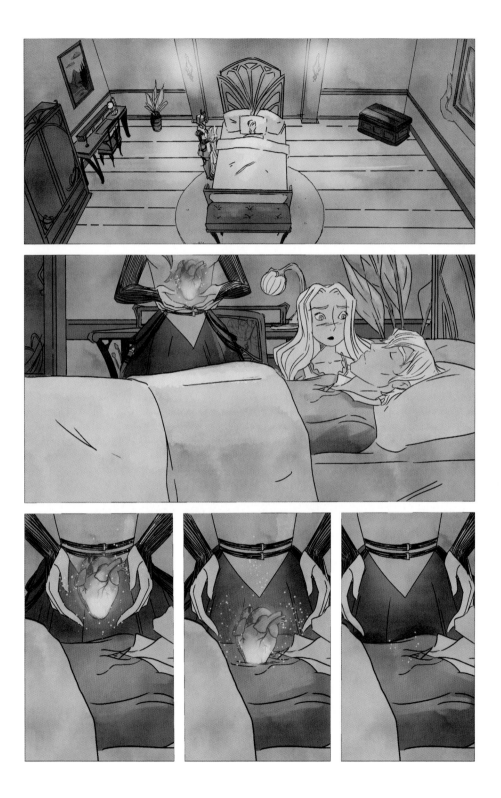

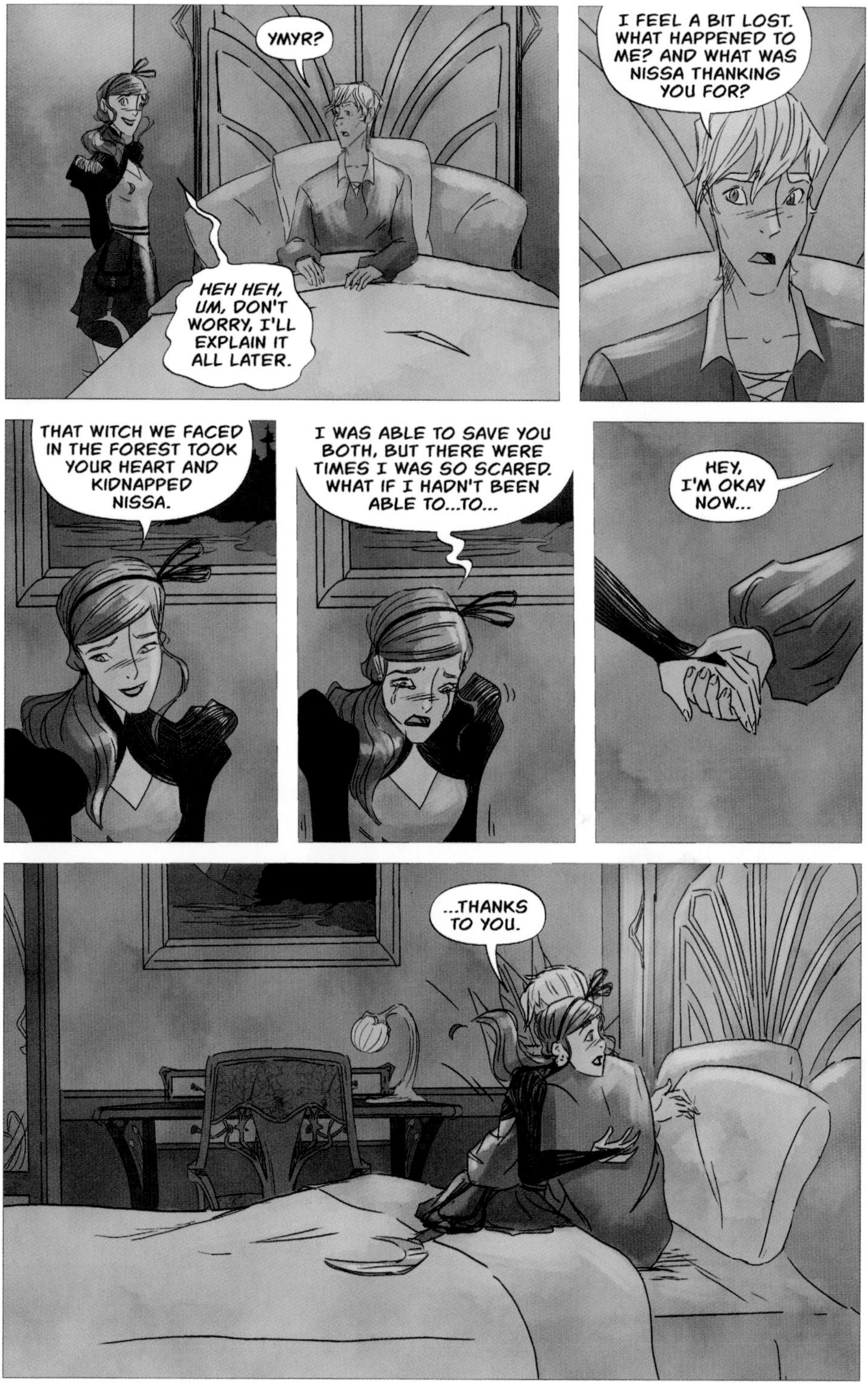
YMYR?
HEH HEH, UM, DON'T WORRY, I'LL EXPLAIN IT ALL LATER.
I FEEL A BIT LOST. WHAT HAPPENED TO ME? AND WHAT WAS NISSA THANKING YOU FOR?
THAT WITCH WE FACED IN THE FOREST TOOK YOUR HEART AND KIDNAPPED NISSA.
I WAS ABLE TO SAVE YOU BOTH, BUT THERE WERE TIMES I WAS SO SCARED. WHAT IF I HADN'T BEEN ABLE TO...TO...
HEY, I'M OKAY NOW...
...THANKS TO YOU.

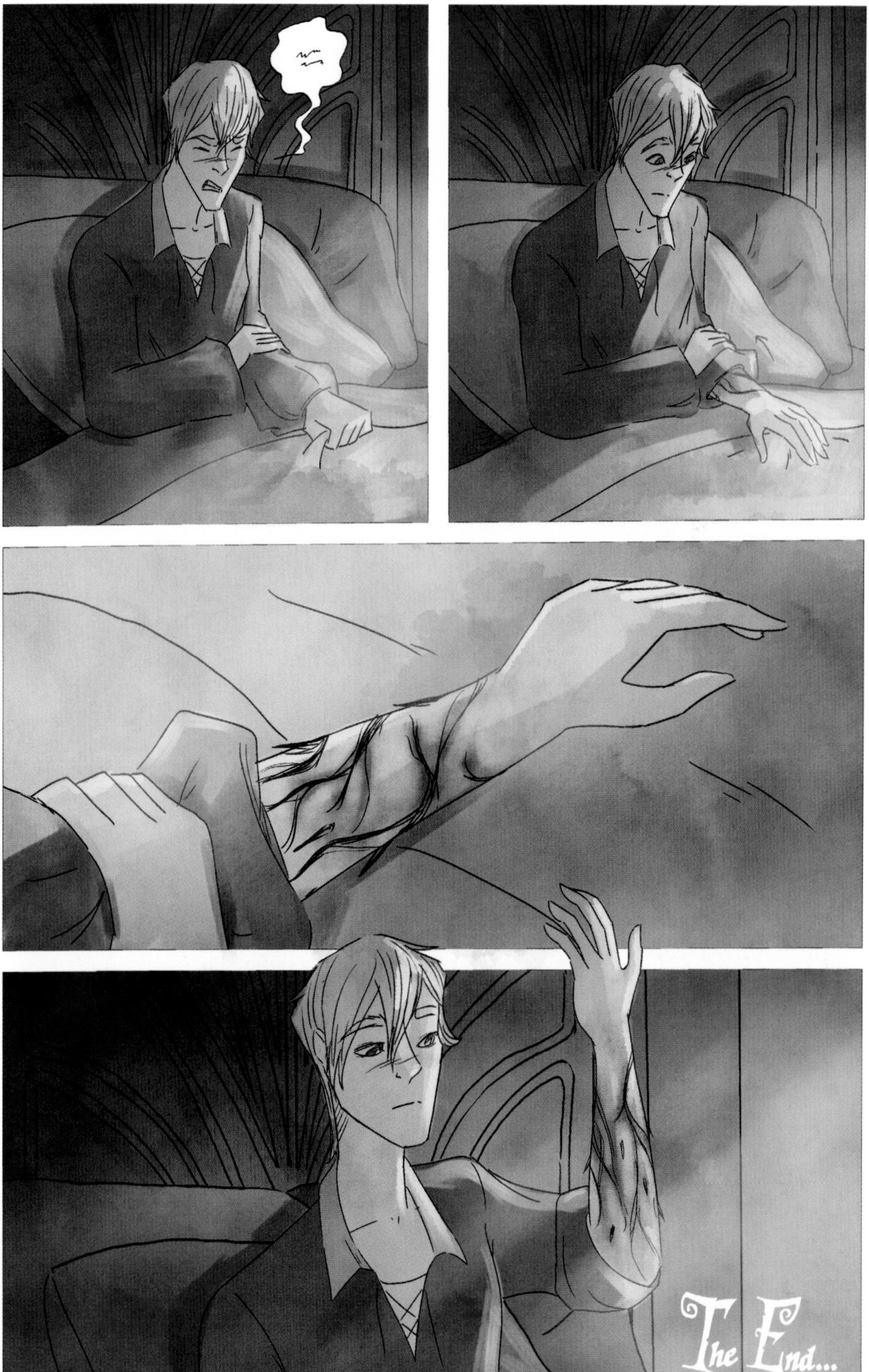
The End...

First Hardcover Edition, November 2021
First Paperback Edition, November 2021
10 9 8 7 6 5 4 3 2 1
FAC-034274-21288
Printed in the United States of America
Colors by Stelladia
Letters by Hassan Otsmane-Elhaou
This book is set in Buisnessland/Fontspring; OutofLine/Blambot; ShakyKane/Comicraft
Library of Congress Control Number for Hardcover: 2021933787
Hardcover ISBN 9781368028356
Paperback ISBN 9781368028363
Reinforced binding

Visit www.hyperionteens.com